SOMETHING
IN THE WALLS

SOMETHING IN THE WALLS

A Novel

Daisy Pearce

MINOTAUR BOOKS
NEW YORK

First published in the United States by Minotaur Books, an imprint of St. Martin's Publishing Group

SOMETHING IN THE WALLS. Copyright © 2025 by Daisy Pearce. All rights reserved. Printed in the United States of America. For information, address St. Martin's Publishing Group, 120 Broadway, New York, NY 10271.

www.minotaurbooks.com

Designed by Gabriel Guma

Library of Congress Cataloging-in-Publication Data

Names: Pearce, Daisy, author.
Title: Something in the walls : a novel / Daisy Pearce.
Description: First edition. | New York : Minotaur Books, 2025.
Identifiers: LCCN 2024028160 | ISBN 9781250334381 (hardcover) |
    ISBN 9781250334398 (ebook)
Subjects: LCGFT: Thrillers (Fiction) | Horror fiction. | Novels.
Classification: LCC PR6116.E168 S66 2025 | DDC 823/.92—dc23/eng/20240724
LC record available at https://lccn.loc.gov/2024028160

Our books may be purchased in bulk for promotional, educational, or business use. Please contact your local bookseller or the Macmillan Corporate and Premium Sales Department at 1-800-221-7945, extension 5442, or by email at MacmillanSpecialMarkets@macmillan.com.

First Edition: 2025

10 9 8 7 6 5 4 3 2 1

For Anne "Professor" Booty, the light of all lights

A strange and terrible wunder.

—Abraham Fleming, 1577

Then the villagers, linked in circles hand-in-hand, danced round the bonfires to preserve themselves against witchcraft, and when they burned low, one person here and there detached himself from the rest and leaped through the flames to insure himself from some special evil.

—Cornish Feasts and Folklore, M. A. Courtney, 1890

ONE

I walk into the pharmacy on Union Street for two things: my photographs and a pregnancy test. As I stand at the counter I feel lightheaded and thirsty. Nerves, I suppose. Or the heat. There was a piece on the radio this morning about a hosepipe ban and water rationing, and Oscar leaned forward in his chair, pushing his glasses up his nose.

"You hear that, Mina?" he said, cutting his toast carefully. "You'll be grateful I put that water butt in the garden last winter now, won't you?"

The temperature on the big digital clock hanging outside the chemist reads 35°C and already the armpits of my T-shirt are dark with sweat. I take my package and walk quickly to the public toilets with my head down and sunglasses on, panting like a dog by the time I duck inside. The toilets are dingy and smell of urine and cigarette smoke, the metal tang of cold tiles. The light that punches through the grimy windows is the color of nicotine. I open the test with shaking fingers and hover over the seat, trying to hold the flimsy cardboard stick steady between my legs.

The insert tells me it will take ten minutes to see a result. I sit with my hands neatly folded in my lap and wonder what I will tell Oscar, how he will take the news. He'll be surprised, I think. He's normally so careful.

Last night, we passed a roadblock at the site of a traffic accident. The blue lights of the police cars pulsed in the growing darkness. I craned my head around to see the wreckage. An ambulance rolled past; no siren, slow moving. A funeral pace. Oscar inched the car forward, frowning.

"Car accident," he said, nodding toward the scene. Glass chips glittering. Hot, bent chrome. He fanned himself with the road map, one elbow hooked out the window. "Looks bad."

"That corner's a death trap," I replied. My skin was sticking to the leather seats. God, it was so hot, still.

"It's not the road, it's the driver." Oscar was frowning. "I've told you that."

I looked at him sideways.

"You don't know that. Maybe a dog ran out into the road, or a child. Maybe the driver fainted. You don't *know* what happened."

He snorted, shaking his head. I knew what was coming. I steeled myself.

"If you're careful, you're safe," he said firmly.

Six minutes have passed, by my watch. I drum my fingers. *If you're careful, you're safe.* Well, on that last night of the holiday, we hadn't been safe, had we? We had one too many ouzos and now here I am, sitting in the cubicle of a stinking public toilet with my head in my hands waiting for the little stick to tell me whether I'm to be a mother. I look down at my engagement ring, wondering where the thrill of excitement is. My mother told me that stuff was for storybooks and young lovers in movies.

"In real life you just want someone who can remember to descale the kettle, pet," she said, giving me a knowing look. *"If you want excitement, take up skydiving."*

I glance down at my bag, remembering the photographs I collected. I'd taken a roll of film to be developed a couple of days ago, mostly pictures from our holiday to Crete and the tour we took to see the Palace of Knossos. Now I pull them out and flick through them, marveling at the blue depth of the sky against the whitewashed houses, the umber-colored alleyways.

I feel something then, an unexpected warmth between my legs, that heavy, sinking sensation low down in me and I know, I just *know*. After all, hadn't I felt that deep cramping in my stomach as I got out of the shower that morning? I wipe myself anyway, surprised but not disappointed to see the smear of dark blood on the tissue. I don't even need to look at the pregnancy test now to know that it is a negative. I snatch up the pictures and cram them back into the envelope, suddenly desperate to be away from this cramped cubicle and the grim fluorescent lighting, cursing as a photo slips from my fingers and slides over the tiled floor. I pick it up and turn it over. It's a photograph Oscar took of me one night in a restaurant high up in the hills. I'm wearing a pale yellow dress, looking beyond the camera to where the swifts were nesting in the rafters of an old barn. A little way behind my right shoulder, partly shadowed, a young man is standing and looking directly at me. His face is slightly blurred, as though he was in the process of turning away as the flash went off, turning his retinas into blank silver pennies. Something sinks in my stomach, as cold and solid as a stone.

"Oh my God," I whisper, brushing my thumb over the figure in the picture. "Oh my God."

TWO

"Did you look at it?"

Oscar doesn't lift his head. He bends over his crossword, long fingers pressing the newspaper flat. His face is hard and angular and built from strong lines; long straight nose, cheekbones like knife blades. He sighs loudly.

"Yes."

"Well?"

A beat. My heart quickens.

"It's him, isn't it?"

"I think you know the answer to that."

He moves as if to write something, counting the boxes with the nib of his pen. Then he sighs again, loudly. It's a tricky clue, five across. *Frighten, as a horse (5).* I snuck a look at the crossword this morning, before he got out of bed and came down for breakfast. I push the photograph over the table again, forcefully.

"Have a proper look. That's Eddie. I'd know him anywhere."

Oscar looks up at me. I haven't told him about the pregnancy scare or the unmistakable relief I felt when I saw the tissue spotted with blood. He wouldn't understand.

"Mina, that's not—"

"Are you looking properly?" The pitch of my voice rises higher, anxiously. "I can't believe you don't see it!"

"This is irrational. *You* are being irrational. He's been dead six years, Mina—I mean, what do you expect me to say?"

Something hard in my throat. I swallow against it.

"I *know* he's dead. I just mean—"

"What? What do you mean? Please explain it to me because I'm struggling to understand." He removes his glasses and stares at me in that way he does, amber eyes unflinching. I roll my hands into fists, frustrated because I get it, I do. I *know* Eddie is dead. But. *But.*

"It's 'spook,'" I snap instead, nodding toward his crossword. "Five across, 'Frighten, as a horse.' Spook."

I snatch the photograph away from him as hot, frustrated tears prick my eyes. Oscar sighs.

"Listen. I'm trying to be kind when I say this—" He reaches for me and I stiffen, but don't pull away. My hands are trembling. "It might be time for you to go back to the group, Mina."

It's been six months since I walked into the church hall on Newham Road with its familiar smells of furniture polish and curdled milk, the flickering light over the doorway which draws all the moths in the dark winter months. Oscar had directed me to it a year ago, after I'd had a spate of bad dreams in which Eddie appeared under a shelf of thick blue ice, screaming and hammering against it as bubbles floated out of his mouth. *"You need to go and talk to other people like you,"* Oscar had told me, handing me a leaflet with a printed heart at the top and below, the image of two hands reaching toward each other. *Hope and Hands Bereavement Support,* it had read. *Let go of loss, not love.*

The group was small back then. Just nine of us sitting in a semicircle on hard plastic chairs, drinking tea out of clumsy, mismatched mugs. Sometimes people spoke and sometimes they didn't, and although I can't say that it helped me much, the bad dreams stopped coming and for a while, it was okay. I met widowers and orphans, victims of tragedies far greater than my own, astonished at their ability to keep going, to persevere. Everyone spoke of empty beds and unworn clothes, the totems left behind by the deceased. We laughed and got angry and rubbed each other's backs when we cried. We fluctuated; the people who joined, left, and rejoined were like the ebb and flow of the sea. That's how Horace, the man who led the group, referred to grief. Sometimes small and quiet and shallow, sometimes a tsunami, cold and frightening. But inevitable, just like the tide. I like Horace. He lost his wife and son in a house fire at the beginning of the decade, still wore the burn scars up his arms, his skin brown and stippled like the bark of a gnarled tree. Even though Eddie had been dead five years by that point, Horace treated me with sympathy and understanding, urging me to pull up a chair with the others and handing me a mug of tea with what I would come to understand was his usual greeting, "You're always welcome here."

As I walk into the room that evening, Horace greets me with a big smile and open arms, my name ringing in his mouth like a bell—*Mina!* A hug, the flat clap of his open palm on my back, his smile so wide it reveals the pink of his gums. He hands me a mug of tea, unsweetened, and I wince slightly at the taste, which makes Horace laugh again. There is a cluster of others here tonight, a few who I recognize but most I don't, new faces all with the same expressions; pinched and haunted, shocked hollow. As I take a seat I see a man hovering in the kitchen doorway, neither in nor out, his face tight with indecision. He is tall and long limbed with dark upward tilted eyes and a scrubby beard, holding a piece of paper in one tightly clenched hand. Our eyes meet briefly and then Horace is touching my arm and saying, "Why don't you tell everyone about Eddie, Mina?" and I'm nodding and saying okay and what I tell them is this:

It was cold the winter my brother had died. Chrome skies and snowstorms which buried the windowpanes and masked the sound of his labored breathing. They said that's what probably finished him off in the end, that cold. As though it had somehow seeped into the hollows of his bones and turned his blood to ice. Eddie had always been sickly, my mother had told me, even as a baby. Later, after the funeral, I would realize she had been in denial about just how sick he had been—her and my father both. His immune system hadn't formed right, couldn't fight off illness. They never talked about it, but they must have known, both of them. They must have.

I settled on the bed beside him, taking his hand in my own. His skin was as heavy and cold and pale as milk. Eddie opened his eyes and smiled at me, weakly.

"I've been thinking about the end," he whispered. He squeezed my hand, just once. "You'll make sure they play the right music won't you, Meens? I don't want Mum screwing it up and putting on her stuff. Not if there's a load of girls from my school there. I don't want to be carried out to Rod fucking Stewart."

I laughed, even though I felt the swell of tears suffocating me, burning the backs of my eyes. The choke hold of his illness, sinking him, shrinking him. He was only fourteen. It wasn't *fair*.

"Of course."

"Iron Maiden or nothing."

"Sure thing, Eddie."

There had been a twinkle about him that day. After days of lethargy he'd developed a flush in his sunken cheeks that hadn't been there in a long time. Of course, afterward, I learned that this is known as "terminal lucidity" and is common in end-of-life patients. A surge of energy prior to the body's shutdown. I took his hand and the silence enfolded us gently, like a soft blanket. His voice was trembling and whispery and I needed to lean in closer just to hear it.

"If there's anything out there, I'll come back and tell you, Meens."

When I finish talking, there is an ache in my chest like something is being crushed, my eyes brimming with unshed tears. I've told this story in this room dozens of times because each telling is a panacea. I don't subscribe to a lot of what Oscar refers to as "new age nonsense" but the idea that grief gets heavier the longer you carry it alone is one that has helped me.

Horace smiles as I excuse myself to go and get a glass of water. In the kitchen, that tall man is still hovering, standing beside the sink with that piece of paper in his hand, a lit cigarette smoldering between his lips. The window is open, the night outside still and humid and pricked with stars.

"I'm sorry about your brother," he says to me, this man. I notice his long fingers. Piano player's fingers, my mum would have called them. I wonder if he is a musician. "It sounds like it happened very fast."

"It did." I pull a glass from the draining board. "It took us all by surprise."

"Your parents must have been heartbroken."

"Yeah," I tell him. Truth is, my mum switched off completely after Eddie died. Staring out the window with nightshade shadows beneath her eyes, fingers worrying at the loose skin of her neck. I was sixteen years old, just scraping through my exams and getting through college by the skin of my teeth. Her withdrawal was abrupt and immediate, and I felt it like a punch to the throat. The day I left home for university, she looked right through me, her face a rictus, holding my gaze long enough to say, *"He should still be with us, Mina."* My dad, on the other hand, found God. It was a rock in a storm, he said. He became fervent and heated when he prayed, started hanging crucifixes around the house. I don't blame him. I don't blame either of them. But I find it hard to be around them, even now. Prayers and paralysis. Old wounds.

The man dips his head. Under the fluorescent lights, I can see glints of red in his hair. I glance down at the crumpled piece of paper he is holding. It is covered in scrawls and loops, scrappy-looking, like something a child has done.

"You should come in and sit down. Everyone is very friendly. You don't have to talk if you don't want to."

"My daughter's name was Maggie. She was seven years old and mad as a hatter. She had hair the color of autumn leaves. I loved her so much."

His voice snags slightly, eyes soft and liquid. I touch his arm, feeling his skin smooth and warm beneath my hand.

"Do you have a photo of her?"

He reaches into his pocket and pulls out his wallet, flipping it open so I can see inside. There, behind the small plastic screen, is a photo of a gap-toothed little girl grinning up at the camera. She is wearing a paper crown, which is slipping slightly over her red hair. Sometimes I wonder how our many-chambered hearts can stand the loss all these years, why it doesn't simply stop beating. I wonder how the grief can still twist inside you like a stitch in your side when you least expect it. The man clears his throat and swipes at his eyes.

"That picture was taken on her seventh birthday. Me and my wife—*ex*-wife now—we made her a Snoopy cake. She loved that stupid dog."

"It's so unfair. I'm sorry. Listen, I'm going to make a cup of tea. Do you want one, uh—?"

"Sam. I don't suppose you've got anything cold, have you?"

"There's juice in the fridge."

"I was hoping for something stronger."

"Like a beer?"

"Vodka. Tequila maybe. My mum used to keep a bottle of brandy under the sink."

I laugh, pulling the mugs down from the cupboard in front of me.

"I think that would be unwise. They have AA meetings here."

"Oh. Tea, then. Thanks."

I fill the kettle and put it on to boil. When he speaks next, his voice is soft and so quiet I could almost have believed I'd imagined it.

"What you just said in there, about your brother—did he—did he ever come back?"

I stand very still. I hadn't told the group about the photograph, the image of Eddie with those unsettling silvery eyes turned toward the camera because the rational side of me knows that it isn't my brother. It *can't* be. It's just some trick of the light, a smear on the camera lens. I know this and yet I cycle back to Eddie's words that day—*"If there's anything out there, I'll come back and tell you, Meens"*—and I wonder. I wonder. Sam clears his throat.

"I went to see a psychic, you see. To try to make contact with Maggie."

"Did it work?"

"You tell me."

He hands me the piece of paper he has been holding. It has been scribbled all over, crumpled and folded from endless handling. Through the looping coils of script some words seem to float to the surface. *Teeth. Heavy. Rust.*

"It's illegible."

"The woman who wrote it claims it's the work of spirits. 'Psychography,' it's called. 'Automatic writing.' She went into a trance right in front of me. It cost me a hundred pounds. She must have seen me coming, right?"

Loops and curlicues, like hieroglyphs. A smear on a camera lens. The dead, walking among us. *"We don't fool anyone harder than we fool ourselves,"* as Oscar is fond of saying. Heat flares in me like a stirred ember.

"I paid in cash. She told me I had to give her something of Maggie's to be able to make contact—a toy or a piece of clothing—so I went up to the attic and I dug through all her old things, all the boxes we couldn't bring ourselves to give away, to find that fucking Snoopy T-shirt she always wore. I was up there half the day. It tore me up to do it, but to take my money on top of that? It's criminal."

I reach for Sam and slide an arm around him. His eyes are gleaming.

"At her funeral—God, the tiny coffin, as light as a feather and the size of a toy but still I don't know where I found the strength to lift it—I told Maggie I would come and find her. I was worried that she would be lonely. That she wouldn't be able to find her way home. You see, I get it. Your brother, that weight you're carrying? I understand."

Something catches in my throat. *"If there's anything out there, I'll come back and tell you, Meens."* Sam and I, orbiting a void, a life suspended just waiting for a sign.

"The worst thing about it is that I basically expose these kinds of people for a living," Sam continues, voice strained and angry sounding, "grifters and con men and frauds. I learned to cold-read before I could fucking talk and I still fell for this crap."

He screws up the piece of paper into his fist and shoves it clumsily into the swing bin beneath the counter.

"You cold-read for a job?"

"I'm a journalist. Figuring people out by what they're purposely not telling me is all part of it, yeah. It's an art form when it's done well."

I laugh. I can't help it. Sam shoots me a sharp look.

"You think I'm exaggerating? Let me tell you what I've learned about you, then. You take sugar in your tea even though you're trying to cut down. You're newly engaged—congratulations, by the way—to a safe, practical man who is quite traditional. He's well-off, and you like to think that your future children will have your looks and his brains. Then there's the *Dracula* connection. Which one is it? Your mum or your dad?"

"How do you—?"

"Mina Harker. The 'light of all lights.'"

I laugh.

"It's my dad. He took my mother to Whitby Abbey while she was pregnant with me. My poor brother narrowly escaped being called Van Helsing."

Sam grins and I feel myself loosening, just a little.

"I saw your face when Horace gave you that tea. There was no sugar in it and you looked like you'd been poisoned. Then there's that sparkler on your ring finger—a solitaire diamond on a gold band. Expensive but not ostentatious, very traditional. It's a safe choice from what I'm imagining is a safe man."

I look down at the ring on my finger. It throws off little sparks of light sharp enough to cut me.

"The only thing I can't work out about you, Mina, is what you *do*. You're early twenties, right? I'm guessing no kids for a few years. You seem quite grounded, quite intelligent. Are you a teacher?"

Normally I'm wary of revealing too much of myself but there's an intimacy here, something formed out of our shared experience, our grief, that makes me be more open than I usually would.

"Close enough. I've just graduated in psychology but I specialize in the clinical aspect of working with children."

"Child psychology, huh? What made you take that path?"

Briefly, I consider telling him how my brother's death had opened a gulf between myself and my parents which had seemed long and black and endless. I think about telling him how it had been a woman called Rebecca Frost who had stopped me sailing over the edge of it, sitting me down quietly in her small office between the school canteen and the cloakrooms with the noisy hiss of water pipes overhead and the sign on the door which read PASTORAL CARE. Mrs. Frost hadn't been a trained counselor but she'd spoken to me with a tenderness and care I hadn't realized I'd been lacking, a box of oversized tissues on her desk that I'd used up in all but an afternoon. I had regular meetings with Mrs. Frost until the day I'd left for university when she'd given me a quick, inexpert hug and told me firmly that Eddie's death was not my fault. I think about explaining to Sam that the impact Rebecca Frost left on me was like a meteor striking the earth but instead I take a sip of my tea, now turning cold.

"Sometimes I wish I hadn't. It's a lot of work in a highly competitive field. After graduation I've got to complete a doctorate and an observational psychoanalytic study—not to mention all the clinical training. Any idea how hard it is to get a work placement without experience?"

"I can imagine. What did you write your thesis on?"

"The effects of complex trauma on undeveloped brains, chiefly in adolescents. It's personal. I'm sure you understand."

Sam nods, lips pressed together tightly. Outside, the pulse and hum of crickets in the long grass. A moth bats against the windowpane. I turn to rinse my cup in the sink, thinking about getting home to an empty house, dinner under cling film in the fridge. Oscar is at the lab till late this evening, sequestered with his group of young students, everything sterile and precise and carefully weighed. All those rocks from outer space held in airtight vacuums. He once brought home a chunk of meteorite and asked me to hold it. I did so, surprised at how little it weighed, full of holes like a pumice stone streaked black and brown and gray. Oscar stared at me, eyes glittering with expectation. I didn't know what to say. He wanted me to say the same thing he would, which is that it made him feel like a god.

"Listen, I have to go. My bus is leaving soon. It was nice to meet you, Sam, I'm just sorry it had to be here, for these reasons."

I hold out my hand to him and he hesitates so long I think he isn't going to take it. When he does, folding his hand over mine and looking me right in the eye, I feel a spark of something, some understanding, shared. The dead like golden threads, pulling us together.

THREE

A week later the hosepipe ban comes into force and the verges and lawns yellow and turn brown while flowers desiccate and shrivel into husks. There is no breeze and the air is dense as velvet. I lie on my stomach in the garden, dozing slightly in the shade, a can of lemonade open at my side. Heavy lidded eyes watching a wasp crawl into the hole at the top of the can, too lazy to lift my hand to swat it away, too hot to do anything except lie and stare with my mouth hanging agape.

I hear the phone ringing from inside the house. I look down the lawn to the open doorway into the kitchen. The phone rings and rings. *Can't be bothered,* I think. *Go away, whoever you are.*

Finally it stops. I can hear the wasp buzzing inside the can, an angry metallic sound. I wonder what it would be like to be

imprisoned in that sweet smelling dark, a pinhole of light overhead, the sides slippery and sticky with sugar. There are worse
ways to go.

When the phone starts ringing again, I sigh loudly, hoisting
myself up onto my hands and knees and staggering to my feet.
Sweat trickles down the backs of my legs and between my breasts,
skin glistening. I'm meant to be going to meet the caterers later
this afternoon to discuss food for the wedding, vol-au-vents and
king prawns on chips of ice, tiny slivers of fruitcake. I'm not
looking forward to it. My appetite has shrunk to nothing in this
weather. Oscar and I are having a winter wedding, like I'd always
wanted. Holly and ivy and mistletoe, the bright red of poinsettias.
The day will be crisp and bright with frost and I will wear white
and my father will walk me down the aisle of the old church with
the tilted gravestones out the front.

Inside, the house is cool, a few flies lazily drawing zeroes in
the air of the kitchen. I bat at them ineffectually as I pass but I'm
hot and slow and they instantly regroup. The phone is still ringing by the time I get into the hallway. Up until last year, we still
had a rotary dial phone but I insisted we replace it much to Oscar's irritation. He likes "old things" as he constantly reminds
me. If it were left to him, we'd still have the old black-and-white
television set with the rabbit ear antenna.

"Hullo?"

"Mina? Is that you, light of all lights?"

I can't place his voice, not at first. Then he laughs gently and
I remember the tall, snaggletoothed man who had stood quietly
in the kitchen of the church hall with a crumpled piece of paper
in his hand.

"Sam?"

"Listen, I don't have long—I'm in a phone box and my money's going to run out any second."

"How did you get this number?"

"I begged Horace for it. It cost me a large donation to Hope and Hands and almost all of my dignity. Are you free? Can you meet me this afternoon, about two?"

I hesitate. My eye falls on the calendar tacked to the wall beside the phone. I can see today's date clearly. Tuesday, June 27. Written in the little box alongside it are the words: *Wedding Menu—Caterers 3pm—bring notebook!*

"What's all this about, Sam?"

I can hear the smile in his voice as he replies, "Ghosts, Mina. I think I have one for you."

Oscar comes through the door that evening, calling my name as he always does—first high, then low. *Mi*-na. I greet him in the hallway, lifting my damp hands to take the bouquet of flowers he is holding out to me. Pink roses and baby's breath.

"These for me?"

"Make sure you add sugar to the water, they'll keep brighter for longer."

"They're so beautiful, Oscar. Thank you."

He snakes an arm around my shoulders and skims a kiss on my temple. Heat radiates from him, making his skin clammy, hair sticking to the nape of his neck. He heads into the kitchen and washes his hands at the sink, scooping a palmful of water over his face. I watch him carefully. Anxiety knots behind my ribs. He glances at the plate of vol-au-vents sitting on the counter.

"Those from the caterers?"

"That's right."

"They good?"

"You tell me."

I watch as he lifts one from the plate and folds it into his open mouth. I hope he won't be able to detect the heat still clinging to it, hope he won't notice the oven door is still warm to the touch. Because if he does, then I'll have to tell him why I missed the catering appointment that afternoon and instead I had to pick up two boxes of frozen vol-au-vents from the supermarket on my way home. I folded the empty boxes into the bin at the far end of our road, a good distance from the house. Sometimes the deceit is so weightless, you barely think of it.

"Nice." He's nodding. "I like this one, what is it?"

"Uh, prawn I think?"

"So will we use them? Did the meeting go okay?"

"Oh, I don't know. There's so much to plan! I wish you'd come with me to these things."

I keep my voice light, even managing to smile a little as I move to the sink, peeling the paper wrapping from the flowers. Oscar slides his hands around my waist so I can lean back into him. It's a wonder he doesn't notice how fast my heart is beating.

"I trust you to get it right," he says kindly. "And you know my mother is just *desperate* to get involved. Why don't you take her along next time?"

I clench my jaw. Oscar's mother is polished and cold and sometimes I see her looking at me askance, the tips of her mouth pointed upward in a taut little smile. When we announced our engagement, she hugged me so tightly that she dug her curved nails into my shoulder blades. *"Wouldn't life be dull if we all married our equal,"* she said, and it had got under my skin somehow, the heat of it.

I turn in Oscar's arms to face him.

"I've been offered some work."

This is how I've chosen to phrase it. An investment. An opportunity. These are the expressions Oscar will recognize.

"Doing what?"

"Research."

I'm speaking with a confidence I don't feel, can't quite meet his eye. Oscar's voice is steady.

"For whom?"

"A newspaper."

"I see." He walks over to the counter and starts looking through the pile of mail. In among it is a circular from the government listing precautions to take in the heat wave. The words *Keep Safe, Keep Cool* have been written at the top beside a cartoon of a thirsty-looking cat. Oscar frowns at it.

"They think it's going to hit thirty-seven degrees tomorrow. I heard it on the radio." He turns the leaflet toward me.

"Oh yeah?"

"It's going to be like seventy-eight all over again. You remember that?"

I did. It had been the summer of skimming stones across the river with my best friend Sharon and rubbing our legs with sunflower oil because we thought it would help us tan quicker. Dad had told us we smelled like a chip shop, which had made us laugh. The sun had been a furnace that whole long summer, the lawn in the garden a strip of yellow, scorched earth.

"It won't be that bad," I reply, filling a vase at the sink, and putting the flowers in, stem by stem. "That was a *drought*. A proper one."

"Which newspaper?"

I frown at the sudden swerve in conversation. Sometimes I think he does it on purpose.

"It's, uh, *The Western Herald.*"

"Hardly a newspaper but go on, tell me what the job is."

"You ever heard of a place called Banathel, Mina?" Sam asked me that afternoon when I'd met him in the café on the harborside. The River Fal moved slowly past, the water brackish, brown, and muddy. I'd told myself I wasn't staying long, ordered a tap water with plenty of ice. Sam put aside his empty plate smeared with ketchup and stirred a sugar into his tea.

"Nope."

"Can't say I'm surprised. It's a tiny village down near Penzance, which barely warrants a mention on the map. Population just over a thousand—on the High Street you'll find a post office, a few shops, and a pub. That's it. Its only real appeal is the medieval chapel there and access to a stone circle further up the valley. The tourists pass the turning to Banathel on their way to Marazion and Praa Sands for their cream teas and don't pay it any mind."

"I thought you wanted to talk about ghosts."

"The paper had a call last week from a man called Paul Webber. He's worried about his teenage daughter, Alice. More than that. He's frightened. You see, just after Christmas, Alice Webber started to get sick. She complained of pains in her sides like needles being pressed there. When they lifted her shirt, there was a pinprick rash and blood welling up as if the skin had been broken. A few days later she started vomiting. By this point Alice was too weak to get out of bed so her mother put a bowl beside it. When she came to empty it, she found watery bile and clots of black hair, like you'd pull out of a plughole. Another time Alice coughed up a handful of sewing pins bent into strange shapes.

She developed a fever which made her start seeing things. She got delusional."

"In what way?"

"Alice told her parents that a witch was spying on her through the chimney breast. She said the witch had a black tongue and her face was 'all on upside down.' Alice shares a room with her younger sister, Tamsin. Their beds are either side of an old fireplace and Lisa—that's their mother—started finding dead wasps in the grate and on Alice's pillow. They think there must have been some sort of colony in the chimney because Alice said at night she heard buzzing and tapping loud enough to keep her awake. After this had gone on for a month, Lisa took Alice to the doctor who declared her perfectly fit and well. Physically, at least. He said the buzzing and clicking she was hearing was likely tinnitus. Harmless but incurable. Nothing we can do, so sorry. Soon, the noises changed. Alice began hearing grunts and squeals which were almost piglike."

I didn't notice the way the time was slipping away from me, the hands of the clock inching toward three. I leaned forward, face flushed with expectation.

"Well? What was wrong with her?"

He puffed out his cheeks, laughing. I recognized it as an expression of bafflement, not good humor.

"No one knows. Alice was sent for more tests, this time at the hospital in Truro. They couldn't find any issues except that she was underweight and borderline anemic. She was prescribed sleeping pills and this appeared to help for a while."

"These tests you're talking about are all physical. Did she speak to any psychiatrists or neurologists?"

"They're on a waiting list, apparently. There's been talk of a brain scan but again, there's a wait."

"Maybe they're hoping your intervention will move them along quicker."

"Well, they'll be disappointed if that's the case. I *was* hoping, however, to be able to offer them access to a child psychologist—albeit a newly qualified one."

He looked at me meaningfully, not quite smiling.

"Me?"

"Why not? Alice needs the help and you need the experience. It's win-win as far as I can tell. Besides, who better to understand an adolescent brain than the woman who wrote a paper on it?"

I stared at him, open-mouthed. I'd come here expecting ghost stories, not this. Excitement ran through me like an eddy in water but I kept my voice steady, remained calm.

"Keep going."

He shrugged again.

"The fever and the vomiting went, after a fashion. But the clicking and buzzing and grunting—the animalistic sounds—they only got worse. Alice said she was most aware of it at night when the house was quiet. That's when the noises became something else."

He looked at me levelly with his pale brown eyes.

"A voice."

I turn the vase in my hands so the late-afternoon sunlight slides over the surface like liquid. Oscar is standing with his head tilted, waiting for me to speak. *"Tell me what the job is."*

"I met a journalist who's working on a story for *The Herald*. They need a child psychologist."

"So why have they asked you?"

A sting, but I hold his gaze. Oscar gives me a weak smile.

"You know what I mean. You've only just graduated. So go on, what kind of investigation is it?"

"It's working with a family, three young childre—"

"Bloody hell, Mina, *what* kind of investigation?"

"A haunting."

He snorts, shaking his head.

"There we are. There's the crux of it. No wonder you look embarrassed. How much are they paying you?"

Tap, tap. His fingernails on the kitchen counter. Impatient. I feel a flush of irritation.

"It's not about the money."

He barks a single, disbelieving laugh.

"They're not *paying* you?"

"That isn't what I said!"

"You don't need to. I can see very clearly what's happened here. You've been finagled. Someone has found a way to use your expertise for free by spinning you some yarn about a haunted house, haven't they? 'Research,' indeed. Goodness me."

He shakes his head, still laughing. My voice is strangled sounding. It's hard to swallow my frustration.

"You spend your life doing research, Oscar. I thought you'd understand how important it is."

"You know I had this conversation yesterday with Lucy. The work we're doing shapes the whole universe, Mina. Known *and* unknown. It's pivotal. Some would call it life changing."

"Would Lucy?"

I'm waspish, can't help myself. He sighs, as if he is suddenly weary.

"Would Lucy what?"

"Would she call it 'life changing'?"

I'm talking through gritted teeth, feeling conflicted and

sad and angry all at once. Then, I see it. The flicker of a smile on his face. This isn't the first time he's mentioned Lucy, the dark-haired undergrad who joined his laboratory in March. I've met her just once, at some austere party she threw last month. I'd worn a short dress and heels, my hair swept to one side. I copied the style from a magazine, which had called it "glamorous." I blotted myself with Opium perfume and wore the gold and pearl earrings my parents had given me for my twenty-first birthday. Oscar was nervous, pacing. Drinking a gin with ice, checking his watch. *"Finally!"* he said, when I walked in. When we arrived at Lucy's flat, it became clear the party was a gathering of other scientists, mostly older men in collarless shirts and tan slacks parlaying the same basic story about research funding back and forth to one another while everyone sipped warm wine. Someone asked me what time I was due on the set of *Dynasty* and Oscar laughed. Other than myself, he and Lucy were the two youngest people there by far. I got too drunk and had to leave early in a taxi, home by ten, feeling the redness creep up my neck, head spinning as I climbed into bed alone. Oscar came home in the early hours, creeping into the bedroom on socked feet. I pretended to be asleep. I am still pretending.

"Put these in the bin, would you?" Oscar is handing me the leaflets that came through the letter box with the post. "I'm sick of this junk mail. We should get a sign up. That's what they've got next door, have you seen? 'No cold callers, no circulars, et cetera.' That's what we need. Make a note to ask them where they got it."

A beat. The air is very hot and very still.

"Mina?"

"I'm going to do it, Oscar."

He leans in the doorway with his arms folded, a look of puzzled amusement on his face. Humoring me.

"You're not serious?"

"Yes, I am. I bloody am. I leave tomorrow."

"Okay, Mina. Okay. Let's just— Gosh, let's just have a drink, all right? Something nice and cold. It's this air, it's too humid. Did you know heat waves are linked to a rise in violent crime? You'd wonder who had the energy for it."

"Oscar, please. I want to talk about this. The train leaves at nine-thirty tomorrow morning and I intend to be on it."

"You won't find Eddie this way, Mina." His voice is so quiet and flat I almost mistake it for the hum of the fridge. "All this expectation. It will crush you."

"What do you mean?"

"You know bloody well what I mean." He sighs. "Look, I get it, Mina. I do. I know how much you miss your brother. I know how much you want to see him again, how tightly you hold on to the idea that he can somehow navigate back to you."

Tears spring into my eyes. The room blurs and then prisms into sharp little points of light. I turn and brush them away. Oscar is still talking.

"But this? You're looking for something that isn't there. You're just prolonging pain."

It hurts, and he can see it, and I know he's trying to be kind but oh, it hurts. I jump as his hand takes mine tenderly, standing so close I can smell the soap on his skin.

"You're in purgatory, Mina. Death by a thousand cuts."

Sam had asked my opinion. As a psychologist, he'd said. As a professional. I admit to having felt a small swell of pride, bright as a red balloon. I straightened up in that hard little chair. It felt good to be necessary.

"Well, it could be that Alice is suffering from some form of temporal lobe epilepsy. That would go some way to explaining some of the states you described—hearing voices, visual disturbances. Or there could be more to it—a tumor maybe? I read once about a man who suddenly woke up only able to speak German. It turned out he had a pea-sized tumor pressing against his pituitary gland. Then you've got any number of psychotic disorders that can cause these symptoms, she'd need to be assessed properly for those. As for the vomiting, you know what pica is?"

Sam shook his head. I took a quick glance at my watch. It was almost quarter to three. I could still make it to the caterers if I left soon.

"Pica is a compulsive eating disorder in which people eat nonfood items—clay, dirt, even soap. It's very common for people with anemia to do this—it's the body's response to a nutritional deficiency. It might explain the hair and the pins, though again, this is just my opinion, and I'm not a doctor. This vomiting, did anyone actually see her do it?"

"No. Her mother just collected the bowl."

"So Alice could have put the pins and hair into it herself, right?"

Sam frowned.

"I guess."

"You're taking a lot of this at face value," I told him, stirring the ice in my glass with a straw. "Aren't reporters supposed to be cynical?"

"There's a story here, Mina, I'm just not sure what type it is yet. It's my job to find out."

I nodded. Sam's voice was strained and it looked as though he hadn't been sleeping, eyes ringed with dark shadows. Besides, I thought, was what he was telling me any crazier than seeing a ghost in a photograph?

"So you think she's faking?" Sam asked. He tapped his cigarette into the ashtray.

"I didn't say that, but yes, that's the assumption I'd start from."

"But it's not normal teenage behavior?"

"There's no such thing as normal teenage behavior."

"You'd need to see her to be sure, wouldn't you? Face-to-face?"

I nodded.

"Yes. Absolutely."

"What about the hallucinations? Could they be linked to this—uh, anemia?"

"Unlikely. But it's been so hot lately—could be dehydration, heatstroke? Even something like carbon monoxide poisoning would cause some of the behavior you're describing, although the whole family would be affected if that was the case. How is she in school?"

"She's been taken out of school. In September she's due to study hairdressing at the local college."

"Ah, okay. What's her homelife like?"

"I mean, I can only go on first impressions but there are five of them living there. Dad works in a factory, Mum's a housewife. There are two young children under ten and a teenage girl. It's hectic. They live in a small, terraced house, council owned, like the others around it. It's a close-knit community, but there's poverty and an air of dissatisfaction with the government and life in general. Unemployment in the whole county is high."

We both fell silent. My glass was empty, the ice melting into miniature floes. Outside, a man was shouting in a hoarse, cracked voice, "She said she could swim! I threw her *in*!" over and over. The heat was sending us all mad, I thought. I checked my watch again. I had to go.

"I hope that's helped you, Sam. For what it's worth, you asked for my opinion so I'm going to give it to you. I think whatever is happening to Alice Webber doesn't have roots in the supernatural. I think it's environmental, almost certainly physical. Something as mundane as hormones, even. If you're considering turning this into a story, I would ask that you go easy on her, huh? I remember how it is to be a teenage girl—I was one myself not long ago—and it's tough. Okay?"

"Sure. Okay."

I stood up, but I didn't leave right away. I studied Sam carefully. There was a blot of color high in each of his cheeks and, when he shook my hand, he didn't quite meet my eye. I wondered why I was not moving out the door and into that bright sunshine, why I was not already calling a cab to an important appointment that I was dangerously close to missing.

"There's more, isn't there? Sam?"

"You'll miss your appointment."

It felt as though someone was squeezing my ribs, making it difficult to draw a breath.

"Sam?"

He sighed, pushing his hair away from his face.

"I was intrigued by this story when Paul told it to me. Last week I went down to Banathel and met Alice Webber and her family. I had low expectations and to be honest, Mina, I wasn't disappointed. Alice is a normal teenage girl, quiet and a bit sulky. Shy. Unremarkable, really. She didn't say much—her father did most of the talking. In the time I was present, I saw no evidence of a haunting or anything untoward. I taped some interviews with members of the family and then I drove home feeling disappointed. I almost didn't bother listening to the tape—it's about forty-five minutes from beginning to end, but I did. I did. And right at the end as I'm packing away there's a voice."

"Whose voice?"

"I don't know. We'd been using the girls' bedroom for interviews, as that's where most of the 'activity' was concentrated, according to Alice. When we were done, I started packing my things away, not thinking about much except how hot it was and the long drive home. By this point I was alone in the bedroom. The recorder picks up a lot of sounds, you can hear me breathing and moving around, zipping up my bag. It's just me in there, Mina. I'd swear it on my life. But when I played it back it's as if something came right up to it and whispered into the microphone."

A chill slipped down my back, breaking me out in gooseflesh. I leaned forward hungrily, caterers forgotten.

"What did it say?"

"You tell me."

He reached into his bag and pulled out a slim black box, plastic and chrome. At first I thought it was a camera but I realized as he passed it to me that I was mistaken. It was a Dictaphone. Sam also passed me a pair of headphones, his face set.

"Play it, Mina."

At first there was nothing but the sound of the mechanism whirring, a hiss of static from the small speaker. I turned the Dictaphone over and found the volume dial, turning it with the pad of my thumb until the hiss became a roar. I pressed the headphones close to my ears, heart quickening, tongue dry and heavy as sand. There was a rustling, voices growing distant as if in another part of the house, walking away. Silence. The hiss and click of the tape. Then, something bled through, distorted. Something with a throatful of splinters.

"Good riddance!"

I dashed the Dictaphone away from me in one deft swipe, whole body stiff with alarm. It hit the ground with a crunch as the plastic casing split. The waitress turned toward the sound, eyes wide. My mouth was working over and over but no words were coming out, and Sam was reaching for me and saying what is it, Mina, what's wrong and all I could think was *tell me about the ice, tell me about the ice.*

FOUR

The parish of Banathel lies in a valley of rich purple heather and high hedges of hawthorn, heavy with bees. Sam drives slowly along the narrow one-way street bordered by a handful of small shops; a café, a newsagent, a butcher with the blinds drawn against the sun. There is a row of granite cottages opposite a pub with tables outside on the cobbled stones. It's pretty, but run-down. Sam had mentioned Banathel was a poor town in a poor county—a result of the closing of the mines and china clay pits—and here and there I start to notice empty shops and houses with newspaper taped over the windows, CLOSED signs in doorways. I notice something else, too, as we make our way through the village—stacks of pebbles with holes worn right through them, strung on beads and ropes and string and hanging in doorways.

"What are the stones for?"

"What stones?"

"The ones with the holes. Outside the houses? Haven't you seen them?"

I point as we pass a small cottage with a recessed doorway. A large iron nail has been hammered into the brickwork from which hangs a cluster of lumpy, misshapen pebbles in grays and blacks and creamy whites.

Sam pulls down the sun visor and smiles at me.

"You know, when I was a kid, my granddad in Yorkshire had a stone hung outside his kitchen window. He told me it was his weather forecaster. When I asked him how it worked, he said, 'If the stone's wet, it's raining. If it's swinging, it's windy. If you can't see it, it's foggy.'"

I laugh, turning back to the window. The newspaper that morning had been full of the weather; sunburn and ozone and a packed Blackpool beach, fears of food shortages, roads buckling in the soaring temperatures. Sam collected me from Penzance station in his old maroon car with the pine freshener hanging from the mirror. We made polite small talk on the drive toward Banathel, heading inland away from the glittering sea and the barking, listless gulls. I leaned out the window to taste the air: the shimmer of salt on my tongue; the softening tarmac; the smoky, parched heat. We drove through hedges of gorse studded with little yellow flowers and jostled over cattle grids and through a dry ford littered with pine needles, tarry with clay. Sometimes the lanes grew so narrow I could hear branches scraping the sides of the car, my skin freckled with sunspots in the flickering light.

We crest the rise of the hill where two roads intersect in a simple X, a signpost toward Prussia Cove to the right, an overgrown churchyard to the left. Sam indicates the left turning and as the car swings around, a small, dark shape darts out in front of us so quickly that I feel the jolt of my seat belt before I can even cry out. Sam stamps on the brakes and utters a single expletive, leaning over the steering wheel to better see the figure that charged into the road, now fleeing through the mottled stone archway of the churchyard beside us. We look at each other in disbelief.

"You saw that, right?" Sam is sweating, running his hand through his hair. "That little girl? She came out of nowhere!"

I nod, unbuckling my belt. Sam looks at me, frowning.

"What are you doing?"

"Making sure she's okay. Wait. I'll be two seconds."

Sam nods, almost panting in shock. He's reaching for his cigarettes before I've even closed the car door behind me. I cross the road in three short strides, ducking through the ivy-clad archway and into the churchyard of crooked, moss-covered gravestones, grass grown long and yellow underfoot. Beside the low wall separating the churchyard from the road, the young girl is crouching and aiming a gun at me, a small, red toy revolver. Spears of sunlight fall through the branches of the large, spreading yew beside her.

"Hey." I take a cautious step toward her, hands raised. "Don't shoot. I'm not armed."

She looks at me with such pantomimed suspicion that I almost laugh.

"I mustn't talk to strangers."

"Very wise," I tell her, crouching down. "Is your mum around? You're very young to be running around like that on your own. We nearly hit you."

She shakes her head solemnly.

"Mum's working."

"You got a babysitter? Anyone meant to be with you?"

She squints along the barrel of the revolver.

"Bert. But he's old and can't run as fast as me."

"Okay. We should probably get you back to him, huh?"

"My name's Stevie," the little girl says. "What's yours?"

"Mina."

"Now we're friends," Stevie says, before adding darkly, "so I s'ppose I mustn't shoot you."

She holds the gun up to my face and mimes pulling the trigger. "Pow," she whispers. I laugh. She's cute, with round cheeks flushed pink and hair as shiny as a chestnut, cut along her jaw. When she smiles, she is missing a front tooth.

"I was wondering, Stevie, do you know what all the funny-looking stones are for? The ones hanging outside the houses?"

"Hagstones." She sniffs noisily and wipes her nose on her sleeve leaving a silvery trail of snot. "To keep the witches out. Witches can *hurt* you."

"Good job you've got your pistol."

"It's not real. See?"

She pulls the trigger and there is a snapping sound and a little puff of smoke escapes the barrel. I'm instantly thrown into the memory of a Christmas morning, Eddie and I in our pajamas, hands trembling with excitement. He pulled a cap gun just like Stevie's from his stocking and when he fired it had smelled just like this: spent matches and a smidge of sulfur.

"All right, Annie Oakley, put it away," I hear a man's voice say. I turn to see a dark figure leaning over the churchyard wall, silhouetted against the sun. Stevie grins and pokes out her tongue, hightailing it around the corner and out of sight, trailing her laughter like ribbons. An older man with a bolt of gray hair extends a hand toward me. His eyes are a rich, marine blue which crease as he smiles.

"There are two types of people in this world." His voice is a rich baritone. "Those who are Cornish and those who wish they were. Which are you?"

"Well, I was born in Devon, so the second one I suppose."

"Well, then, you have my condolences. Next best thing to being Cornish is being here, so you're a step in the right direction."

He shakes my hand, his grip firm and steady.

"Bert Roscow. I'm guessing you're part of this circus on Beacon Terrace, aren't you? It'll be television cameras next."

I stare at him blankly. *Circus? Beacon Terrace?* I've no idea what he's talking about, so it is with some relief that I realize Sam has parked the car a little farther up the road and is walking toward us. Bert sees him and grunts, planting his big hands on the wall and leaning a little farther forward.

"I was just saying it'll be television cameras next!" Bert calls to him. His voice is loud but he doesn't seem angry, although it's hard to tell. I can't seem to place his age—his hair is white and his face netted with wrinkles—but he's sprightly and hale, well-dressed. Sam smiles at him, shaking his head as he speaks.

"I shouldn't think so, Bert. They're all too busy filming this weather, aren't they? Half an hour of it on the news last night. I almost lost the will to live."

"So you've come back for another go, have you?" the man asks. "You must think there's something in this story."

"I do, as it happens." Sam nods. "Public interest. Last year *The Herald* ran a story about a gray monk haunting the site of an old friary—pure fiction of course, with a few blurry snapshots— but our readership increased threefold and we got more post that week than we could manage. People came down from all over to visit the supposed Friars Walk behind the big Tesco."

"I meant about the girl. Alice. You think there's some truth to what they're saying?"

Sam laughs uneasily. I can't help feeling that he has been caught out somehow. Like a child pointing out to a magician that he can see the mechanism of the trick up his sleeve.

"You're asking if I think the house is haunted?"

"I'm wondering what could possibly have brought you here if you didn't. I'd hate to think you were pursuing a story without a thought for Alice's welfare."

"Ah," Sam says. "On that note, let me introduce you to Mina Ellis. She's a child psychologist and she'll be assessing Alice to see if there isn't some more, uh, fundamental problems at hand. Mina, this is Bert. He lives next door to the Webbers."

"Number Twelve," Bert tells me, eyes twinkling. "Me and my wife, Mary, the light of my dreary old life. We both watched Alice grow up and she never gave us a jot of bother. Seems like one minute she was playing with her dolls under the kitchen table and now I'm being told she's a high priestess who can communicate with the dead. I told her, I said, 'Alice if you're in touch with the spirit realm, speak to my brother and ask him where he put the keys to his bloody garden shed.'" He laughs, looking from me to Sam and back again. "I'm sure I'm showing my age here but who was it who said ghosts were a product of digestion? 'A blot of mustard, a crumb of cheese—there's more of gravy than the grave about you,' something like that?"

"Dickens," Sam says, lighting his roll-up. "It's from *A Christmas Carol.*"

"That's right! Good man. Good man."

A little way behind him I see the young girl again, holding her gun against her hip. Stevie is watching us cautiously and when I smile at her she dashes behind a gravestone in the shape of a Celtic cross. Before I know it Bert is shaking my hand warmly and saying, "Well, whatever's going on in there, I hope you both get to the bottom of it. Give us a knock if you need anything and you can meet Mary, if she's having a good day."

As Sam and I walk back to the car he calls after us, "You know I used to be in the newspaper business myself, Sam—might be able to give you some tips!"

"What was all that about a circus?" I ask Sam who frowns and shrugs.

"Not a clue," he tells me.

FIVE

Outside 13 Beacon Terrace a knot of people are standing, sweltering in the heat. Their shadows spill over the pavement and pool in the road like melted tar. Sam pulls my suitcase from the car, faking his shoulder giving way with the weight of it. We both laugh politely.

"Who are they?" I ask, nodding toward the group ahead.

"Huh. Don't know. They weren't there last week."

I notice he has unbuttoned his shirt a little and catch a glimpse of damp skin and wiry coils of chest hair. He removes his sunglasses and fixes me with a stare.

"Last chance," he says.

"For what?"

"To back out. There's a train heading back to Plymouth in an hour. I'll make your excuses—I can tell them you got sick."

"Why would I want to do that?"

"I don't know. Maybe you're having second thoughts. Maybe you're scared but you're too proud to tell me."

"Oscar always says it's not the dead we ought to be afraid of, it's the living."

He smiles thoughtfully, extending a hand for me to walk ahead of him.

"Okay, Mina. Okay."

I'm wary of the crowd—there is a strange, glimmering energy coming off them—not excitement exactly, but close to it, just beneath the surface. Feverish, maybe. A few heads turn as we approach and a voice floats out of the small mass, "It's the reporter again, look." Questions bubble, their voices low and suspicious. They part, but only a little, so we're forced to squeeze through. An elderly woman in a sun hat and hard white shoes steps forward, one heavily knuckled finger floating up toward me and stabbing me in the chest hard enough to make me stumble backward.

"I see fires on the horizon," she says, mouth twisting with the words. "They're burning red!"

A tall man squeezes close to me, his bony hip pressing into my waist.

"Can she find Donald? Ask her to look for him. Please! Ask her."

"Sam?" I say weakly, as the crowd tightens about me. The tall man presses something into my hand. "Please," he persists. A boy on a BMX is performing bunny hops down the road, his mouth sliced into a grin. He calls something out, I don't quite hear it but heads turn toward him and he laughs nastily. The weight of bodies against me is suffocating.

"Sam!" I say again more sharply, feeling a wave of dizziness lift from the base of my skull. I think I can hear Sam's voice saying "Hey, cut it out," but it's overlapped by the press of a body in front of me, musty breath in my face.

"You need to salt the ground," the man says, towering over me. He must be at least six foot seven, long limbs, stubbled jaw. His eyes protrude from their sockets in a way that show the whites all around. "You need to protect yourselves. Rosemary and hemlock!"

He has a handful of something that he scatters in front of me. I don't look down, I don't stop. I push past him and fumble the latch of the little wooden gate. The sun beats down on the tops of our heads like a fiery halo. I can feel my scalp contract with the heat of it. The gate opens and I stumble through it into a yard of scrubby concrete. A potted plant outside the front door is brown and wizened and long dead. Beside it, molten stumps of candles have been left next to a small wreath of bay leaves. There is a teddy bear slumped between them. It reminds me of accident sites, the tributes that appear there. I hear Sam behind me, voice raised as he follows me through the gate and latches it against the press of bodies.

"Behave yourselves! Jesus!"

"You didn't warn me about this," I snap, turning away from the rash of faces hovering, open-mouthed and bulbous eyed like a shoal of hungry fish. "Who are these people?"

"I don't know, Mina. Honestly. They weren't here last week."

I look down at what has been placed in my hand. A dog collar of faded green leather. The little brass disc on it reads *Donald*. Sam is knocking on the front door, flushed with urgency. I risk another glance behind at the people milling by the gate, their glassy eyes fixed at the house. It's only a small group—a dozen maybe, it barely constitutes a crowd—but that strange aura ra-

diating from them is a voltage slowly increasing. The weight of
their expectation makes my skin itch.

The door is opened by a young boy—Billy, it has to be—
wearing a pair of tracksuit bottoms. No top. His skinny ribs
press against pale skin. There is a graze on one of his elbows,
another on his chin. He looks from me to Sam and his expression
of irritation and annoyance dissolves. He grins, rubbing a hand
over his shorn head.

"Sam! My man!"

"That's right, Billy-boy. Are your parents home?"

"Mum is. Dad's at work."

He looks up at me, face twisted in thought.

"This her?"

"This is her, Billy. Can we come in? You've got a mob out here."

Billy runs off yelling and Sam steps aside so I can enter the
house first. Indoors it's gloomy, all the curtains drawn against the
prying eyes outside. The hallway smells like the ghosts of cooking;
of boiling and roasting and frying, spitting oil, burned fat. Charred
skin. Underfoot, the carpet is a sickly yellow color, thin and scuffed.

"Hi. It's Mina, isn't it?"

A woman appears in the doorway to my right. She is lean
and pale looking, her voice hoarse.

"That's right. You must be Mrs. Webber."

"Lisa, please. Mrs. Webber makes me feel so *old.*"

I take her in: a stony face that could seem cruel in the wrong
light, shoulder-length hair, a tight smile that doesn't quite touch
her eyes. Her gaze darts over me.

"They still out front? We thought the heat would drive them
away."

"What's going on?" Sam asks, placing my bag at the bottom
of the stairs. "Who are these people?"

"Did you ever tell me where you were from, Sam?"

He hesitates as if anticipating a trap. Then, "Bristol."

"Ah. Well, then. Banathel is a very small town you see, and in small towns people talk. After your visit down here last week, word got round that Alice was going to be in the paper 'cos she could speak with dead folk. We had a lad knock to see if she could ask the ghosts where his bike was. Said it got nicked last week and his mum was going mad. Paul sent him off with a flea in his ear but by midday half the county were on about it. Next morning a few people pitched up outside. Then a few more the day after that and the next day even more."

"Herd mentality," I say. Lisa frowns.

"Some of them drive over every day from Bodmin in a minivan. Some church or other, I don't know. They don't want to talk to me. Just her. Yesterday they started leaving stuff out there. I clear it away but they put it back. They light candles but they're just melting in the sun. *And* they keep putting things through the bloody letter box. We've had to tape it up!"

"What kind of things?"

"Little notes, photographs. They're all wanting something. They seem to think Alice can perform miracles."

I look down at the dog collar the tall man had passed me. *"Can she find Donald?"* he asked.

"Come through," Lisa is saying. "I'm afraid we've only got juice or milk but I can put the kettle on?"

"Tea's fine."

I follow Lisa down the hallway and into the cramped kitchen. There is a pile of washing in a plastic basket, a puddle of brown water beneath the sink. Lisa disappears into the pantry and reappears with a biscuit tin. She levers it open and holds it out to me.

"Go on," she urges, almost whispering. "That lad of mine will have heard that lid come off from a mile away. They'll be nothing left soon."

"They eating you out of house and home, Lisa?" Sam asks, pulling his cigarettes from his pocket. Lisa smiles tightly.

"It's the summer holidays. I don't know how we'll get through it. They're a plague of locusts, my kids. Roll on September. They'll be the school's problem, then. Oh, here he is. Couldn't hear me calling him through for a bath last night but no problem hearing the lid come off the biscuit tin, ay?"

She scruffs Billy's neck affectionately as he runs into the room, diving his hand into the tin and pulling out a handful of custard creams, laughing and ducking and running away. Sam watches him, then turns back to Lisa who puts the tin on the middle of the table and fills the kettle. The pipes rattle noisily.

"Are the girls here, Lisa?"

She nods, wiping her hands on her apron. Lisa Webber is only nine years my senior but she moves slowly and her face is netted with lines. *She's tired,* I remind myself. *She has three kids. You'd be tired, too.* But it isn't just that. It's a weight, a gravity. Like something is dragging her down. I hear her spine creak as she reaches for the tea caddy, the sigh as she bends to the fridge. I wonder if she is ill. Arthritis maybe.

"Tamsin's upstairs doodling. Alice, she's outside sunbathing. She'll look like a leather handbag in ten years if she keeps it up but there's no telling her. I suppose I ought to be grateful she's leaving the house at all after— well, after the last few weeks."

She takes the cigarette Sam offers and sits opposite me at the dining table. It is Formica, like the one my parents have. I dig my finger into the blackened crater of a burn mark in the plastic, feeling awkward and out of sorts. Lisa blows a plume of smoke toward the putty-colored ceiling and looks askance at me.

"He's told you, has he? What's going on."

I nod. She smiles.

"I know it must seem mad. Paul said—that's my husband—Paul said maybe the heat is melting all our brains."

I'm suddenly reminded of the man outside the cafe shouting *"She said she could swim! I threw her in!"* in his hoarse voice. Maybe Paul's got that right, I think. Lisa leans back on her chair and opens a drawer in the dresser, rummaging through it, her cigarette clasped between her fingers. Smoke uncoils toward the water-stained ceiling.

"Here you are." She pulls out a small wad of papers and places them in front of me. They are bound together with an elastic band. "That's what we've had to put up with. We didn't ask for none of this, you know. We just wanted someone to listen to us about our little girl."

I slide the elastic off and sift through the pile. There are old photographs, some in grainy black and white; wedding pictures, children, dogs. A folded newspaper clipping shows a young man astride a motorbike, helmet in hand, grinning. The headline reads DEATH-TRAP CORNER CLAIMS ANOTHER LIFE.

"That's Patrick Trevail. He died last summer. Him and his bike went right under a lorry. His poor mother. I've heard she collapsed at the funeral. He was her only child."

"It's heartbreaking," I say, opening up a folded scrap of paper. It has a series of letters and numbers and below it one word printed in ink. *Kittiwake.*

"Far as we can tell it's a boat," Lisa says. "Those numbers

along the top are nautical coordinates. Paul said there was a *Kittiwake* lost in the fog down by Mousehole but that was over a hundred years ago."

"All these people," I say, more to myself than anything. Babies in christening gowns, a man in a hospital bed with his head bandaged, a woman lying on a beach and laughing, her face tilted toward the sky. *Linda, Algarve, '78* is written on the back in a sweeping hand. Among it all is a star-shaped medal on a striped and faded ribbon.

"That's a Burma Star from the Second World War." Sam sifts through the pile, picking it up and holding it to the light. "What you've got here Lisa are psychometry tokens."

"They're what?" Lisa snorts, but I think I might already know. I remember when Sam told me about his visit to the psychic; she had asked for something of Maggie's in order to make contact.

"It's an object belonging to or representing someone who has passed on," I offer, and Sam nods. "Apparently it can help to make contact with them."

"Well, someone needs to tell them it isn't going to work," Lisa says crossly, crushing her cigarette out in the ashtray. "It's just taking up space in my bloody drawer."

"Why do they think she can speak to the dead, Lisa?"

Lisa frowns, thinking. Two bright spots of color burn high in her cheeks.

"She was saying such odd things. At school, then here at home. Sometimes it was like she was listening to music you couldn't hear, you know? I'd catch her just staring at the fireplace and her lips were moving but no sound was coming out. When I asked her what she was doing, she said"—here Lisa sighs, fretful and ill at ease. It's clear she isn't comfortable talking about this— "she said that the dead wanted her to open her throat."

Sam casts me a brief, concerned look. Lisa waves smoke away from her face and gives a tired, dry laugh.

"One of the specialists at the hospital mentioned schizophrenia. All this hearing voices and that. It's frightened me to death. Then there's all the other stuff."

"What other stuff?"

At that moment the back door opens and a tall girl with wavy hair the same muddy blond as her mother walks in.

"Alice." Lisa gestures toward her. "Come and meet our guests."

I'm not sure what I'd been expecting but the Alice I'd pictured in my head had been willowy and slender and goth-looking, face a pale slice between two long veils of black hair. I'm almost embarrassed at how far off the mark I am. Alice is blond and tanned, wearing shorts and a T-shirt printed with the words POBODY'S NERFECT! tied at her midriff. Her small, rounded belly is just visible over the waistband of her cutoffs, legs long and coltish. She's the girl you see giggling with her friends at the back of the bus or fooling around in the arcades. Normal. Unexceptional. I'm almost disappointed. How can this be the haunted young girl Sam and Lisa have been describing?

Alice walks barefoot to the fridge and opens the door, crouching down to peer inside. I can hear the tinny sound of music through her headphones.

"Hi, Alice," I say. "My name is Mina Ellis. I'm hoping we'll have the chance to get to know one another while I'm here."

Nothing. She pulls out a carton of orange juice.

"Alice!" Lisa snaps.

Alice looks over at us dumbly. She slowly removes the headphones. I notice she has a wad of chewing gum stuck to one finger, which she eases back into her mouth.

"What?"

"This is Mina. She wants to talk to you."

Alice takes three quick gulps from the carton. She looks at me with a slow, sly smile and just for a moment I wonder if maybe there *is* something about her after all, some strangeness baked into her like clay. It's in the curve of her smile, that quick flash of teeth. Like something is hiding there under the surface. I tell myself to get a grip. It's the heat. All those stories Sam told me, they're getting to me. I turn toward her in my seat, unfolding my arms. I smile to show her I'm not a threat.

"We have something in common, Alice."

"What's that, then?"

"Our names. They're both from books."

I keep smiling, even as she slides her headphones back up again, gaze lingering on me for a moment. Her gum snaps between her teeth as she walks back out through the open doorway without another word. "I'm sorry," Lisa says evenly. "It's that age, I'm afraid. She's got worse since the sickness started. I used to get rotten headaches that seemed to last for days at her age and now it looks as though I've passed them on to her. What shitty luck. Do you have any children, Mina?"

I shake my head.

"One day, maybe. I'm getting married later this year." I hold up my hand so she can see the engagement ring on my finger. Lisa coos, leaning toward me to better see it.

"A winter wedding? How lovely. How long have you been with—?"

"Oscar. Uh, about three years. Engaged for one. I met him at university."

I actually met Oscar in the student union. I was drunk, he was sober, and he escorted me back to my room on campus, making no attempt to kiss me, even when I desperately leaned in for it. Older than me by ten years, he was a mature student with a degree in physics who had just received a grant to begin research into zodiacal dust clouds. When he finally asked me out a week later, we drove to the coast to watch a meteor shower up on the cold, windswept cliffs. With his frank, open gaze and his surety, so certain in himself—in *us*—Oscar was unlike the other people I'd dated, other students, boys my own age with empty wallets and heavy, probing tongues in my mouth. He drove an Austin Metro with an interior of bright paprika orange and took me to the observatory at Herstmonceux and for dinners in Rye and Bath, places rich in history. I took my first foreign holidays with Oscar, visiting Gothic abbeys in France and Germany and the ghostly ruins of Pompeii. While all my peers were listening to the Eurythmics and Gary Numan, Oscar introduced me to the Carpenters and Joni Mitchell who sang that we are stardust, billion-year-old carbon.

"Whatever you have has to be better than mine and Paul's wedding." Lisa laughs, interrupting my thoughts. "Me, eight months pregnant and wearing one of Mum's old dancing dresses with taffeta frills and the number seventy-nine pinned to my back. The registrar getting my name wrong, calling me Laura. I thought Paul was going to run out halfway through, just right on out into the road and keep going, never mind the flippin' traffic."

I nod, suddenly wrung out and homesick. The heat, this unfamiliar house, those strange people outside the front door—I have a frightening feeling that I have made a terrible mistake coming here. *Should've listened to Oscar,* I tell myself sternly.

"Why don't you take your things upstairs, Mina? We've put

you in Billy's room at the front. He's in with us. The girls share the room next door. Sam, I'm afraid you're on the sofa. It's a bit of a squeeze but we'll manage."

"Thank you," I say, as another wave of that homesickness washes over me. "You're very kind."

SIX

Upstairs I find myself in a gloomy hallway with scuffed skirting boards and faded floral wallpaper. At one end, a doorway leading into the small bathroom with a mustard-yellow bathtub and a narrow window of frosted glass, the upper corner gaffer-taped where a crack runs through it. At the other, Billy's room. It's a box room, small and dark and stuffy, with a narrow bed pushed against a wall covered in posters of footballers and racing cars, the wallpaper scraped away in long, curling strips. I unfasten my suitcase and lift out my washbag, putting it carefully on the bed. Inside it is the small package the doctor gave me the previous day. I hadn't told Oscar about the doctor's appointment. It hadn't gone on the calendar, or in the notepad next to the phone. I'd kept it a secret, barely believing I would be brave enough to attend, even as I'd stood outside the surgery in the sweltering heat, my heart palpitating. "I had a pregnancy scare," I told the doctor, knitting my fingers between my knees and leaning forward on the leatherette chair, "and I really ju— I *can't*. Do you understand that? I *can't* be pregnant, not now."

The doctor looked at me sympathetically, eyes dropping briefly to my engagement ring. She did not ask me any further questions as she filled out a prescription for the pill, and I was relieved. After all, how could I explain that the thought of having a baby with the man I am due to marry fills me with anxiety? That the idea of Oscar being a father—cautious, dutiful, resigned—makes me feel cold with a dread which I can't name and daren't examine, afraid of what it might mean? Instead I silently carried the little white box home from the chemist wrapped in a scarf and hidden in the bottom of my handbag. After all, if you're careful, you're safe, right? I turn back to my case and push aside the folded clothes, reaching into the small inner pocket. I pull out the photograph, carefully and reverently folded, the one taken in a restaurant in Crete with my brother in the background, appearing just over my shoulder. I study it, pressing my fingers gently to Eddie's form. A psychometry token of my own, I think.

"That your husband?"

I jolt, looking up to see a young girl in the doorway. She is barefoot, pressing her toes deep into the carpet. With her denim cutoffs and wheat-colored hair, she's a miniature version of Alice, only she has a frank, open gaze and a curiosity I hadn't seen in her older sister.

"No, it's my brother. You must be Tamsin." I quickly fold the photograph away. "You gave me a fright."

"You're in Billy's room. Poor you. He farts like mad." She covers her mouth to hide a muffled laugh.

"Oh dear. But I think he's sleeping with your mum and dad, so I should be safe. Do you share a room with your sister?"

She nods, chewing one of her fingernails. A soft toy hangs over her forearm, limbs dangling.

"That must be nice. I used to share a room with my brother when we were younger."

"Alice hates it. Said she can't wait to leave home."

I study her. All three of the Webber children have a confidence I never had as a child; a willingness to look adults in the eye without fear of their scrutiny. It's slightly disturbing. I've always assumed most children had been whittled into quiet obedience like Eddie and I had. It's a shock.

Tamsin steps right into the room. It's only small, and she is suddenly very close to me, enough that I can smell her breath, slightly sour. She looks around her with unconcealed distaste for her brother's toys and clutter. She hooks her hands into her pockets, one leg wrapping around the other like a yogi.

"You're here because there's something wrong with Alice. Aren't you?"

"Yes. But that's not quite—"

"Will we be in the newspaper?"

"It's not up to me, Tamsin. We'll have to see what happens."

"Huh." She loses interest then, reaching for one of Billy's toy cars. She spins the wheels of it with the palm of her hand. Her nose wrinkles. "I don't like this room. It's too small. My dad says when we get our new house we can have a bedroom *each* and I'm going to get a cat of my very own."

"Is that right?"

"Yeah. We'll have enough room for a pinball machine and a pool table, he says. Mum said she wants a tumble dryer with lots of different settings. Will you come live with us, too? You won't have to sleep in Billy's disgusting old room neither."

"Well, I'll be married by then, Tamsin, so I think I'll need to live with my husband."

"He can come, too, if he wants."

She's grinning, excited. I'm surprised. What has happened to Alice so far sounds quite traumatic, although it's possible their parents have shielded Tamsin from the worst of it. Still, though, I expected fear, concern at the very least.

"But won't you be sad to leave here? This is your home, after all."

She looks up at me and holds my gaze.

"Nuh-uh. This town is scary."

"Okay, Tamsin, that'll do." It's Lisa, coming up the stairs, a pile of laundry in her arms. "Let the poor woman unpack."

Tamsin lingers a moment longer in the doorway, perhaps waiting for me to say something, to contradict her mother maybe. *No, it's all right, let her stay.* When I don't, she slowly lifts up her hand and waves goodbye to me. I wave back.

"She'll talk the hind legs off a donkey, that one," Lisa says as Tamsin heads for the stairs, trailing her hand along the wall. "Do you think you'll be all right in here, Mina? It's a bit cramped."

"Oh yes, I will. This is so kind of you. Thank you."

"No, thank *you*. Coming all the way down here, giving up your time. Here." She holds up a silver mortise key, sliding it into the lock on the bedroom door. "We tend to hide these away from the kids; otherwise they're a nightmare for locking each other either into or out of their rooms, but we thought you might find it useful for privacy. I know it must be a bit of a shock for you coming into this madhouse."

I start to protest and she gives me a sympathetic smile.

"Don't worry, Mina. I realize how it must seem to you, all this. I don't know how much Sam's told you but I'm really hoping you might be able to give us some answers about Alice. We've all been worried sick."

"He mentioned you've pulled her out of school."

"We had to, Mina. We didn't have a choice. The things she was saying were scaring people—not just other kids, teachers, too. It got to the point where she had to be isolated at lunchtimes. No one would sit next to her in class."

Her voice is quiet and slightly strained. She plucks nervously at the pile of laundry with her fingers, unable to meet my eye.

"I'm so sorry that was her experience. Adolescent mental health is something I'm really interested in, especially how it—" Lisa interrupts me by laughing softly and I tail off, confused.

"What?"

"Sorry, it's just—'mental health.' Like Alice has got a broken brain or something." I nod, and give Lisa a reassuring smile. I've been expecting this defensiveness, this disbelief. "Mental health" is a frightening term if you're unfamiliar with it outside a clinical environment, seeming to conjure up images of a brain which is diseased or defective. I match the tone of my voice to hers, lean closer.

"It's just a term to describe any number of conditions."

"You know, I was always told there was a history of mental illness on my mother's side because my great-grandmother found herself in St. Lawrence's but it turns out she wasn't mad, she was just poor. You know that used to happen a lot? Women being sent away to institutions for not having children, not wanting to get married or for having too little money? Makes me wonder if people would still like things to be that way."

I speak carefully, can feel her agitation.

"I didn't mean to suggest that Alice needs to be locked away."

"It's like already you've decided there's something wrong with her. In the head, I mean."

"Listen, Lisa—I'm here because Sam asked me to come and assess Alice from a psychological point of view. It's my job to determine what's underpinning her behavior and there are tests and methods I can use to do that. I don't have any preconceptions about what this is."

Lisa looks past me out the window. Downstairs, the front door slams and a male voice calls out. Immediately Tamsin flies out her bedroom yelling, "Dadd-eee!" and Billy's feet clatter up the hallway. Lisa turns her head toward the noise.

"Ah!" she says, brightening. "Sounds like Paul's home. Every day this happens. He comes in, winds the little ones up, then wonders why they're too overexcited to sleep. Come on down and meet him when you're done."

I watch her leave, feeling hot and uncomfortable. Outside, the *whump whump whump* of helicopter blades passes overhead. They are dampening down the fields and heathland where the heather is dry as kindling and prone to sparking into quick, destructive flame.

SEVEN

It's a squeeze around the small dining table. Two folding chairs have been brought in from the garden to accommodate everyone. The children are eating fish-and-chips straight from the wrapping, Billy smeared with ketchup, barely chewing, grabbing fistfuls of chips with both hands, much to his mother's dismay. The room is high with the smell of vinegar and salt, the heat of so many bodies packed around the table. Paul, Lisa's husband, is short and dark and stocky, with a tanned, weathered face like scrunched-up brown paper. His hair is curly, coiling long at the back of his neck. With that and his mustache he reminds me of that boxer my father likes, Barry McGuigan. He is watchful, taking big gulps from a can of Coke between mouthfuls. The other Webbers, Lisa and the children, have been interested in me, even curious, but accepting of my presence. I don't get that feeling with Paul. There is a challenge in his eyes as he folds the paper back over the remains of his dinner and lights a cigarette, blowing the smoke out through flared nostrils. His gaze fixes on me.

"You're a psychologist?"

"That's right."

"You've just graduated, Sam said."

I nod. It feels as though his gaze is pinning me to my seat and I resist the urge to squirm.

"Yes."

He points his fork at Alice.

"Well? What's wrong with her?"

Alice flushes uncomfortably.

"That's not something I'm willing to discuss over dinner," I say. I try to give Alice a small, reassuring smile. Even though her headphones are looped around her neck, I can still hear the soft percussion of the music.

"She's good, is she?" Paul asks Sam as if I've suddenly left the room. "Knows what she's on about?"

"She does, Paul. Yes."

"You know the *Sunday Mirror* have been in touch?" Paul leans his chair back against the wall, watching Sam slowly chew his food. "They've said they think it'll make a great story. Maybe even front page."

"Good money, too, I'll bet," Sam answers. "You should consider it."

I feel a slight throb of tension and sense there's a power struggle going on, although I can't seem to work out the depth of it, not yet. Paul turns his gaze back to me.

"So. Mina. You're the one he's brought to try to catch us out, huh?"

I look from him to Sam, raising my eyebrows.

"He thinks you're trying to discredit their story," Sam says.

"Well, I wouldn't do so without reason," I tell Paul, smiling. I think of Lisa saying *"It's like already you've decided there's something wrong with her."*

Paul snorts, tipping his chair back onto two legs and scratching his underarm. He is skinny and leathery with muscle.

"You think it's tricks."

"I think it needs verifying."

"What's 'verifying'?" Tamsin asks.

"It means she doesn't believe us," Paul responds, eyes fixed on me.

"Give her a chance," Sam says, laughingly. "She's only been here two minutes."

"She's got a photo of her brother!" Tamsin says suddenly, bouncing in her chair. "I've seen it. You were looking at it earlier."

"I hope he's not as annoying as *our* brother," Alice sneers.

"Hey!" Billy protests.

"You got a picture of that fiancé of yours, Mina?" Lisa asks me, voice barely audible over the sound of Tamsin squealing as Billy kicks at her under the table.

"Not with me."

"How comes you carry a picture of your brother around with you but not your fiancé?" That's Alice, spearing a chip on her fork. "That's weird."

"I know it must be hard for you to believe, Alice, but in *some* families brothers and sisters can actually like each other," Lisa chides, putting an arm over Billy to stop him squirming out of his chair. It's so noisy in here I feel like covering my ears.

"Ewww, imagine carrying a picture of Billy around! Gross!"

Tamsin singsongs and Alice sniggers, even as Billy turns beet-red and starts yelling in protest.

"Are you going to marry your brother, Mina?"

"Do you put the picture under your pillow at night?"

That heat in me kindles, flames.

"I wouldn't even wipe my *arse* with Billy's photo."

"Hey!"

"He's dead," I say, flatly. The words fall out of my mouth like old stones. Silence falls heavily, and all eyes turn on me. I didn't mean to do it. I didn't mean to shock them. I'm just flustered. I'm not used to this noise, this press of bodies so close together, the smell of them, sour sweat and hot breath, suntan lotion. There's something else, too, a darker odor. Riper. It has a tang like old pennies. I'm not used to people talking over each other, biting off the ends of each other's sentences. It's just me and Oscar at home. "He died a long time ago. Nearly six years now."

"How old was he?" Tamsin says.

"Fourteen."

Gazes swivel toward Alice. It's jarring when you realize death doesn't just come for the aged or the sick. Alice shifts in her seat but doesn't look up. Her shoulders are sunburned, her nose and forehead turning a raw, burnished red. There is a ringing in my ears like static.

"I'm sorry, Mina. Your parents must have been heartbroken," Lisa says.

"They were. They are. Still, I mean." I notice Billy looking up at me with sad, round eyes. I force myself to smile. "Long time ago now. All in the past."

Paul's eyes are bright, hot coals sunk into snow. He points at Alice.

"She's had to leave that school, you know. We couldn't keep sending her in, not how she was. Talking gibberish, fainting in the toilets. That's not right, is it? She needs to be out with her friends, like I was at that age."

"Paul—" Lisa begins gently, but he shrugs her off, turning back to me.

"You reckon you can help her, then, do you?"

"I'll do my best," I tell him. He snorts, balling the fish-and-chip paper up in his hands.

"Well, I hope so. You look clever. Doesn't she look clever, Lisa? Could've sent us someone with a bit more on top, Sam, though, eh?"

As he cups his hands at the front of his chest and laughs, I flush, heat staining my skin a bright pink. Lisa tuts and glares at Paul.

"Ignore him," she tells me. "He was hoping you'd look like Sam Fox."

"She knows I'm only joking. Don't you?" He doesn't wait for me to answer. He crosses his arms and looks at Sam. "Do *you* think we're lying an' all?"

"It's irrelevant what I *think. The Herald* have sent me to find proof of a haunting, they don't want my opinion."

"But you must think it's a possibility, or you wouldn't have come back," Lisa says, her voice tremulous, hopeful. The room suddenly seems very quiet, very hot. Suffocating, almost. Through the back door the yard is dusky with a shimmering heat.

"I'm trying to keep an open mind, Lisa."

Paul looks at me, then back to Sam again, his lip slightly curled as if in distaste.

"You know I remember a while back reading about that

poltergeist in Enfield. That family had a whole team of ghost-hunters and experts come in to investigate the story. It was national news."

Sam laughs again. "Well, I'm afraid you're just stuck with me and Mina for now. If we find real evidence—that is, if we can establish an active haunting—you'll be in a better position to get the help you need."

Paul leans forward hungrily, elbows on the table. "What kind of help?"

Sam shrugs. "In the very worst case scenario, I've heard of people having the place exorcised or being moved from their homes."

"Dad—" Alice says, but Paul holds up his hand.

"What'll it take? For a worst case scenario?"

"We're a long way from that, Paul, don't worry." Sam brushes his hands together. He looks relaxed, almost insolent. He's still smiling, revealing those crooked teeth, slightly discolored.

I look over at Alice. Her hands hold the sides of her plate so tightly her knuckles turn white. She does not lift her head. Paul pitches his cigarette out in the sink. It hisses.

"Well, welcome to Beacon Terrace, Mina. Hope you brought your bell, book, and candle."

EIGHT

The house is quiet, the night air sticky and close to the skin like a hot, damp breath. Thin curtains hang lifeless in front of the open window as I climb into bed and lie there in the dark, hands folded on my chest. It's hard to fall asleep, my brain clicking and whirring and jolting like a broken clock. A little past one I must start to drift off because I'm woken what seems like seconds later by a sound outside the closed bedroom door.

I lie for a moment, half-conscious. It had sounded like scrabbling claws, pawing at the wood. I lie still, my mind turning to Eddie in an absent, somnolent way. The two of us in our old house in Clovelly, sitting on the beanbags in that sunlit spot of the attic that had always smelled a little like mothballs and damp. "Mouseshit Corner," Eddie had christened it, because we'd regularly find mice droppings up there no matter how many traps our mother put down. We'd take up our father's copy of *Mysteries of the British Isles* and pore over the stories about demons and ghosts in quiet, awed wonder. Eddie was particularly fond of Black Shuck, the legendary devil dog that prowled the dark Suffolk lanes with flaming red eyes, his appearance a portent of death and disease.

Then the noise comes again. It sounds like an animal is out there. A big dog, mouth laced with drool. Grunting, panting. Scratching at the wood. There is a wet snuffling sound along the bottom of the door like it is seeking ingress. Hunting me. I force my rigid muscles to move, hearing the click of my spine, the sharp, shallow breath in my lungs. I think of calling out for Sam but he's downstairs and I can't alert him without waking the whole house. My eyes fall on the key Lisa handed to me earlier. I didn't lock the door when I went to bed and now, seeing a large shadow briefly blot out the light in the gap along the bottom, I wish I had. I wonder if it's possible a stray dog has broken in somehow (*"Can she find Donald? Ask her to look for him. Please!"*) and as I edge slowly toward the door, I can't help feeling that whatever is out there is low to the ground, predatory. I hear that hoarse panting again, like an animal caught in a snare. Close-up, the sounds are heavier, more primitive. Porcine. It makes me think not of a dog but of a beast covered in wiry bristles with thick, ugly tusks that scrape along the floor.

I press a hand to the door and the movement seems to pause, as if sensing me. *It knows you're there, Mina,* some quiet, internal voice tells me. I take a short breath and then another. I am a statue, perfectly still. I wonder if it can hear how fast my heart is beating. Then I open the door.

The hallway is empty, the air still. In the darkness there is a static that lifts the hairs on the back of my neck and tightens my lungs. I stare into the gloom, eyes strained for movement, but no shadow darts across the hallway or peels away from the wall, no creeping hand clamps around my ankle. There's nothing there, I tell myself after a moment, closing the door and climbing back onto Billy's narrow, sagging mattress. Nothing there, silly.

Still, though. I lie awake a long time afterward, eyes peeled open in the dark, listening for the rattle of the doorknob or the quiet *click* of the latch as whatever I thought I heard out there finds a way in.

NINE

The next morning, I open the front door to find a middle-aged man standing at the gate. He has an arm missing, the empty shirtsleeve pinned to his chest. His face is hard and gnarled with knots of pink scar tissue that reach all the way to his hairline. He watches me as I step outside, the ground already warm beneath my feet. The crowd today is small, only a handful of people. But it will get bigger. Already it has the feel of something building. Pressure, like a storm. Incense sticks burn in the gaps between paving slabs. Someone is carrying a placard which reads GIVE THE DEAD THY TONGUE. The mood is somber, pale faces rubbing tired eyes. A woman in a flowered sundress lets her dog urinate against the gatepost. The dark stain spreads onto the pavement, steam rising into the air.

"What are you all doing here?" I ask them. "What do you want?"

The man with the placard watches me approach. His voice is very deep and has no inflection, his lips barely moving.

"We're here to see the girl. Bring her out so she can speak with us."

"Absolutely not."

"Is it true?" Another voice on my right. I turn toward it. It's the woman with the pissing dog. She looks me up and down, assessing me. "What they're saying about her."

"Depends what they're saying, I suppose."

"That she's got powers," the man with the placard says.

"You'll need to be more specific," I reply calmly.

"I've got a limp." That's another man, older and slightly twisted at the hip as if by polio. He leans on a stick. "I'm not able to work. Can she help me do you think? She's been telling me to come here and she'll heal me."

"I lost my wife in the crash." That's the man with one arm and scarred face. His eyes are a sketch of misery. "After the funeral her jewelry went missing and I think my son has took it and sold it. Will you give her this? I need to know what to do!"

He's holding something out to me but I don't reach for it. I don't want it. I think of all those psychometry tokens lying in the kitchen drawer with a feeling of such profound sadness I think I might start crying and never stop.

"This is madness," I tell them, staring around at them all. "Please, go home. She's a young girl, just a teenager. She's not special, she's just sick."

The woman with the dog narrows her gaze. She has beady eyes that gleam like sunlight on metal.

"Aren't you that reporter?"

"I'm not, no."

"You come here with him, though?"

"Yes."

"Why?" That's the man with the walking stick.

All their faces are looking at me expectantly, round and blank as moons. I swallow.

"I'm here to assess Alice."

"She's here for the same reasons we are," the woman says. The dog is panting, unfurling a long, pink tongue. She jerks the lead. "To see if all that they're saying is true."

I can't meet her eye because she's right, isn't she? That *is* why I'm here, with my photograph and my expectations and my fragile, beautiful *hope*. I told Oscar it was research and told Sam it was a learning experience, something to shore up my qualification—but underneath it all I'm just like these people, needing answers. I suddenly feel exactly as Oscar told me I would. Unprepared and overwhelmed.

Lisa opens the door for me. She casts a single disparaging look over the small crowd before ushering me inside.

"They've been out there since six o'clock," she says, bitterly. "One of them reckons Alice is sending him messages in his sleep. He's cut off bits of his hair and put them in an envelope."

She opens the little paper package to reveal twists of wiry, black hair. I flinch away, revolted.

"I dread opening these things when I find them on the doorstep, now. What will they send her next? Where does it stop? I don't know how much of this I can take, Mina. It's like living in a goldfish bowl. I've got to fight these weirdos just to get to the corner shop."

I attempt a sympathetic smile. Unmoved, she fixes me with her cool gray eyes.

"Honestly, Mina, what's happening to her? What if it's serious? What if there's something wrong with my little girl?"

Her voice cracks and her hand covers her mouth. I put an arm around her narrow shoulders, feeling her bony shoulders shudder as she stifles a sob. She hides her face against me, presumably so the younger children don't hear. I speak quietly when I say, "Lisa, whatever it is, I'll find out. I promise you. That's why I'm here."

"I know, I know." She sniffs loudly, taking a couple of long, deep inhales until her throat crackles. "I'm sorry. It's all this horrible business—the heat wave and Alice and now the phone's gone down and they're talking about power failures all over the country. I'm just so tired."

Sam appears in the kitchen doorway. His hair is damp as if he has just showered, a cup of coffee in his hand.

"They'll have to go inside soon. Legally, I mean. It's just been on the news."

"What has?"

"Curfew. They just announced it on the radio. We've all got to stay indoors between noon and four. Hottest hours of the day, apparently. The next few days, temperatures are going to soar, according to the weather."

Lisa and I exchange a wide-eyed glance as Sam continues, "If they stay out there all day they'll either be arrested or hospitalized with heatstroke. Either way, they'll be out of your hair."

I don't find the thought comforting. It makes me think of all those desperate people going to ground, waiting for dark to emerge again and collect in the shadows of the evening.

TEN

As Sam sets up the video camera in the sitting room to prepare for interviews with the other members of the Webber family, I find myself standing outside Alice's bedroom door. My mouth is tacky and dry with nerves, heart fluttering in my throat. I'm holding Sam's Dictaphone in my left hand, a notebook in my right. He wants everything documented, right down to the dreams we're having. I haven't yet told him about the noises outside my room last night or the dense, empty silence as I yanked the door suddenly open. I want to speak with Alice first.

I knock softly, and when there is no reply I gently push open Alice's bedroom door. I'm instantly struck by the same thick odor that I noticed last night at dinner—a coppery, mineral-rich smell, like sunless water in a still lake. It's stronger here, in this airless, gloomy room, and almost sweet like marzipan. Alice is sitting in bed, leaning against the headboard with a magazine on her knees. Her skin is burnished a dark and ugly red except in the places where her sunburn has started to peel; the bridge of her nose, her shoulders. Her hair is loose and unwashed and even though she smiles at me as I walk in I notice how tightly the tension is drawn on her features. She lowers her headphones and straightens up as I close the door behind me.

"What star sign are you?" she asks brightly.

"Sorry?"

"Your star sign, Mina. What is it?"

She indicates the magazine open in front of her. The curtains ripple slightly as I walk past them and lower myself onto the end of her bed.

"Um, Pisces I think. Why?"

She clears her throat and reads aloud.

"Your horoscope for July. 'Tough times call for tough measures, Pisces, and we all know how much you hate difficulty. A man with red hair will catch your eye but he could spell danger.'"

She lifts her eyes to meet mine, smiling slightly. "Woah. 'A man with red hair.' Spooky! Who do we know with red hair, I wonder?"

"Alice—" I keep my tone light, but the look I give her is firm.

She ignores me, practically curling her toes with pleasure at my discomfort. "I'm just saying." A beat. "Would you say Sam's hair is red, or just *auburn*?"

"Very funny. I'm engaged, remember?"

She's laughing, giggling almost.

"You must love your fiancé a lot to want to marry him."

"Of course."

"I bet you've got a beautiful house. Is he handsome? Oh, of course he is. You're so pretty."

"Your dad seems to think I could do with being prettier."

She licks her finger and turns the page of her magazine.

"You mustn't mind him. He always gets like this when he's on the killing floor."

Something about the way she says those words—"the killing floor"—so light and airy and distracted, it chills me to the bone.

"The what?"

"It's the part of the factory he works in. He says you need a strong stomach and a steady hand to put a bolt gun to a cow's head and pull the trigger. You can only work there a little bit at a time. Three days on, four days off. It does something to the brain otherwise. Something bad."

I study Alice carefully. She's still flicking through the magazine, touching the pad of her finger to her tongue. Her tone is so strange, almost as if she is on the cusp of laughter.

"The killing floor is where all the messy stuff happens. Blood and guts and stuff. He tells us stories sometimes. They're horrible, but he thinks they're funny. One day, one of the other workers put a cow's tongue in his lunch box and Dad laughed so hard he nearly passed out showing us. Mum says that the job has made him mean. That's why you shouldn't mind what he says to you. His jokes and that. He doesn't know he's doing it."

She searches my face with a perceptiveness that is almost uncanny, eyes glittering. I set Sam's Dictaphone on the mantelpiece, red light glowing, reels inside turning with a slow clicking sound.

"I'm going to be making some notes while we talk, Alice. It's just to help me remember our conversation."

"Sam said you were a psychologist."

"That's right. Do you know what that means?"

"I'm not stupid, Mina." She sniffs. "It means you think I'm crazy."

She's drawing into herself, pulling her knees toward her. Alice's voice has taken on a flat, weary affect as she pushes her magazine to one side and I realize she is already tired of having this conversation, of the focus being on her. I don't blame her. I give her a smile and close my notebook.

"You know, Alice, I happen to think you're very much sane."

"So what's happening to me, then?"

"Well sometimes the answers aren't always straightforward. It's why I'm here. To look at your homelife, your health, your friendships—all the things that shape you."

I smile encouragingly. Her knees are still drawn up to her chin but she's watching me from under her lashes and I take that as a good sign. She's interested.

"How have you been sleeping, Alice?"

"Not great. I have bad dreams."

"Can you tell me about them?"

She shrugs. "It sounds dumb."

"Thing is, Alice, dreams can sometimes be a tool to unlock a problem. Even the bad ones."

She thinks for a moment, her hands folded across her chest.

"Are you recording this?" she asks me. I nod, pointing toward the Dictaphone.

"It's just to help me remember the things we're talking about. I can stop if you want."

She doesn't answer, just looks down at her painted toenails.

"Can you tell me about the dreams?"

Alice shakes her head miserably, drawing her knees a little closer toward her.

"Alice?"

"I can't," she says quietly.

"Why?"

Silence. The whirr of the tape. Alice looks up at me and whispers, "She watches me through the cracks in the bricks. She's in there now. That's why we can't talk about this."

I nod, trying to keep my voice neutral. I'm not afraid, not yet, but there is a spidery sensation creeping up my back.

"Who is 'she,' Alice?"

Alice doesn't say a word. I try again.

"Is it the one you've talked about before? The witch with the upside-down face?"

"Yes," she murmurs. "She lives up in the chimney."

Alice stares straight ahead, her whole body practically vibrating with tension. I can feel the air thicken around us, dust motes shift into strange, twisting sigils.

"Your mother mentioned something to Sam about this. There was a wasp's nest found up there, wasn't there? Do you think that could have something to do with it?"

"I see her eyes in the holes."

"In the dream?"

Alice licks her lips. The soft, muggy heat of the day is rising, the sunlight slicing through the gap in the curtains a sickly orange color, like sodium lights. Sweat beads my brow and rolls down my collar. I uncross my legs, suddenly aware of how fast my heart is beating in the notch of my throat.

All the time, she mouths. Something about the way she says it makes my skin turn cold. She lifts a finger and points to a spot just behind my head. *Right there.*

I turn my head so slowly I can hear the tendons in my neck creak. There is old, faded wallpaper peeling away from the chimney breast. In the places where the paper has peeled away, there are small black gaps between the brickwork. I lean closer, teeth clenched against the feeling that my racing heart might just burst out of my throat, palms tingling. I stare into the narrow space.

What will you do if something looks back at you, Mina? That voice again, panicky. *If you see an eye gleaming in there in the dark?*

"I don't see anything," I tell Alice, pulling away with some relief. "I think this is probably one of those things we can chalk up to your brain playing tricks on you. It happens more often than you'd think."

Just then, the slightest sound, maybe just wind in the chimney, maybe a bird landing on the roof. I laugh uneasily but Alice doesn't smile.

"Am I going mad, Mina? Are they going to take me up Bodmin?"

"What's that?"

"It's the loony bin, only you don't call it that no more. They call it St. Lawrence's Community Hospital so it doesn't frighten people. It means the same thing though. It's where they lock up all the weirdos. Like me."

St. Lawrence's. Lisa had said her great-grandmother had been taken there, hadn't she?

"Do *you* think you're mad, Alice?"

The magazine slithers from her knees and onto the floor. I take her hand—God, her skin is still so *warm*, she must surely have a fever—and squeeze it gently. She looks at me, her eyes wide and wet.

"That's what hearing voices means, doesn't it? Everyone said so."

"Like who?"

She looks upward, toward a series of photographs tacked to the notice board that hangs over her bed. I move closer, leaning in to see the faces of this group of teens clowning around for the camera—there's Alice, long hair swept over her shoulder, sitting on the lap of a tall, brown-haired boy. There she is again, pouting in a bikini with a friend wearing mirrored sunglasses. There are several photos of Alice and what appears to be the same girl, hair coiled into tight little curls, skin pale. All freckles and teeth and neon bracelets. Bright young things.

"Who's this, Alice?"

"Vicky."

Her voice is dull, and she doesn't offer any further information. I lean closer to read the words scrawled on the bottoms of the photographs. *Best M8s 4 Ever!* in coiled, swirly writing. Another reads *Feelin' Gr8 in '88!*

"Those people outside the house, the ones that have been hanging around the last few days—they say I'm *holy*. They write me letters and post them through the door. They've left things out there, little statues, toys. Did you know that?"

I think of the small offerings I saw when I arrived at Beacon Terrace; the wreathed bay leaves, dried to a dark green, the ratty-looking teddy bear leaking stuffing. I nod.

"But people at school don't think that. They don't think I'm special. They all think I'm a nutjob. Even the teachers."

"I'm sure they don't," I tell her, but it isn't true. I know how it can be. School wasn't kind to me, the girl with the dead brother and the father who handed out religious pamphlets outside the shopping center in his brown shoes and coat, face a study in grief. I suffered, too.

"Besides, you're not at that school anymore, are you? Sam told me you were going to college in September."

She brightens a little at this, picking at the chenille bedspread with her fingernails.

"Yeah! I'll be studying hair and beauty. They have the classroom all set up like a salon, it's so cool."

I nod and smile and pick my notebook back up. During my studies I learned that teens value self-determination. *"Let them set the agenda,"* the professor told us, rolling up her sleeves, *"and engage with them on their terms."* Besides, I don't want to keep thinking about that chimney breast and the dark cracks in the brickwork, the way Alice whispered to me, *"I see her eyes in the holes."*

"Have you always wanted to do that? Be a hairdresser?"

"For sure. I was cutting the hair off all my Sindy dolls as soon as I could hold a pair of scissors. I cut poor Tamsin's hair when she was a toddler, took off all her beautiful baby curls. Not sure Mum will ever forget it to be honest but she asked me for a trim the other day so I hope that means I've been forgiven. I've been cutting our neighbor Mary's hair and at Christmas her and Bert bought me my very own proper hairdressing kit to take to college."

"I met Bert yesterday, up at the church. He mentioned his wife was ill."

"Yeah. It's a real shame. Mum said she had got really sick a few years ago and she'll never get better. She talks funny now, like her voice is all mushy, and she needs Bert's help to get around. I still cut her hair but I don't know if she even knows I'm there sometimes. It makes me feel sad. Especially for Bert. He loves her more than anything."

She looks up and gives me a weak smile.

"They used to look after me and Tamsin a lot when Billy was born. It made Mum sad having Billy. She cried every day. Bert said that some women feel like that sometimes, after having a baby. That the pregnancy can make them unhappy but they get better in time. Billy was a proper handful, he was wild. Still is, although I don't notice it too much anymore. He doesn't mean it, but some days it's like the Devil got inside him, that's what Bert says. At the time I didn't mind too much because Bert and Mary used to make us nice dinners and let us help ourselves to the choc ices in the freezer. It was a bad time but not a bad time, does that make sense?"

I tell Alice it makes perfect sense.

"A few years ago, I started going 'round some evenings to set Mary's hair and Bert would come in and play his old records for us. I sort of pretend I don't like it but I don't mind really. He made us funny little cocktails out of orange juice and pineapple from a tin. He calls them *Bertinis* and puts little paper umbrellas in them. It always makes Mary laugh. Sometimes he plays a song that was the first dance at their wedding but it's slow and Mary always falls asleep before the end of it."

She sighs, hugging her knees to her chest.

"After I started cutting Mary's hair, I had other people want me to do theirs. People in our street mainly, friends of my mum. I'd go to their houses and I didn't charge much—I just needed to practice. At Christmas I had a booking for an address on the other side of town. It was raining that evening and I remember thinking maybe I won't go. I couldn't really be bothered, and I didn't want to get wet. I wish I hadn't gone. I really, really do."

"What do you mean?"

Alice swallows loudly.

"I don't want to talk about this now, Mina. I'm tired."

Ah, I think. Here it is. Alice folds her arms, jutting out her lower lip. It's a sulky, petulant posture that would seem like artifice in anyone else but this exhausted young teen, her eyes suddenly hooded and cold. I lean forward, keeping my voice calm, trying to hold her gaze.

"Alice, I can't help you unless you give me the information. Otherwise I'm just out here working in the dark."

She thinks for a moment, leaning back against the pillows, eyes closed.

"The address was out on Tanner's Row, just on the edge of the village. It's probably only about a ten-minute drive but on the bike it takes a bit longer. I should have known all those houses were empty—Dad was talking about nothing else for weeks—but I was just thinking about the money. I'd been saving for a new stereo, because the one I've got is knackered. Of course once I got there, cycling all the way in the sleet and the cold with my fingers so numb I could hardly feel them, I realized right away. There were no lights on for one thing. Not even a streetlamp. No one goes in or comes out of Tanner's Row anymore. All the cottages there got sold to a developer and now all six of them are just sitting there falling to bits, waiting to be knocked down. That's what Dad gets so mad about. Good Cornish granite going to waste, he says. The last house on the row, number six, was where I was headed. When I got there the front door was already standing open."

A pause. Her eyes flick to the collection of photographs again, her and that girl and those hundred-watt smiles.

"There was someone standing there, calling me over. It took me a while to realize that it was my friend, Vicky."

I glance up at the photos again, Alice and Vicky with their faces pressed close together, eyes shining with bright adolescent fervor.

"Vicky had a flashlight in her hand. 'Come on,' she was saying, like something exciting was happening, 'come on, we've been waiting for you.' She was laughing. I wasn't laughing. I was pissed right off. Confused, too. Something still didn't feel right, but you know—I'd gone all that way in the cold. Might as well see what was going on. I leaned my bike against the wall. As far as I know it's still there. I haven't been back to get it.

"When I went inside the house, I had to duck because of the way the ceiling was sagging. Everything stank, like dirty water. There was carpet but no furniture and so the people inside were sitting on plastic bags on the floor."

"What people?"

"From my school, mostly. It was hard to see in the dark. Vicky's brother was there, he's at college, and some of his friends I suppose. A few girls from my class. They had flashlights and were drinking bottles of Thunderbird. They were obviously all in on the joke because when I arrived someone said, 'Who ordered the hairdresser?' and they all just about wet themselves laughing. Even Vicky. She offered me a go on the wine but I didn't want any. I wanted to leave. The house was gross, so dark and damp. There was graffiti all over the walls and empty cans everywhere. One of the girls stood up then, a bit pissed. They all were, I think. She held the money for the appointment out to me. Five pounds. Said it was only a joke, that they were still going to pay me. Only I had to do something first. Before she'd give it to me, like."

"What did they want you to do?"

Alice sighs, hands plucking at the cover. Her voice is soft and almost slurring, so deeply buried is she in the memory. Her eyes are wet and distant, mouth drawn down.

"I had to get something out of the chimney. I didn't want to do it. I told them that. 'Absolutely not,' I said. 'Whatever it is I'm not putting my hand up there, why couldn't someone else do it?' That's when Vicky stood up. She came right up close to talk to me and she said, 'Come on, Alice. It's only a bottle. Just take it out and then they'll pay you. Please, Alice, you're the only one brave enough.' On and on like that until I said, 'Fuck it, fine, I'll do it.' Everyone cheered. One of the boys even put his arm around me which was, you know, nice. They shone their flashlights up there so I could see. Lit up like that I wasn't scared at all. It was only a chimney. Bricks and cobwebs and soot. It smelled bad but the whole house smelled bad, like everything in it had drowned. I couldn't work out why they'd all been so afraid to do it. I reached up all the way to my shoulder—it was awkward, and it ached for a long time afterward but in the end I found it in a hole in the bricks, right where they said it was."

A beat. I watch her carefully. There is the slightest tremble in her hands, voice wavering as if on the cusp of tears.

"Go on, Alice."

"It was a bottle." She swallows, her eyes deeply socketed and ringed with shadow. "I managed to pull it free but I suppose my fingers were so cold I couldn't hold on to it properly. I dropped it and it smashed on the fireplace.

"Everyone screamed. I think Georgia said, 'Oh my God. I'm going to be sick.' One of the boys ran first but most of them followed, straight out the front door. Only Vicky hung back, and she was so frightened I could hear her voice shaking. I kept asking her what the matter was, why everyone had freaked out. She said, 'You broke the witch's bottle, Alice,' and then she ran. After that I don't think we said two nice words to each other—*and* I never got my fiver."

I sit breathless, watching her. Her knees are drawn right up to her chin as if she were receding into herself.

"Alice, when I was studying psychology, I wrote a paper on mass psychogenic illness. It's the theory that an idea or a feeling—particularly a strong one like terror or excitement—can spread through a crowd like a disease. It can even change the way people behave."

As I lean toward her, I feel the slightest pressure on the back of my neck as if someone is watching me. Some oculus perhaps, cracks in the brickwork. I ignore it, threading my hand into Alice's own.

"It's what happened in the Salem witch trials and the dancing mania of the Middle Ages. It's even been observed in animals, that's why they call it 'herd mentality.' It doesn't mean there is something wrong with you. Quite the opposite. It's a shared experience, that's all."

I reach out and turn off the Dictaphone. I almost feel disappointed. Teen fever, a whipping up of emotions. There was a case recently in an all-girls school in upstate New York—hundreds of girls came down with a 'fainting sickness' despite tests showing there was no medical reason for the mysterious fits. It's a social contagion and even though it's fascinating it's also normal. I need to go and talk to Sam. At last, I think, we might have an answer to what's happening here. It's only as I stand up and cross the room, one hand reaching out for the door handle, that I hear her say, "You didn't ask me."

"Ask you what?"

"How it feels."

"How what feels, Alice?"

"When dead people start talking to me. You didn't ask me what it feels like."

My mouth floods with the taste of hot metal. Fear, polluting me.

"What does it feel like?" I ask her quietly and she looks right at me.

"Like biting into ice," she says.

ELEVEN

A little before midday I find Sam standing in the front porch, his hands in his pockets. A cigarette burns in an ashtray beside him. He has a strange look on his face that I initially mistake for boredom, but it isn't boredom. It's a sort of wonder.

"Look at that, Mina," he says, nodding toward the road. "It's like the Rapture."

I follow his gaze. The street is deserted, the small crowd having dispersed presumably because of the curfew and the flat, stifling heat. A few toys litter front gardens; bikes and balls and water pistols, a Hula-Hoop hanging from the branch of a tree. There's a can of drink spilled on its side and an empty car parked at the side of the road, all the doors left open. Someone has been drawing in pastel chalk on the ground just outside the front gate—strange symbols, tadpole-like, with bloated heads and long, tapered tails. The same chalk has been used to write *bE Not afrAId* along the wooden fence. I notice more offerings have been added to the pile just outside the front door; flowers wrapped in cellophane, a foil chocolate heart softening in the midday sun. A laminated Bible verse has been propped against the wall. The heat makes the pavement shimmer, a fine hazy mist floating over everything. My father would be thrilled. *The End Is Nigh.* He's been hoping to get swept up in the Rapture ever since we put Eddie's body into the ground.

I shiver despite the way the small glass porch traps heat and holds it like a miniature greenhouse. There are no plants in here however, just a tumble of assorted shoes and boots and a stack of yellowing newspapers.

"They must've gone indoors."

Sam grunts.

"Hopefully for good. Did you see that guy throwing salt on the ground? You know why people do that, right? It's protection against witches."

"How do you know that?"

"In my job I've met a few ghost-hunters, Mina. It's part of the kit. Salt, for the doorways and windowsills. Talcum powder for the halls."

I must look puzzled because he laughs. It is a rich, easy sound.

"They dust the ground with it to catch footprints."

"I don't think Lisa would want us sprinkling talc around the house."

His face becomes serious again, eyes darkening.

"No, you're right. Listen, stay away from those people out

here, Mina. Not just the salt guy, all of them. There's something not quite right about the way they've been drawn here, I don't like it. I don't like *them*."

There is a pause as we both turn to look out through the dusty glass. There is no breeze to stir the trees or the long, yellow grass.

"Did you listen to the tape?"

I handed Sam the Dictaphone after I came downstairs from Alice's bedroom.

"Sure. I thought it was interesting what you said about, uh, what was it? 'Psychogenic illness.' It would make sense that Alice thinks she's the victim of some sort of curse; plus it abdicates her of any responsibility."

"Did Tamsin and Billy reveal anything?" I lean against the glass. It is hot as sin against my back and makes me think of Alice saying *"It feels like biting into ice."* Sam thinks on the question for a moment, still looking out into the road.

"Billy seems to treat the whole thing like a bit of a joke. I get that, he's five years old. Tamsin on the other hand, she had a little more to say. She mentioned about Alice dropping out of school, the episodes of sickness. There's this belief that Alice can talk to the dead, which I think has come more from those folks in front of the house than any actual evidence. Tamsin said she hadn't seen any proof of it. She did say one thing though."

This pricks my interest. I peel away from the window.

"What?"

"She said, 'The witch watches Alice through the cracks in the bricks.'"

"Okay, well—we know that. Alice told us that."

"Exactly, and Tamsin used the exact words Alice did. It's on the tape you just gave me. She doesn't say 'the hole in the chimney,' or 'the witch looks through the cracks.' They both say it the same way—'she watches through the cracks in the bricks.'"

"So?" I shrug, as Sam rubs his throat thoughtfully and sighs.

"A more suspicious man would suggest the words were rehearsed. A *very* suspicious man would bet if we compared my interview footage with your tape there'd be more of that same phrasing." He looks at me, his eyes avid. "They're being coached, Mina. I'm sure of it."

Sam doesn't tell me who he thinks is coaching the children but I could hazard a guess. I saw the way Paul's body language changed last night at the mention of being moved from their home, the intent way he'd leaned forward asking, *"What'll it take? For a worst case scenario?"*

Sam checks his watch, face suddenly earnest.

"It's eleven-thirty. Curfew starts at twelve. I don't know about you, Mina, but I need to get out of this house for a bit. Do you think Lisa has a map of the local area?"

"I can ask her. Where are you thinking of going?"

"Tanner's Row. There's a house there we need to take a look at."

TWELVE

Lisa is ironing and smoking a cigarette when I walk into the kitchen to ask her for a map. The iron hisses as she sets it down, jettisoning steam. She doesn't question what we need a map for, and doesn't offer directions of her own. It's clear she hasn't slept well—her eyes are bloodshot, hair scraped away from a face which is tight and brittle with worry. She crosses to the dresser and slides open a drawer. I notice it is not the same one she reached into for the psychometry tokens the previous day, and I don't realize she is deliberately blocking my view until I try to stand beside her. Then she turns her back to me, angling herself just right so that I can't see past her. I don't say anything, and when she finally pulls the map out and hands it to me I notice how her eyes skim over me, how fast she slams the drawer closed.

I think about mentioning this to Sam as we head into the silent street, but I'm struck dumb by sunlight so bright it saturates everything. Smoke thickens the air, a perfume of burning heather and dry kindling, something peaty and rich. We walk without speaking, passing a house with a paddling pool in the front garden, two teenage boys lolling in it, stripped to their waists, heads back, sunglasses tilted up to the sky. It is so quiet. No birds, no dogs barking, no insects. Just that still, heavy air already blossoming into torpidity.

We reach the little parade of shops just beyond the Village Green and stop outside the video store, peering at all the posters in the window. There are handwritten notices, too: cleaning jobs and missing pets and a Raleigh racer for sale. As we stand there, a woman appears in the dusty window and fixes another little card down in the lower left corner. She sees us and grins, poking her head out the doorway.

"Interested in the Scarecrow Competition, are you? First prize is a carvery dinner for two."

Sam looks at me, eyebrows raised as if to say, *What do you think?* I laugh.

"Ha, no thanks. I got stuck in a corn maze when I was a little girl and cried until I was sick. I had nightmares about scarecrows for months."

The woman grins, stepping out the doorway and into the sunlight. She has coppery hennaed hair growing dark at the roots and a soft, plump figure draped in fringe and tie-dye, a skirt studded with little round mirrors. Her eyeliner is sharp black wings.

"Hang about, I know who you are. You're that reporter from the paper I heard about. The one writing about Alice Webber."

"Yup. Sam Hunter." He holds out his hand and she shakes it warmly. There is a mesh of thin scars on her forearm, just below the elbow crease. Like she has dragged a razor blade there, or the edge of a scalpel. "This is Mina Ellis. She's a child psychologist, and very much the brains of our investigation."

The woman laughs and takes my hand but I notice the way her eyes linger on Sam a little longer. I'm surprised at the small frisson of jealousy I feel in my gut.

"I hope you don't mind my saying so but you look very *young* to be a child psychologist."

"Technically this is my first case."

"Ah!" The woman arches a brow conspiratorially. "But what an *interesting* one."

Sam lifts his chin toward her. "Do you know her, then? Alice?"

The woman looks at him, eyes moving up and down. Assessing. She tilts her head. When she smiles, dimples deepen in her cheeks.

"My name's Fern, if you want to print that in the paper. F-E-R-N. The plant spelling, not the Scottish one."

"Oh no, this isn't— This is off the record."

"Well, here's the thing. It's a small town and everyone knows the Webbers. I used to live by them, when I was younger. They're good people, especially Lisa. I babysat Alice when she was a little girl, before the other two were born. She was a normal kid, just like any other. Up to last Christmas she would come in the shop, her and her friend renting videos at the weekends. Like a pair of parrots they were—bright and loud and a bit wild. Always laughing."

I think of the photographs above Alice's bed, the two girls with their faces pressed close together, laughing. *Best M8s 4 Ever!*

"That must be Vicky," I say. "Alice has talked about her."

"Well, like I said, they were joined at the hip right up until the cold weather blew in and Alice got sick. Why don't you come on in out of the sun for a moment?"

Sam and I exchange a quick glance as he follows Fern beneath the awning into the cool of the store, me trailing behind them. Inside, it is cramped and fairly run-down—the carpet bulges in places and the glass lid of the freezer is cracked and clouded like a cataract. The videos are stacked on shelves that reach the ceiling, blocking out most of the natural light. I notice another of those strange stone arrangements hanging on a nail inside the doorway. "Hagstones," the little girl had called them. To keep the witches out. I reach out and touch it.

"Huh. I keep seeing these. It's the equivalent of putting garlic on your door to ward off vampires, is that right?"

Fern looks at me, head tilted. She gives me a small, pointed smile.

"I suppose."

"It's unusual though, isn't it? To see them everywhere like this. Most of these old beliefs, they . . ."

A pause. She holds my gaze, still smiling.

"Go on."

"Well, they die out, don't they? There's no need for them anymore. Old superstitions."

"Really? You never wished on a shooting star? Never knocked on wood or thrown salt over your shoulder?" She leans on the counter. "Never got told stories about witches as a kid?"

"Fairy stories? Sure."

Fern shakes her head. Her voice is soft, buttery almost. She looks at Sam and me with real intention, as though she is spelling something out.

"No, I mean real stories, about real witches. The kind with the black throats and tongues. The ones who creep into your house through all the cracks and crevices."

"Not those stories, Fern, no." I glance toward Sam to see what he is making of this, but his expression is closed, hands in his pockets.

"I can tell, else you wouldn't be asking me about the hag-stones. They're protection, just like locking your door."

I'm convinced she is teasing us, can imagine her laughing later about how gullible we are, how naïve. Fern keeps right on smiling that same, impish grin as Sam picks up a video box, turning it over in his hands.

"What kind of films were Alice and Vicky renting? If you don't mind me asking?"

"Huh, let's see. *Dirty Dancing*, that was a big one. Reckon they hired that about six times a month. Mostly fun stuff, you know? *Teen Wolf*, *Cocktail*. What I think of as bubblegum movies."

"But no horror? No *Exorcist* or *Nightmare on Elm Street*?"

"Well, I'm going to overlook what you're insinuating about my ID checks on teenagers but no, at least not from me. That isn't to say they haven't seen it elsewhere, or got someone older than them to hire them out. That happens a lot."

Sam nods. He puts the box back on the shelf.

"Okay. It was just a thought anyway. I need to find out what her influences are, I suppose."

"Well you could do worse than speaking with her friends. If you can find any, that is."

"What do you mean?"

"Like I said, this time last year I'd see her and Vicky Matherson going everywhere together like conjoined twins. Then, nothing."

I nod. The timeline fits with Vicky luring Alice to Tanner's

Row last winter. Alice said the two of them hadn't spoken since. Sam looks at me and taps his watch, mouthing the word "curfew." I nod and we say goodbye to Fern, who waves at us airily as we step outside. According to the map, Sam tells me as we cross the road, Tanner's Row is just fifteen minutes away.

THIRTEEN

We walk along the High Street, up the hill and past the church. The heat makes it hard to speak and after a while we are comfortable with the silence. By the time we take the turning onto Tanner's Row, the street sign eclipsed by a sharp tangle of nettles and bramble, the church bell is chiming out the hour. The cottages are a small row of six granite-built houses in varying stages of dilapidation. They are gloomy and dark bricked, addled with rot. Window frames buckle and swell and old iron drainpipes are streaked with rust. A skinny-looking cat watches us from one of the overgrown gardens, eyes narrowed. It has a mouse hanging from its mouth, pink tail still twitching, beads of blood on its whiskers.

"Which one is it, Mina?"

Sam's voice is hushed in the still, heavy air.

"Alice said it's the one on the end. Number six."

I feel tension ratchet up my spine as we pick our way down the narrow lane spiked with weeds and cow parsley, long tongues of nettle.

We find Alice's bike still leaning against the low stone wall of the last cottage along the row, just like she said it would be. I don't know much about bikes but it occurs to me that even a cheap bike would be worth something to someone with nothing and wonder why she has never come back for it. Sam bends down to check the tires and looks up at me frowning. "They're flat."

"I'm not surprised. It's been here about six months."

We're talking in big, exaggerated whispers and now we exchange a glance, laughing nervously. Sam holds out his hand toward the last cottage on the row and steps aside so I can enter. After you, no after *you*. We laugh again.

Alice was right about the smell in here—it's fetid, as though something is putrefying in the walls. A cloud of flies moves in drowsy circles in the hallway. Through the doorway I glimpse graffiti on the walls, a tide of litter swept into the corners. The ceiling bulges. The old sofa is askew, all the stuffing ripped out like dusty white entrails. Sam brushes up beside me as I hesitate on the threshold.

"You going in?" he whispers.

"Yes, I'm just—"

"Just what?"

"Don't you feel it?"

I'm not expecting him to say yes. I'm expecting him to play dumb, to say, *Feel what, Mina?* and tell me I'm being paranoid.

But he does say yes. He does. Then he reaches out and squeezes my hand with his own, drawing a quick, sharp breath from me.

Stepping through the doorway is like stepping into a vacuum, as if all the air has been sucked from my lungs. The room is dark and cool with blotches of damp crawling down the walls. Torn curtains hang limply on skewed rails. In the farthest corner a pile of stained material—clothes or a sleeping bag, maybe—has been heaped. Something small and fleeting, glimpsed from the corner of my eye, scurries behind the skirting board as I cross the floor slowly, heading for the large fireplace. A floorboard creaks overhead, like a weight settling and I freeze, looking upward.

"It's an old house," Sam mutters. Still, his grip tightens on my hand just a little before he pulls away. He reaches up and traces a finger along a line of carvings on the wooden beam over our heads. "Look at these. Is that writing?"

The rafter is covered with a cross-hatching of scratch marks. They're not new—the scarred wood has already darkened with age—but they run deep, as if carved with a heavy, deliberate hand. Sam is cursing himself for not bringing the camera when I see the scorch mark a little farther along the beam. I reach up on tiptoes, brushing aside a net of old cobwebs. The mark is small and black, almost invisible against the old wood. The shape resembles a tadpole, with a round head and curved, narrow tail. Like a comet. I rub it with my thumb. The old wood is worn smooth.

"I've seen this before. Outside the Webbers' house. Someone drew it on the ground."

"Looks like it's been burned in." Sam peers at it, so close

his nose is almost touching the wood. "See the way it's been branded? Like a hallmark on silver."

Another creak overhead, a floorboard shifting. This time, Sam does not smile.

"Do you think there's someone here?" he asks, in a low, husky voice. His eyes glimmer in the dusty room. "Squatters maybe?"

I incline my head and listen. There is no more creaking, no sighing of old wood or rustle of movement.

"I don't think so. Let's hurry anyway, it's already gone twelve."

I turn away from him and on my next step something crunches beneath my foot. I slowly lift my heel to see broken glass glittering on the dark wood. There is more of it just ahead. I pick up a small chunk—it's milky green and smooth, like sea glass—and cup it in my palm.

"This must be it," I say simply. "The witch's bottle Alice found in the chimney. There's more of it over here, look."

It's like putting together a puzzle. The bottle has mostly broken into large fragments, some as big as my palm, and it's an easy job to bring most of the pieces together. I find the base of the bottle nearest the fireplace—it must have bounced and rolled as it had fallen out the chimney—and inside it is a little liquid, tacky to the touch. I sniff it cautiously, recoiling at the sharp, bitter odor.

"Urgh." I hold it out to Sam. "Does that smell like urine to you?"

He looks at me evenly, mouth curved in a slight smile.

"Are you trying to seduce me, Miss Ellis?"

"All right, all right. Pass me that newspaper, would you?"

It's not a newspaper, as we discover when Sam lifts it by the corner with a pinched finger and thumb. It's a crumpled porn magazine. He hands it to me gingerly and watches as I rip out a couple of pages, trying not to look at the topless woman standing on the deck of a boat with frosted hair and a high-cut thong, tiny pink nipples like hard candy. I start arranging the pieces of broken glass onto it, wrapping them carefully in the damp pages so they don't get damaged. I collect another piece of glass from the tiled hearth, half-buried in soot. It is the color of a blinded eye spotted with droplets of a gummy red wax. The largest of these droplets is about the size of a hazelnut and heavily dimpled, as if it were stuck with pins. I pick it free of the glass and turn it between my fingers thoughtfully.

"Mina?" Sam's voice has a worried note in it. "Do you hear that?"

I look up.

"Hear what?"

We wait. The flies have drifted into the center of the room as if drawn by some obscure corruption. Sam looks anxious, staring up at the large, curved chimney breast. I open my mouth to speak and that's when I hear it, too. A scratching sound inside the chimney. We both turn our heads toward it mechanically, eyes wide. In that dark, gloomy enclosure it feels as if the walls are suddenly rushing toward us, sealing us in.

"Maybe it's a bird," I say. A thread of soot patters into the grate. "It's an old house, right? Stands to reason there would be all sorts of stuff nesting here."

"We should go, Mina."

"Okay, okay." I wrap up the broken bottle and I notice, right at the back of the fireplace, another piece of that milky glass.

"Oh wait, one more."

"Mina—"

Another scratching sound. It's not panicked, like a bird or a squirrel would be. It's as if something is slowly working its way loose.

"Just let me—"

I'm leaning into the fireplace and it's big, bigger than I thought it would be. Alice could have fit her whole self in here easily, and it smells cinereous, like cold ashes long dead. I reach out for that scrap of glass, my fingers outstretched and trembling, the chimney rising above me like a long black throat, and as I feel a cold draft on the back of my neck I have one simple thought. *Don't. Look. Up.*

A scraping overhead and a fine scrim of powder trickles onto my bare shoulder. I almost cry out at the feathery touch, pinching the glass between my fingers and lifting it away hurriedly. Beneath it there is something half-buried in the soot and ashes. A child's shoe. Something about it stops me cold, stirring the hairs on the back of my neck. My teeth snap closed. Sam is behind me now—so close that I can smell the sweat on his skin, the mint gum he is chewing—but I can't move. I just stare at it—a tiny leather shoe with yellow stitching and a strap with a silver buckle.

"Hey, what the hell?" Sam croaks. I know what's going to happen as soon as he sees it. He is going to reach in there for it. "Maggie had those shoes."

"Don't." I put my hand on his arm. His skin is shockingly cold. "Don't. It's a trap."

"Huh?" Sam's brow knits together, his face drained of color, and I don't know how I know it but I do, it's a trap set just for him. It's bait. It's a fucking *lure*.

A scraping comes from above us in the chimney and I have a vision of the witch folded in up there, eyes wide and luminous in the dark, arms knotted over her head, legs crooked and bent, knees jutting somewhere up near her ears forming impossible angles. Her broken bones grind as she moves, desirous to be free. Her tongue will be long and black and spongy like a cancerous lung, and in her hand a piece of fishing wire, the end of which is tied to that single child's shoe, half-buried in the soot. She is drooling with excitement.

"Come on." I tug Sam's arm, practically hauling him away from the fireplace. The scratching sound has resumed with more intensity than before. "We have to go. Now!"

Sam hesitates but only for a moment, his face still drained of color. I dig my nails into his skin, as if trying to break through his captivation.

"Now, Sam!"

That seems to do it. His expression changes from that haunting, slack-jawed shock to something almost like comprehension. We leave at a run, shins stung by the nettles in the overgrown yard, almost slamming into Alice's discarded bike left leaning askew against the wall. We only slow down as we pass the sign for Tanner's Row at the top of the lane, hearts bright and quick in our throats.

FOURTEEN

Sam and I walk fast until we are past the church and into the sun-light between the houses, when our pace finally slows. Cheeks flushed and breathless, I catch Sam's eye and we both snicker at ourselves, slightly embarrassed.

"You know, I read once that a cat was found up a chimney that had survived seventeen days just drinking rainwater. All kinds of things get stuck up there I bet. Seagulls or bats or foxes, even. It happens all the time in these old places."

I can't tell if I'm trying to convince Sam or myself. Either way it doesn't matter. He scuffs his foot against the curb, hands deep in his pockets, chin to his chest. Buried in his thoughts.

"The bike's bothering me," he says finally, as we turn onto the High Street. I glance over at him. "I'm surprised that no one has tried to steal it or dismantle it for parts. If what Alice told us is accurate, that means it's likely *no one* has gone up to Tanner's Row since that day last winter. Not kids, not squatters, not the developers. No one."

"We can't know that," I tell him, but I'm being punctilious. I've been wondering the same thing. Of course, I tell myself, there's no reason that people would *want* to go up there—the house smells bad and there are obviously dangerous structural issues with the buildings—but I don't think that is all it is. I remember what I told Alice about mass psychogenic illness earlier that morning and how easy it is to seed ideas into soft minds. All it takes is one person to whisper a story and soon the whole town hears about it. A witch in a bottle, a girl hearing voices, hagstones and amulets and *bE Not afrAId* written in pale colors.

There's something wrong with that house on Tanner's Row. I felt it the moment we stepped inside the hallway with its peeling wallpaper and swollen, bulbous ceiling, those tadpole shapes burned into the rafters. The air inside was oppressive; hot and heavy as treacle. Oscar had once told me about a disaster which took place in Boston back at the beginning of the twentieth century. A large storage tank had exploded and flooded downtown Boston with millions of gallons of hot, sticky molasses. He'd described how people and horses had drowned, thrashing about in the boiling viscous liquid. The harder they'd struggled, the deeper they were ensnared. That's how it felt inside that house. Slow moving, suffocating. Like drowning in tar.

We don't speak again until we've nearly reached the video shop. There are a couple of figures waiting outside it, one tall, one short. I recognize the short figure immediately, even at a distance: the bowl haircut, gap-toothed smile, and that sweet, doughy face. It's the little girl we nearly hit with the car outside the churchyard, the one who grudgingly decided not to shoot me.

"Mummy!" she is yelling, jumping up and down. "Come on! Quicker! It's almost starting!"

There's Fern crossing the street and hurrying toward her, a big, welcoming smile on her face and I realize the little girl—Stevie, she told me her name was—is her daughter. I don't know how I didn't see the resemblance before. Stevie catches sight of Sam and me, and her face changes, just for a moment.

"You're the Mina lady," she says thoughtfully. Then Fern is lifting her up into her arms and swinging her giggling through the air. The taller figure steps back to give them room and I see it is Bert Roscow, the man who lives next door to the Webbers. He nods a greeting to Sam but it's me he turns toward, his eyes gleaming with interest beneath silvering, bushy brows.

"Ah, Mina! I was hoping to see you. How are you finding things? All this has been rather a baptism of fire for you, I imagine. I hope Alice is okay. They should turn the hose on those ghouls outside the gate."

"She's doing her best to ignore them," I tell him. *The people outside the house say I'm holy.* "Alice speaks very highly of you and Mary."

"Ah, Bert and Mary have been my saviors since Stevie was born," Fern says, lowering Stevie to the ground. "Being a single parent *and* having a business to run? Forget it. Honestly, I couldn't do it without them."

"It helps that Stevie is easy-peasy-pudding-and-pie," Bert says and laughs softly when Stevie wraps her arms around his legs. "Just like you were."

Fern catches my eye and winks.

"He's being generous. I was a troubled kid."

"You were a delight," he says, as Stevie reaches for the door handle, urging, "Mummy come on, it's starting! Ninja Tuttle is starting!"

"See you later, Stevie-Beans."

Stevie yanks the door open so hard she staggers backward, her face comically alarmed. Then she's laughing and through the door, kicking off her shoes, feet pounding on the stairs. "Bye-bye, Bert! Bye-bye, Man and Mina-Lady!" over her shoulder.

Sam waits until Stevie is inside before saying, in a low, confidential voice, "Mina and I just paid a visit to Tanner's Row."

Bert and Fern exchange a bemused glance.

"Whatever for?"

I tell them both a brief, condensed version of Alice's story of the previous winter. When I reach the bit about the bottle in the chimney, Bert nods solemnly.

"Witch's bottle."

"A what?" Sam shields his eyes from the sun, stepping under the shade of the awning.

"Witch's bottle. It's an old folk magic. Traditionally they were filled with sharp metal objects and vinegar or urine. Sometimes they'd pack them with hair or thread. The idea was that the thread created a maze that the witch would get lost in, trapping her inside. Did you say Alice broke it?"

I nod, fanning myself. It's so hot, so close. The air is thick in my lungs. I think of that shoe just lying there buried beneath the ash and feel sick and dizzy.

"Mind, it's a shame they're knocking those old places down," Bert says sagely. "They're full of history, you know."

"There's old marks on the rafters, and the ceiling has come down in the kitchen, but I caught a glimpse of the floor in there,"

Sam tells him. "It's proper Cornish slate. Someone should re-cover what they can before the developers move in."

"They won't stop building work for some old graffiti," Fern spits, her face flushed with what looks like real anger. "These money-grabbing bastards will raze the lot to the ground without a second thought."

"Not graffiti, Fern." Bert grins, giving us another flash of his dentures. "'Apotropaic marks.' I've seen similar before in old farmhouses. Those *are* historically significant. They should take those beams out and put them in a museum."

I think of the little tadpole shape, burned into the wood.

"What were the apotropaic marks for?" I ask Bert. He looks animated, as if he has been waiting to talk about this subject for years. It reminds me of Oscar when someone asks him to explain black holes. That flare of excitement and enthusiasm.

"*Belief,* Mina. The marks were protection against the witches and devils. Look around you, we're still doing it even now, hundreds of years later! Hanging hagstones and saluting magpies, hoping it will keep us safe from bad luck and bad dreams."

"Mummy!" From inside the house. I can see Stevie's shadow on the stairwell. "Tuttles is on!"

"I better go," Fern tells us all, smiling apologetically. "One day I'm going to cook those ninja bloody turtles into a big old soup. Thanks, Bert."

She kisses him affectionately on the cheek and waves good-bye to Sam and me. I smile, but I notice Sam is more subdued, pained and lost in his thoughts. I think again of that shoe with the yellow stitching—*Maggie's shoe*—just waiting to be found.

FIFTEEN

The air is heavy with fragrant heat; melting rubber, hot clay. The tails of smoke. Sam, Bert and I walk slowly down Beacon Terrace, washed in a vast blanket of stillness. We talk quietly about the curfew and the heat wave. I tell Bert about Oscar and our impending marriage and he congratulates me. Bert tells me he's just celebrated his seventieth birthday and laughs when I tell him he looks like Des O'Connor, adding, "You must tell my wife that, she'd be thrilled!"

As we draw up outside his house, directly next door to the Webbers, we all fall silent, looking at the chalk markings on the ground, the small pile of offerings by the door. A votive candle has been left, guttering in a glass. Bert sighs.

"That poor girl. She must be scared stiff. I hope you can help her, Mina."

"Mina thinks that breaking the witch's bottle triggered an intensely psychological reaction in Alice." Sam is smoking, leaning against the fence where the chalked writing reads *bE Not afrAId*. He looks more settled now, less like someone peering over the edge of an abyss.

"Ah, interesting that you think it's a psychosomatic symptom. It's amazing what the mind is capable of. You know my grandfather fought on the western front back in the First World War? He was a stoic man, very brave but very quiet. He came back with tinnitus and a limp on his left side but at least he came home. A lot of men weren't so lucky. Right up until he died, my grandfather insisted he and the other members of his battalion had seen an angel with long white hair walking across the battlefield on a cold November morning. One of the soldiers had actually called out to her, 'Hoy there, are you mad?' but she had kept on walking, smiling as if she knew a secret. My grandfather said she was barefoot and that's how they all knew she was divine."

"Wow."

"There's a lot of those stories that came out of the war. They became a tool for propaganda, a divine providence that served to boost morale. Angels and ghostly bowmen and riders with flaming swords. But my grandfather, and the ninety other men that were with him that morning, would swear on the Bible that what they saw was a guardian angel walking through the barbed wire and the mud and bodies with no shoes on her feet. How do you explain that?"

"I wouldn't try to," I answer. "It's a form of collective consciousness, it doesn't need explaining. What it needs is dismantling, slowly. Taken apart bit by bit so that the lack of plausibility becomes evident."

"Is that what you intend to do with Alice?"

I think of that soft scratching in the chimney.

"Perhaps. But this town doesn't help. Hagstones, apotropaic marks—Banathel has a real problem with witches, doesn't it?"

Bert laughs softly. "Once upon a time, maybe. The witches were drawn here by the Devil, if the old stories are true. About a mile west of here is a ring of stones, said to be a coven turned to stone for dancing on the Sabbath. Thirteen stones for thirteen bewitched women. As kids we always kept away from them, even on bright and sunny days. There's something about them that is . . . sunken, I suppose. There's just some places that feel like that, isn't there? Like there is a thinness to them, something unreal."

I think of the house on Tanner's Row and nod. "You a historian, Bert?"

He laughs, slightly abashed. "God, no. I'm something of an amateur at best. I dabbled in it when I became interested in genealogy—people and places are often tied together, so researching one naturally led to looking into the other, I think."

Bert turns to look at his house, the garden neat and tidy and squared away, lawn trimmed to a dark green inch, and sighs.

"I'd better go and see how she is. Mary likes having Stevie over—she always did enjoy the company of children—but it exhausts her now."

"Have you any children of your own, Bert?"

"No. We just took in the waifs and strays. It's not so easy these days with Mary so ill and my arthritis playing up but we manage. It fills the house, having children there."

He looks morose for a moment, deep in thought. I wonder what it must be like to watch the person you've spent your life with—your love, your comfort—fading away. It must be a soft pain, slowly blooming. Flowers and thorns.

I watch as he walks up the pathway to his house and lets himself in through the front door, raising a hand to Sam and me as he closes it behind him. Then I tilt my head back and look up. A plane is slowly crossing the sky, trailing a white cloud of vapor. I watch it a moment and think of Crete, and swifts' nests and yellow dresses and my dead brother reaching for me in a photograph, his mouth partly open as if saying *Tell me about the ice.*

SIXTEEN

There is a frozen lump of meat on the kitchen table, wrapped tightly in plastic. A leg of something. A haunch. Paul brings them back with him from work, Lisa said. Hocks and cheeks and briskets, flabby pink snouts. The haunch is a livid pink color, marbled with fat. It is so tightly wrapped that I can see the blood slowly defrosting and pooling against the plastic surface. Sam moves it aside so that I can unpack the witch's bottle carefully, spreading it out across the table. The house is quiet, the two younger children in the sitting room, Paul at work. Sam leans over me, cigarette clamped between his teeth.

"Do we tell Alice about this?"

I pick up a piece of thick, blue glass and hold it up to the light.

"Yes. That's the reason I brought it back here. So she can see for herself it is a material object and nothing else."

"A broken bottle of piss and wax. We sure know how to have a good time, huh?"

"*Shhh,*" I say, not unkindly. I'm concentrating, turning it over in my fingers. The glass is old and ridged, some raised lettering still visible on the broken neck.

"You know who else pisses in bottles? Truckers. Drunk kids." He is grinning, eyes narrowed against the smoke as he reaches down and picks up one of the small balls of wax. It is pricked with holes like a pomander but only as big as a holly berry in his palm.

"What's this?"

"I don't know. It was stuck to the glass on the inside. There's a few of them, look."

He examines it, scraping at the wax with his thumb.

"It looks like voodoo, all these holes. Maybe a curse of some sort. What's inside it?"

My head snaps up. I hadn't considered that the wax was concealing anything. I feel that strange sensation again, like cotton stuffed into my throat.

"Don't."

"Don't what?" he says.

"Put it down. Don't open it."

"Why not?"

I don't know, I want to tell him. It's just a feeling. A bad feeling, like the one you get in a cold spot in the sea, legs cycling over a long depth of frightening, terminal dark. It's the same feeling I had in the house on Tanner's Row standing beneath the chimney and seeing that small shoe in the drift of soot. *Because it's a trap.*

At that moment the kitchen door opens and Lisa is standing there, hands twisting together in front of her, face strained. Her eyes pass over me and settle on Sam, her lips drawn in a quivering frown.

"There's trouble," she says.

I don't recognize the two boys out there, but I know the girl with the dark curly hair and long eyelashes, her round face tilted toward the upper windows of the house. I saw her photo in Alice's bedroom.

"That's Vicky Matherson," I say, peering through a gap in the curtains. "That's her? That's Alice's friend?"

"That's Alice's friend?" Sam is leaning close to the glass, his arms folded.

"*Was* Alice's friend," I correct him. "She's the one who tricked Alice into going up to Tanner's Row and getting that bottle out of the chimney. Before that they used to hang around together all the time."

Sam looks at Lisa who is hanging back in the darkened sitting room, one arm around Tamsin, another around Billy.

"Where's Alice?" he asks her. She points to the ceiling.

"Upstairs. She hasn't come out of her room all day."

There's other people out there, too, massing outside the gate. Someone lets off a firecracker and there is a loud whooping cheer. Music is playing from a car somewhere farther down the street, muffled bass like a heartbeat, furry and distorted. I can feel a crackle of hostility. This isn't like before. These people, they don't think Alice is holy. Sam and I exchange a glance.

"Lisa, take the kids upstairs," Sam tells her, as another firecracker blasts outside. One of the boys with Vicky is wearing a vest that reads TUFF SHIT and has a skinny, malnourished look about him. He might be eighteen or twenty even, older than the others. Mean-looking. The other boy has a buzz cut and flat, expressionless features. There is a scrim of fuzzy hair above his upper lip. His voice is deep and surly as he calls out, "Where's your broomstick to, Alice?"

"I've got a broomstick she can ride on!" Tuff Shit yells, grabbing a handful of his crotch. There is a ripple of sneering laughter. Vicky looks around her and just before she lifts her hand, I see she has something round in it, something white. I think at first it is a stone—a *hagstone*, maybe—but as she launches it toward the house I realize it is an egg. It hits the window with a wet, ugly sound. More hooting. Snotty yellow yolk drips from the glass.

"What do they want?" I ask Sam, feeling the white heat of adrenaline building in the pit of my stomach.

"Mina, listen. We have to—oh *shit*." Sam jerks upright, his gaze darting beyond my shoulder and out toward the hallway. "No, Alice. Stay where you are! Don't go out there!"

Alice has appeared at the foot of the stairs. Neither of us heard her come down. It's as though she just materialized there, wearing that baggy T-shirt over a pair of denim shorts. *Crack!* Another egg hits the front door.

"Alice?"

She doesn't turn to look at us but she smiles and it's all teeth. Her lips slough back wetly. The top half of her face barely changes, her eyes hard and flat and utterly empty. The smile doesn't touch them. It just stretches the skin. I feel something cold tighten around my spine. Outside they have begun chanting her name, *"Ah-liss, Ah-liss, Ah-liss."* Sam moves toward her but hesitates. Perhaps he sees that vacancy and, like me, is afraid. There is a cracking sound as more eggs are pelted, knocking over the offerings that have been left outside the porch like skittles. The candle rolls over, flame winking out, glass cracked. Someone cheers, stamps their feet. I hear that deep voice again, hoarse with a barely controlled delirium. "Wrap her up in barbed wire, coming to set your hair on fire!"

Vicky is cackling, climbing up onto Buzz Cut's shoulders, dress hitched around her waist. I turn to call out to Alice but she is already walking toward the front door, hands raised to open it.

SEVENTEEN

The heat slams into me as I push past Sam and chase Alice out into the yard. She is barefoot, golden hair unraveled from her ponytail like some febrile Lady Godiva. The crowd of teenagers—more than a dozen, I'd say at a brief glance—jeer and bark and whistle as she steps out of the house. The noise is jolting and provocative and I expect Alice to shrink away, maybe turn back and run inside. She does neither. She simply stands there, absorbing it, her face a blank and bloodless mask. I'm almost pleased to see that empty expression. Anything is better than that ghastly smile.

"Alice, come inside," I tell her, grasping her shoulders so that she is forced to look at me. "You're doing exactly what they want you to do. You have to ignore it."

Her eyes are glassy and don't flinch as the first egg snaps

against her in a wet spray. I see it happen almost in slow motion; the spatter of albumen, the jerk of her shoulder, Vicky's face contorted into a sick, dazzling smile.

"We know what you are!" she's screaming, face raw and strained with the effort. "We know what you are, Alice Webber!"

Then another egg, and another. That music, still. *Thud, thud, thud.* Farther down the road a few neighbors are opening their doors, presumably to see what all the commotion is. An egg hits Alice square in the chest, causing her to sway backward. Beside her I'm splattered with yolk, stringy and viscous. Vicky is shrieking laughter, hands held high in the air. I grab Alice's arm and I'm astonished how cold her skin is, like grasping wet cement. A wasp lands on her hand, crawling over the ridges of her fingers. Eggshell crunches under her bare feet as she takes a couple of steps forward, ignoring me.

Vicky hawks up a mouthful of phlegm and splits her fingers into a V shape, spitting through them at Alice and laughing wildly, looking around for approval. Tuff Shit has reappeared, cigarette behind his ear, hand reaching down the front of his trousers. He's belligerent but it's all for show: the swagger, the cocky sneer, the pecking motion of his head. I've seen it before in other boys his age. In my experience, there's a vein of fear running through them as hard and bright as crystal.

"Alice," I say firmly, trying to be heard above it all, "Alice, come on. Come back inside."

But that smile has resurfaced and there is nothing behind her eyes. She doesn't hear me. She is as cold and distant as Venus. For a moment I think she is speaking—I can see her shoulders twitch, her mouth slowly moving—but the voice I hear is slurring and thick, heavy. Like a throat full of molasses. It is a language I don't recognize, Germanic maybe. The words spread like a ripple, like oil on water, dark and tainted. It fills me with something icy and unknowing and I taste the bitterness of bile in the back of my throat.

"Alice," I'm pleading with her, my voice high and taut as string, and I don't know what I'm begging for but I know something terrible is coming, I *know* it, and I want to stop her. "Alice, don't—"

Vicky is on Buzz Cut's shoulders and then suddenly she isn't. I watch her fall with a sickening thud, toppling as if she were struck. Everyone goes very quiet, eyes big and round as zeros, heads turning. I reach the gate at a run, bursting out onto the pavement and pushing through the dense mass of people to where Vicky lies twitching in the road. The neck of her T-shirt is torn. Behind me one of the boys starts laughing. It's breathless, slightly hysterical, and when no one joins in he stops.

I kneel beside her. I'm the only one. No one else seems to want to go near her. The crowd steps backward in an almost uniform motion, eyes seeking each other out for reassurance. Vicky must have been holding an egg when she hit the ground because there is eggshell all over the pavement and in the curls of her hair. At first I think it is flecks of bone as if her skull has shattered like porcelain and my stomach turns over queasily. The bitumen is hot and sticky and bites into my knees. Vicky's hand is reaching for her throat. She makes a noise. *"Urrrk. Urrrk."* Like a seal. Like she is gargling mouthwash. Her back arches and her feet drum into the ground. One of the boys says her name like a question, "Vicks?" His voice sounds small and frightened, very sober. I don't know if it is Tuff Shit or the other one. They are all looking at her with wonder, as if they can't believe their own eyes.

Vicky's lips are turning blue. She grips the neck of her T-shirt and tugs as if trying to be free of it. She twists and bucks but can only dig her heels into the road so hard they have started bleeding. Her eyes bulge. One shoe has flown off her foot, landing a few feet away.

"Alice, call an ambulance! Alice!"

My voice doesn't sound like my own. I sound stretched thin, exhausted. I'm getting frustrated with all these people standing and watching and doing fucking nothing. Can't they see she's dying?

"Call an ambulance! Someone, call an ambulance!"

I switch and turn on the crowd behind me, hands outstretched toward them. Most of them look away. The ones who don't are bug-eyed with terror. I don't blame them. I think Tuff Shit is laughing but then I realize he isn't laughing, of course he isn't. He's crying. I hear a long ripping sound and see Vicky is tearing into the neck of her T-shirt so violently she has pulled it apart. I glimpse the strap of her bra underneath, the flash of a gold St. Christopher necklace. Her hands circle her neck as if she is trying to choke herself, eyes seeking me out helplessly. No sound comes out of her mouth. Such dark eyes she has, like pools of ink. *Poor Vicky,* I think as I use my fingers to lever open her stiff jaw, trying to get a look inside. By now people are drifting away. They didn't want a part of this and I don't blame them. Vicky's throat is bulging like something is stuck in there, her tongue a fat wet slab that reminds me of that haunch wrapped in plastic on the counter. I think of Alice saying *"the witch's tongue is black"* and I feel sick and cold all over. Vicky's whole face is dark now, almost purple. Next time I look at her, she doesn't see me. Her eyes are gone, gone all the way back into her head.

EIGHTEEN

The next morning I wake to bright sunlight, shrill as a scream. It's late by my watch, just gone eleven. I've slept for nearly twelve hours. Downstairs the radio is playing and I can hear the clatter of cutlery. I take my contraceptive pill in the bathroom with a cupped handful of water, feeling tension knot my shoulders. I'm still shaken by what happened yesterday. The way Vicky fell, as if she'd been pushed by invisible hands right off that boy's shoulders. I can't get the images out of my mind—they rattle past like a slideshow: the wasp crawling over Alice's fingers, the eggshell nestled in the curls of Vicky's hair, the way Tuff Shit's mouth curved down into a horrified, quivering rictus. Something about the whole thing feels volatile, like a stoked flame. Today though, the street outside is empty. No incense burning, no placards declaring GIVE THE DEAD THY TONGUE, no small huddle of afflicted-looking people.

It's a relief. I hope they stay away. Alice went silently to bed the previous evening even as the blue lights of the emergency vehicles had pulsed outside, the sickle moon bone-white in the sky. When I tapped on her bedroom door, Dictaphone in hand, she called out for me to leave her alone.

I open the front door gingerly and peer out into the white heat of late morning. The little shrine which had been building is cleared away but crusts of egg are still spattered across the downstairs windows, drying to a paste. In the kitchen, behind the closed door, I can hear a radio softly playing. Maybe it's Sam, sitting with his cigarette burning the insides of his fingers yellow, tea stewing in the pot. I hope it is. I could do with someone to talk to. My mood lifts a little.

At first, I'm not sure what I'm looking at on the kitchen table. There are small mounds of pale flesh threaded with veins, slit open like crimson petals, deepening to purple. The newspaper beneath them is stained pink with blood.

"Rabbits," Paul says, without looking up at me. He's sharpening knives on the back step the same way I used to see my grandfather do, sweeping the blade along the stone. "I've skinned them and taken off the legs. The fur comes off clean, like peeling a banana."

He stands and looks at me with his narrow, serious eyes. He is shirtless, the hair on his chest soft and dark like a pelt. He looks tired, and I wonder if he has just finished his shift. If he has, it looks as though he has brought his work home with him. I burp queasily.

"Where is everyone?"

"Lisa's taken the little ones to her parents'. We thought it best to get them away for a while. Sam's up at the Green trying to find a phone box that hasn't been pissed in, I should think. He's been trying to call the hospital."

"About Vicky?"

"You know, we used to have her here for tea not so long ago? Vicky was a sweet kid, always polite. Please and thank you and she called us Mister and Missus Webber no matter how many times me and Lisa told her to just use our names. Her and Alice were born on the same ward just two days apart. Some girls just get the Devil in 'em."

"What about Alice? Is she okay?"

"You tell me. You're the expert." He smiles tightly.

"I haven't been here long enough to form an opinion, Paul." He snorts.

"You been here long enough to make a guess?"

I stare at him over the table, the smell of blood thick in the air. His voice sounds as if it is taunting me, somehow.

"Uh, okay, then. In my opinion I see a level of emotional disconnect in Alice. Certainly there's a distorted perception of reality." I think of the way Alice looked at Vicky the previous day, that bloodless smile. "I'd like to assess her properly though, before I say any more."

"Can you give that to me in English?" He's smiling but it's taut and mean. He thinks I'm patronizing him.

"I mean she's delusional."

"Ah. The witch."

A beat.

"That's part of it, yes."

"What's the other part?"

I shift uncomfortably.

"Some of the symptoms I'm seeing in Alice—the withdrawal,

the intrusive thoughts, even the hallucinations—can be traced to a trauma in childhood. Can you think of anything that may have affected her, Paul?"

He looks at me a long time, a drop of blood swelling and fattening on the knife tip. I watch it sway pendulously, hypnotized.

"What are you trying to say, Mina? That I can't protect my own kids?"

His voice is very quiet, very measured. But there is a tremor in it, just enough for me to know how hard he is trying to control his anger.

"Of course not," I say, thinking of the house on Tanner's Row, Alice's friends shrieking with laughter, hysteria. "But you can't always know what your children are doing, especially teenagers."

Paul considers this quietly before grunting and wiping the knife with a bloodied cloth.

"Huh. You don't believe in witches, then, Mina?"

"No."

My eyes return to the bloodied little cadavers on the table, smeared with fat. A fly lands on one and Paul swats it idly away.

"What was it you said your fella did again?"

"He's a researcher."

"What of?"

"Space."

"Oh yeah? Can he skin a rabbit?"

I lick my lips nervously.

"No."

"Lisa's grandmother always told her to marry a practical man. She was teasy as an adder but that was one thing she got right." He lifts up the hind leg of one of the skinned rabbits on the table. "You want me to save you a lucky rabbit's foot?"

"That's a misconception. In the old Celtic tradition it was a hare."

"That right? Huh. My family were all hare coursers. All looked like the lurchers they used, too, all skin and teeth and bones like they hadn't enough to eat. Them hares got so scared sometimes their hearts would just blow like a faulty gasket. Don't sound very lucky to me."

Sweat bites into my skin, stinging my eyes. The smell in here is clotting, turning greasy.

"I suppose not."

"I remember hearing stories about hares. How they were witches who had shape-shifted and couldn't change back. Maybe they'd forgotten how. Maybe they just liked living wild. Running fast, fighting, fucking in the moonlight. Ha! I wouldn't mind."

He looks up at me and I see a flash of something heady—lust maybe, or desire. His pupils look fat and swollen. I think of Alice saying *"The killing floor does something to the brain . . . something bad,"* and even though my pulse is fluttering like a trapped moth, teeth clenched, I hold his gaze fast.

"People 'round here Mina, they believe in witches. This town is built on their bones. If you reckon on the stories from back in the old days, witch's blood ran through Banathel's gutters and it was black as tar." Paul lifts one of the small, headless bodies nearest to him and pushes his index and middle fingers into the bloodied slit in its stomach. I wince. "You know who Matthew Hopkins is?"

"The 'witch finder general,'" I say. "We studied him briefly at university. He's analogous with witch hunts and mass panic, although 'witch finder' is a euphemism really, isn't it? He tortured women. Nothing more."

"I suppose you could call it that. But he thought he was doing the right thing, didn't he?"

"The right thing for who?"

"For the community. For God. He was frightened, lots of people were. Superstition ruled over religion and reason. These people needed to be *appeased*." He lifts the bloodied tip of the knife level with his lips and for a frightening moment I feel sure he is about to lick it.

"You saw yesterday what happens when fear gets out of control. People get hurt."

"But all this superstition, it just feeds the myth. Surely you see that?"

Paul is silent a moment, working his fingers farther into the cavity with a meaty ripping sound, exposing a muddle of coiled intestines and a glimpse of bone, greasy and slick with fat. He tugs the innards from the body of the rabbit and my stomach turns slowly over.

"I taught my girls how to skin rabbits. When Billy's old enough, I'll teach him an' all. They've got to learn. No point being squeamish. No point pissing about. If you can't look an animal in the eye when you kill it n' gut it n' skin it, then you've no business eating them."

A bead of sweat rolls down his temple.

"I learned that my first day on the job. On the second day I learned how they get the work done, day in, day out. Do you know what the secret to it is?"

I don't, I tell him. I can't imagine.

"We put our thoughts into boxes. We have to. It's the only way. It's serious work, hard on the hands, hard on the brain. Not everyone can do it. I've seen grown men—and it's always men, believe me—just turn on their heels one day, no warning, and walk out the door. They get right in their cars and drive through the gates and they don't look back, even though the blood is still dripping off their boots. Scared people do strange things. I had one kiddy, couldn't have been more than seventeen, Terry, his name was. He drove a Ford Escort. That car was his pride and joy. Terry was always joking, always messing around. He put a cow's tongue in my lunchbox once, just laying there on top of some iceberg lettuce like a big pink worm. Terry just about laughed himself stupid over that."

I realize with sick dismay that I can see where this story is going but Paul has momentum now. He squeezes a glossy sac out from the inside of a rabbit—a liver maybe, or a kidney—and throws it into a bucket by his feet. It makes a wet slapping sound.

"Terry's been working on the killing floor about a month when I find him in the office one morning. He's white as a sheet. He's wiping his mouth with the back of his hand again and again until I grab hold of him. His lips are raw and bleeding like he's pulled all the skin off them. I ask him what's wrong. He said, 'It's the smell, Paul, I can't get rid of the smell.' I knew what he meant of course. You work there for a while and you get used to it but it's always there, spoiled and sweet, like—"

"Marzipan," I say flatly. I'm thinking of the sickly odor I'd encountered when I'd first met Paul and again yesterday in Alice's room. The chimney in the old house on Tanner's Row had smelled like it, too, like hot iron and rotting pork. Sweet and coppery. It's how true fear smells, close-up and visceral.

"Terry said he'd tried all sorts to get it off. He'd even bought some of that—what's it called—carbolic soap, like they use in the hospitals. Scrubbing at his skin with a nailbrush till it bled. It was in his clothes, too, he said, even after they were washed. One morning he'd woken up and the whole room had smelled like it, as if it was just oozing out of him. But the worst thing, he said, the very worst, was that now his food was starting to taste like it, too. Like everything was too sweet and gone rotten. He'd bite into an apple and it was all he could taste, the killing floor. 'It's haunting me,' he'd said, and I've never seen such a look of horror as I did that morning on Terry Jenkin's face. I would've told him to go home but he did the job for me, handing in his notice on the spot. Good lad, I remember thinking. You got out before this job did for you what it does to the rest of us. Turns us numb."

I watch as he uses the tip of the knife to lever out a tiny rabbit heart, dark as a bruise, and drop it onto a plate. Flies swarm over it with a low, somnolent buzzing.

"Terry *did* walk out and get right in his car. Only he didn't leave. They didn't find him until that evening, just before they locked the gates. He'd slit his wrists with the broken edges of a Coke can. There was so much blood it had pooled in the footwell by his feet. The car—Terry's pride and joy, the one he'd saved and saved for—got towed away and crushed and that was the end of it. That was the end of *him*. The problem was, Mina, that Terry didn't know how to compartmentalize. You heard of that before? 'Compartmentalize'?"

"In psychology it's described as a defense mechanism."

Paul grunts again, shaking his head a little. He's sweating, his voice hard and sharp-edged. Like I could cut myself on it.

"Well, I don't know about that, but it sounds about right. For most of us in the abattoir, being able to compartmentalize means that we're not all ending up rocking in a corner or turning the bolt gun on ourselves. Because it's death we're dealing with. Sure, there are standards and levels of care. But when it comes to the bones of it—heh—it's death."

"Why are you telling me all this, Paul?"

He looks at me, carefully holding my gaze. His eyes have lost that hazy, muddy look and there is a small, knowing smile hitched at the corners of his lips.

"Because you can't predict what fear will do to people. You don't know which way it will send 'em. Some people don't have the stomach for it and it drives them mad."

There's something about the intensity of Paul, his steady, unflinching gaze, that casual butchery, that makes my nerves jump like oil on a skillet.

"Take Sam, for instance. He came in the kitchen earlier and when he saw me working here he turned around and walked straight back out again. Said looking at all this blood made him feel sick."

His voice is rough and husky, eyes glinting beneath the dark overhang of his hair. Gently, he taps the knife against his temple.

"He doesn't have the stomach for it, see? *You* do though, Mina. You've been standing here for half an hour like it's nothing. What does that tell you about yourself?"

NINETEEN

Sam is agitated, bouncing on the balls of his feet. He'd found a phone box and, after being passed around the switchboards of the hospital, he finally spoke to the ward Vicky had been placed on.

"I told them I was her cousin," he says. "She's in a coma. They're treating her for anaphylactic shock. Some insect crawled into her mouth, they think. Probably got right to the back of her throat before it stung her."

I think of the wasp that crawled over Alice's fingers. There is a deep feeling of menace, sleek and slippery, uncoiling inside me. Sam shakes his head, as if in wonder.

"It's taken me fifteen minutes to walk back here on account of every bugger stopping me and asking what's going on. All asking if I thought Alice did it on purpose."

"'On purpose'? How could she have done that?"

Sam shrugs. "I don't know, Mina, I'm just telling you what they told me."

"You sound like you're starting to believe it yourself."

My voice is firm, and I'm surprised how angry I feel when Sam hesitates, looking down at his hands.

"Do you remember, Mina, what I told you about desperate people? How they're driven to do desperate things? Mothers finding the strength to lift cars away from trapped infants, the Donner Party eating their own in the snow to survive—climbing into the attic for your dead daughter's clothes in the hope that a psychic might somehow be able to reach her."

He gulps, as if he is suppressing a laugh but it's a bitter, icy sound loaded with grief, and I wish I hadn't heard it. I nod.

"When I first heard that voice on the tape, I felt something I hadn't felt in a long time. Hope. 'Course I know now why they describe it as a 'glimmer of hope' because that's exactly how it feels, like a narrow chink of light through rock. A flame burning low, on the verge of guttering out. I came to Banathel because I felt hopeful, Mina, but maybe hope is just desperation dressed up in fancy clothes because I still haven't found Maggie, I haven't found proof of any kind. Just a sulky teenager and that fucking shoe in the fireplace."

"So do you want to stop? Do you want to go home? Sam?"

I'm surprised how much this thought bothers me. The idea of going home without digging a bit deeper, without helping Alice out the other side of whatever she's going through. I pull at his arm and he looks at me, his face creased in misery.

"I need answers, Mina. I want Alice to stop hiding in her room and come and fucking talk to us. I want *proof*."

He hooks me with his gaze, scowling. I understand his agitation but I'm not convinced. Alice seemed genuinely afraid when

I sat with her yesterday morning. Whatever it was she thought was in the chimney, she believed in it as much as the people gathered outside believed in her. Perhaps Sam reads this on my face because he snorts and shakes his head.

"I know you want to think this is genuine, Mina. I do, too. Because the alternative is that Maggie and Eddie are gone and that's unbearable, isn't it? Almost impossible to get your head around. But you have to, otherwise you'll end up like me in a few years, chasing spooks in the dark."

"I just— I don't think Alice is capable of any great deception. It's not just that she's so young, it's—"

—she watches me through the cracks in the bricks . . . I see her eyes in the holes—

"—a lot to put on her shoulders. I don't think she'd be able to maintain it this well for this long."

"Well, let's prove it, then, shall we?"

"How?"

Sam's flushed, sweating slightly. I can see how hungry his expression is, all mouth and glittering eyes. He gives me a fervent, wolfish grin.

"We're going to hold a séance, Mina."

TWENTY

I'm watching the little red light winking on a video camera, which has been positioned at the end of the dining table. The rabbit corpses have been cleared away and the table wiped clean but the smell still lingers, the one Paul spoke of, the one that had haunted poor Terry to the end. Iron and pennies and marzipan.

"Are you sure you want to do this?" I ask Alice a third time, turning to look at her.

Paul coaxed her out of her gloomy bedroom with a promise of pizza but she still looks nervous and unsure, winding her long hair around her finger. Alice is wearing the same baggy T-shirt she wore the day I arrived (POBODY'S NERFECT!) and now she is beginning to smell stale and slightly sour. Her blond hair is dark with grease.

"Because you don't have to, you know. No one is forcing you."

"I know," she tells me.

Paul smiled unpleasantly when Sam had told him his idea, eyes pricked with a bright gleam. He said, *"Whatever you need to do to make it work, Sam,"* and patted him on the shoulder with something like fellowship. It made me think of Masonic rituals and a sly, unscrupulous brotherhood. I reach out to Alice and squeeze her hand briefly, just once. Sam's eyes slide to me and then to the camera, speaking in a loud, clear voice.

"It's just gone twelve-thirty on Friday, the thirtieth of June, and I'm here with Alice Webber and Mina Ellis at Beacon Terrace. We are about to conduct a séance in which we will try to contact the so-called witch that Alice released from the bottle at Tanner's Row."

He looks back to Alice.

"Okay, Alice, let's begin."

Alice drops her chin to her chest. I watch the slow rise and fall of her shoulders. A minute goes by in silence, then another. Sam and I exchange a nervous glance.

"Alice? You okay?" I ask in a voice that is almost steady. Almost.

Nothing. Just the tightness of her fingertips pressing into the table, turning her nail beds white. In the silence I'm intensely aware of the strip light buzzing like high-voltage tinnitus. I glance up at it and what I see repulses me. Inside, the casing is crawling with wasps. It *bristles* with them.

"She's here," Alice says and I feel it, right in that moment. A sensation of kinesis; the skin tightening on my bones, a stomach drop like a descent. It's a similar sensation to driving over a humpback bridge. Sam must feel it, too, because he shifts uncomfortably, looking around as if someone has just walked up behind him.

"Who?" he asks. "Who's here?"

Alice lifts her head. Her pupils are fat blots of ink. She stares at Sam and her lips curl slowly and with menace. I've heard of your blood running cold before but I haven't believed it was a real thing until this moment. When she speaks, her voice is silky and soft, slightly lisping.

"Little Maggie. Margaret. She didn't like it when you called her that though, did she? It used to make her mad. She has your hair, the same color. Like autumn leaves."

Sam swallows. I see it, the expression on his face. Like a wince of pain.

"Maggie?"

"Yes."

"Can you see her, Alice? What does she look like?"

Alice hesitates, swiping her tongue across her lower lip. Perhaps it is a trick of the light but just for a moment it looks stained black, the color of bruises.

"Not how you remember her."

"Oh?"

"When we shed our corporeal forms, the dead become transformed."

"Into what?" Sam is up, hovering an inch away from his chair now, leaning over the table. I'm studying Alice. *Corporeal?* I think. It's hard to equate this cold, toneless girl with the one who was giggling and reading horoscopes to me. If it's a trick, it's a very clever one.

"Sam—" I say, warningly. He doesn't even look at me, simply waves me away.

"Into *what*, Alice? Transformed into what?"

"Your daughter has become a creature of bone and light. Her skin is a cage, rattling teeth in an empty, eyeless head."

"Jesus," I whisper, and in that moment Alice turns her knife-gaze to me and I shrink away from her. An insectile itch crawls up my spine and into my scalp. It burrows and slithers and makes me want to rip off my fucking skin.

"Careful, Mina," Alice says, and the way her voice curls around the letters *hurts, it hurts,* like the sound of my name coming from her mouth is barbed and I can't move. She pins me against the chair with one foot in the other world, *beyond the veil,* the wasps buzzing in the light shade. Alice peels her gaze back to Sam and my chest expands, filling with air. Relief.

"You abandoned her. Little Margaret. Why did you do that, Sam?"

He looks briefly at the camera and then to me. His voice jolts, too loud, fingers gripping the edge of the table.

"Don't. Don't say that. I didn't abandon her."

I cast a glance over my shoulder. That sensation of weirdness, of something being a little *off-center* is growing stronger. I can hear those sounds again, the ones I heard on my first night in the house that made me think of Black Shuck the hellhound, panting and snarling and spewing white foam. I wonder if the camera will pick it up. Sam doesn't seem to notice. His cheeks are slowly reddening, becoming inflamed. He rakes his fingers through his hair.

"All those wires," Alice says playfully. "They came out of her like tentacles. Poor Maggie. The hospital floors made your shoes squeak, didn't they? Sometimes you still hear it, at night. Soft-soled shoes on polished floors, the echo of the ward. Maggie heard it, too. You thought she didn't, but she did. She heard all of it, even at the end."

Sam's face twists into a grimace. He locks his hands together in a pleading gesture and says in a low, trembling voice, "Tell Maggie I'm sorry. I didn't mean it. I was afraid."

Alice smiles but her voice is full of menace.

"You left her to die in a strange bed in a frightening place."

Sam looks at me desperately and I don't know what to say. No wonder he has gone to such lengths trying to find her, I think. *It must hollow you out, the guilt.*

"It was the hospital. I don't— I was so afraid of—of seeing what was happening to her!"

I want to comfort him, to put a hand on his arm, say soothing words. But I'm too afraid that Alice will turn and look at me again with that baneful stare. I don't know how Sam is managing it, the weight of her judgment. He repeats himself, "Tell her, Alice! Tell her I'm sorry."

The noise at the kitchen door has changed texture, deepening to a scratching as if something is digging its way in. Sam slowly turns his head.

"What is that?"

"Don't," I warn him, as he rises from his chair, one hand rubbing the back of his neck. Alice's lips pull back from her teeth. It's how I imagine someone would try to smile if they have only ever had a smile described to them. Her eyes swivel in their sockets and a bubble of something black swells and pops between her parted lips.

"Don't open it, Sam. It's not what you think."

I'm reaching for him too late, he's already brushing past me. He looks as if he has aged a decade, unsteady on his feet.

"Is it her? Is she here? Alice? You said she was here."

Fear leeches all the saliva from my mouth because I see what he is about to do. Sam walks across the kitchen toward the door.

The scratching is becoming more frantic and now the door seems to be bowing inward as if something of a great weight and force were pressing in on the other side of it. The wood groans under the pressure.

"Sam, that isn't her, it's not Maggie. Sam!"

He's not listening. He is standing in front of the door with his T-shirt untucked and his hands opening and closing into fists. *Her bones are a cage, rattling teeth in an empty, eyeless head*, I think, and when I look at Alice her eyes have cleared, her face slack with shock.

"What's happening, Mina?" she asks, in a voice that finally sounds like her own. "What's all that noise?"

"Sam!" I jolt out of my seat, meaning to stop him but even now I can see his hand is reaching for the doorknob, his ghastly smile, caught in profile, painfully happy and relieved and earnest. He thinks it is his daughter, his Maggie. He thinks she has returned.

"Sam, don't—"

Too late. He swings the door open. A silence descends like an axe falling, heavy as lead. I feel the abrupt sensation of a connection severed, the shock of it. Out there the hall is empty, sickly yellow sunlight slicing through the frosted glass in the front door. Sam is panting as if winded, his expression tortured. He switches around to look at Alice and spits as he talks, seemingly unable to restrain himself.

"Where is she, Alice? Where's Maggie?"

Alice looks from me to Sam, her expression blank and uncomprehending. Overhead, the wasps toil against the light shade.

"Where's my little girl?"

Sam's voice breaks and he bows his head. My nerves are shot, my voice trembling as I ask, "Alice, hey. Hey, look at me. When you said 'she's here,' who did you mean?"

"Her. The witch woman," she whispers, barely audible. "She left her mark on the door."

I stand up slowly, chair scraping over the floor. Sam lifts his head and pulls the door inward so the whole panel becomes visible. There is a moment of long, spun silence before Sam says very quietly, "Get the camera, Mina."

I pull it from the tripod, holding it with both hands to keep it steady. The video camera is bulky and noisy, with PROPERTY OF THE WESTERN HERALD stamped on the casing. I fill the frame with the image of the outside of the kitchen door, brushing past Sam who is standing motionless, mouth hung slightly open in shock. I linger on the places where the paint has been gouged all the way down to the wood, the places where the panels have splintered and cracked. I think of those snarling, grinding sounds, and my whole body turns cold, skin raw with gooseflesh. Out here in the hallway that sweet smell of spoilage is rich and soupy. I turn the camera so that the whole door can be seen, motioning to Sam to step aside so I can capture it all. It's that comet shape again, the one I saw burned into the rafter on Tanner's Row and chalked on the pavement outside—the witch's "mark" Bert had called it—and now here it is, rendered so large the long tail scrapes beyond the doorframe and into the wallpaper, ending about a foot down the hall. Some of the scratches are raked so deep the plasterboard is starting to peel away. I lower the camera, stunned into silence. Sam looks at me and I can't read his expression. His face is pained, deeply lined. He looks like he's just woken from a nightmare.

"I need to take a walk," he says, not looking at me, not looking at Alice. "I need to get out of this house."

TWENTY-ONE

Just after four I walk up to the green, my head spinning. I can't stop thinking about the way it felt when Alice looked at me, as if my skin were flayed and my nerves exposed, how her gaze had substance, the texture of sand in an open wound. Alice, saying *"the dead become transformed"* and me wondering with softly growing horror what Eddie has become in his transformation. Some shade perhaps, with pinprick white eyes. Hands of ice and glass. I came here hoping to reach him somehow, to reassure myself he was not suffering, that he was not gone. *"If there's anything out there, I'll come back and tell you, Meens,"* he'd said.

Please don't, Eddie, I think now. *I don't think I can bear it.*

I reach the phone box and sift through the change in my purse, beginning to dial our home number before reconsidering and dialing the number for the laboratory instead. I wait while the call connects, gazing out over the green. In the late-afternoon light it looks dusky and soporific, the water of the large village pond gleaming like mercury. The tall reeds and rushes that surround it are brushed with pollen, giving it an almost misty aura.

"Baldhu, eight-nine-four," a voice says in my ear. Female. My heart sinks a little.

"Hi! It's—I'm looking for Mr. Simmons. Oscar. It's his fiancée."

I hear it. Just before her hand covers the mouthpiece, I hear it and I can picture it with such startling clarity that for a moment I am somewhere else entirely; Oscar's small, modern lab with the sanitary surfaces and the bulky computers and the hooded white suits they wear which rustle as they walk. One word, softly spoken. Oscar's voice.

"No."

"I'm sorry, he's unavailable," the female voice tells me and I have to fight an urge to ask: *Is he fucking you, Lucy?*

"When will he be back?"

A brief pause. I imagine they are exchanging another glance, him signaling to her with his eyes, a wave of his hand. Then, "I believe he's left for the day."

I hang up. I don't know what I'll say otherwise and even though I've long suspected it, grown accustomed to it almost in a reflective, weary way, I am surprised to find my cheeks are wet with tears. I stand very still and hold my hand over my mouth, struggling to hold back a sob. *"No,"* he said and that was so evident, so final. I don't need anything more.

"Mina!"

I turn reluctantly, swiping at my cheeks. It's Fern, crossing the grass toward where I am standing outside the phone box on the pavement, one hand on the door for support. Her smile fades as she gets closer and, by the time she reaches me, has been replaced by a soft expression of concern.

"Oh man," she says. Fern steers me gently away, sliding an arm around my shaking shoulders. "I know me and you don't hardly know each other but come here. Have a hug. I'm sorry for whatever upset you, honey. Life's shit sometimes, isn't it?"

I sniffle and nod, unable to find my voice. She looks at me carefully as she pulls away.

"Want to walk back with me? Bert's bringing Stevie home about now."

We link arms as we cross the grass, the sun low in the sky, a faint tinge of smoke on the air.

"You know I heard about Vicky," Fern tells me gently, "and they're saying the paramedics got to her in time. She'll be all right, they reckon."

We carry on in silence for another moment.

"Everyone's saying Alice cursed her," she continues. "Poor Alice. This must all be such a headfuck for her. She could do with getting out of that house, even just for an afternoon, 'cos if enough people start telling you you're a witch, then sooner or later you're going to start believing it."

"I think maybe that's what they want. The dad, certainly. He'd love her to be a witch, to get a headline out of it. It makes me wonder—"

"Wonder what?" Fern asks, looking at me askance. We pass a honeysuckle bush singing with scarlet blossoms.

"Oh, I don't know. I feel like I'm losing sight of what I'm here for."

"To help her."

"Right. But it's like this whole town wants the opposite. They're feeding into the delusion. How am I meant to convince her it's all in her head if people are outside demanding she talk to their dead relatives?"

Fern conceals a small, secretive smile and squeezes my arm.

"We're not all bad."

"Oh Fern, no. No, of course not, I'm sorry. You've been lovely, and Bert, too. Alice just needs to get out of that fucking house."

"Take her to Bert and Mary's for an hour or two. It's right next door."

I think of Alice saying *"They used to make us nice dinners and let us help ourselves to the choc ices in the freezer."* How they looked after her and Tamsin after Billy had been born. Then I think of what Bert said about taking in waifs and strays, and something clicks.

"You stayed with them, too, didn't you? When you were younger. You hinted at it yesterday."

Fern gives me a small, pointed smile.

"Yeah. Between the ages of thirteen and fifteen, I was too much of a handful for my parents, and Bert and Mary took me in. Lisa, too, when she first got pregnant with Alice, and her mum kicked her out. Me and Mary, we used to drink these cocktails on sun loungers in the garden—"

"*Bertinis*." I laugh. "Alice told me about them, too."

"Ha! *Bertinis*! That's right. Pineapple and orange slice on the rim. I thought I was so sophisticated with my straw and my cocktail glass. It was so sweet it hurt your teeth but at the time it tasted like sunshine. Mary would doze off in the sun and me and Bert, we'd—"

She smiles, puzzled.

"What?"

"It's funny, but I'm struggling to remember. He used to put music on the old record player. Old jazz records. The records sounded scratchy, I guess because they were so old. Huh. My memory is shocking. Last week I called Stevie's teacher the wrong name and yesterday I nearly burned the flat down because I forgot the chops under the grill—and yet I can tell you the name of every fucking Ninja Turtle! What's all that about?"

We laugh. It feels good, slowly walking in the sun, leaning into each other as if there are delicious secrets to share. I'm trying to pinpoint this sensation and realize with a hollow shock that it is kindness. No, more than that. It's *friendship*. I hadn't noticed the absence of it before but for so long it has just been Oscar and me and no one else. I'm worried I'm about to start crying again so I'm relieved to see Bert and Stevie standing on the edge of the green. Stevie is jumping up and down with excitement.

"Bert took me to the park! We fed the ducks!"

"What else did we see?" Bert asks her encouragingly. His silvery hair is swept back from his forehead. "A swan!"

"Wow!" Fern easily matches her daughter's excitement. "Did you know swans mate for life, Stevie-Beans? That means they stay together forever and ever. Isn't that cool?"

Stevie's smile falters a little and her face clouds over. She looks at her mother with narrowed eyes.

"Don't call me that, Mummy. No one's allowed to call me that 'cept Bert."

"Oh!" Fern laughs uncertainly as Bert gives her an apologetic smile. "Of course. Sorry, Stevie."

Stevie smiles then, big and wide and generous, and tells her mother about the duck pond and all the bread they threw in and then at one point, in a loud, strident voice, she declares, "And there were piles of bird *shit* everywhere!"

"Stevie!" Fern laughs and then Bert's laughing and so am I, and Stevie grins at me in that way she does, and that's when I notice her hands are dusted with chalk in pink and green and blue. I frown, thinking about those words outside the house scrawled onto the ground, and an ominous, frightened feeling lights up in me like a match head.

TWENTY-TWO

As I turn onto Beacon Terrace on my way back from the green, I see an elderly woman with a shopping trolley on the same stretch of pavement as me. I don't think too much about it, other than supposing she is going for her groceries now curfew has been lifted for the day. It's only as she nears the Webber house that I realize the woman has swerved out into the road, walking in a large semicircle and only mounting the curb again once she is past the front gate. All the while she is staring at number thirteen with such suspicion and fear that it takes me straight back to Paul skinning rabbits and saying scared people do strange things. I scuff at the faded chalk markings with my feet. I think of Vicky lying in a coma, intubated, throat stung fat and swollen. Someone has wiped away the words on the fence and written

new ones, not in chalk but in thick black paint. It no longer says
bE Not afrAId.

It now reads *Burn The Witch.*

Paul is smoking restlessly in the doorway when I reach the
porch, as if he has been looking out for my arrival. He looks
amped up, muscles twitching under his skin. "Who's up there
with her, Mina?" he barks at me. I can see sweat glistening on his
skin. "Who's she talking to?"

I follow him slowly to the bottom of the stairs, listening. I
can hear Alice's voice, strident and loud, like a burned-out priest
administering last rites. I climb a little farther up the stairs until
I can see through the gap in the banister. Alice's bedroom door
is closed. I catch a trace of that smell, so dark it is almost bloody.
Her voice rings out, now singing a song.

"This is a shit show. I thought you were meant to do something! I thought you were here to help her!"

He runs a hand over his face, Adam's apple bobbing convul-
sively in his throat. His voice is hard-knuckled, ugly.

"Paul, you have to calm down."

"I'll calm down when you fix my daughter!"

I bite back the urge to tell him Alice doesn't need fixing, that
she isn't broken. Instead I say, "Where's Sam?"

Paul shrugs.

"God knows. He took off after that séance, didn't he? Probably halfway over the Tamar by now."

I climb the stairs barefoot and silent, trying to catch what
Alice is saying but her voice is so slippery and the words are a
language I no longer recognize. Her voice dips and rises like a

spring tide and by the time I'm pushing open the bedroom door and saying, "Alice, I'm coming in," I'm almost sure she is speaking an old, eldritch language, something buried in a peat bog or dug out of the ice.

Alice is sitting on her bed with her back to the room. She is cross-legged, T-shirt sticking to her spine in damp, sweaty patches, the sunburned skin of her neck visible with her head bowed forward. Her hands are clasped over her ears, voice loud and unmusical. I open my mouth to get her attention when a flicker of movement catches my eye. My heart ratchets up, throat tight. My head turns toward the fireplace where I could have sworn a clutch of pale fingers has quickly withdrawn into the black throat of the chimney; nails dirty and rimed with soot, skin limpid and gray. My pulse ticks at the back of my eyeballs, my breath fish-hooked in my throat. There is nothing there.

No. No. I'm tired. My mind is playing tricks on me.

Still, though. Still. It's as if my synapses have been deadened and cauterized. I stare at the fireplace and when Alice turns her head stiffly and looks at me I wonder if she knows just how frightened I am.

"Did you see her, Mina?" she whispers.

"No," I say. "I didn't see a thing."

I step toward Alice, noticing the Walkman on the floor beside her, headphones spooled messily.

"The batteries have died," she says softly, lowering her hands. "Now I can hear her all the time. I've tried everything but I can't drown her out."

I stare at her. Sitting this way with her feet tucked beneath her, she looks younger than her years, her face a portrait of misery. I wonder if we pushed her too far with the séance, if our very presence here has simply made things worse. I hear Oscar's voice telling me I wasn't ready for this, that I was unexperienced, unprepared. Alice looks up at me.

"I just want to be normal," she whispers. I take a step toward her.

"Alice, you need to listen to me. Yesterday I went up to that house on Tanner's Row. I gathered together all the broken pieces of the witch's bottle and brought it back here."

"Why?"

"So I can prove to you that it's just a bottle. You need to see that with your own eyes. Yes, there's some gross stuff inside it—pee and hair and bent pins—but that's all it is."

My heart is still beating uncomfortably fast and I'm not convinced my voice is quite steady. I don't like being so close to that fireplace, the dark void above it. I wonder if I will see those fingers tonight in my dreams, pale and arachnid.

"We choose how much power we give others over us, Alice. Right now, you're handing over all the power to nothing more than broken glass and bad intentions. You think you're not in control but you are, you *are*."

Alice laughs. It is somehow both gentle and horribly mean.

"Sure, Mina. Okay."

I draw level with her. The floorboard creaks slowly under my weight. Alice doesn't look up at me as she speaks.

"You know one night, just after I got sick, I woke up and Tamsin was sitting here on the floor right about where we are now. Just sitting there smiling and looking up at the fireplace. I was half-asleep and I must have said something like, 'What are you doing, it's the middle of the night,' and Tamsin whispered, 'There's a kitten stuck up in the chimney. Can you hear it?'

"And I could, Mina. I could! A tiny mewing like a little cat was trapped up there, sad and hungry. *Poor little thing,* I remember thinking, and then Tamsin started to move forward as if to reach out for it and that's when I saw the witch's black eye gleaming through the hole and I got out of bed pretty quick after that. I grabbed hold of Tamsin and I dragged her away from the fireplace. At the same time that mewing started to change. It began sounding like squealing, like a pig stuck in a trap. *Urgh.* Just thinking about it makes me feel cold all over. Tamsin started shouting 'get off me' and twisting her arm so fiercely I thought it might just snap. I think I still would've held on to her though, even if it had. Even if the bone had come through the skin I would've kept her away from that black hole and that horrible noise that didn't sound like a kitten no more. You see, the witch, she was trying to draw Tamsin in, and if she did that I wouldn't see my sister ever again."

Alice looks over to the fireplace, her face waxy-looking and stricken with fear.

"I know you all think it's pretending, like I'm a dumb little kid, but you can ask Tamsin, it happened. She was so mad at me she just about screamed the house down until everyone woke up and Mum come running in saying 'what's wrong what's wrong' and all I could tell her was the witch in the chimney wants to eat Tamsin. That's about when Mum started crying. She said, 'I can't take much more of this, Alice, it has to stop.' Like I was doing it on purpose."

She stops and takes in a long, shaky breath. I think of Tamsin saying *"I'm going to get a cat of my very own,"* and the shoe in the grate, just waiting for Sam to reach for it. The bait, the lure. Gooseflesh creeps over my skin. I open my mouth to say something reassuring and that's when my gaze drops into Alice's lap and I see for the first time what she is holding. It's my photograph, the one taken in Crete. I stare at it.

"Alice, where did you get that?"

She looks down at it with mild surprise.

"It's him, isn't it? Eddie. Your brother."

"Have you been going through my things?"

I hear a strangled, gurgled laugh. I can't be sure it came from Alice, not really. Her limbs draw closer to her chest, her eyes turned upward to look at me.

"She tells me things, you know. The witch. She tells me about how my daddy sometimes thinks about taking his deboning knife to one of us kids and opening up our ribs on the kitchen table. He thinks about that *a lot.*"

Alice's lip curls, like a snarl. Her tongue slides along her teeth and my heart jolts. I reach toward her.

"Alice—"

"She told me about Maggie, Sam's little girl. She told me about you, Mina. You and Eddie."

I'm suddenly filled with an urge to scream. It balloons in my throat until I can't breathe. Alice lifts the photo and holds it up to face me.

"I know about the pond with the bad ice in the middle, how it had looked rotted and sunken somehow. Like a bad tooth. It was winter and the trees didn't have any leaves and there was snow on the ground. You don't like going home anymore, do you? Because of that day. Because of what happened."

Fear, fattening in the cave of my heart. I feel it now, crawling all over my skin, tightening my scalp. I want to put my hands over my ears just like she had. I want to be at home watching Oscar fold the newspaper along the creases with tedious precision. I want to crawl under the bed and hide.

"Have you been talking to someone about me?"

"*She* told me. She tells me everything."

I feel breathless, rocked back on my feet. There is a buzzing sound, like a swarm of wasps, only it's in my head, in my *skull*. Like they are nesting in there.

"My brother died a long time ago of pneumonia, Alice. There was nothing we could do." I can feel myself growing anxious, it gnaws at me. "I didn't know the ice was going to break. I thought it would hold!"

A beat. Alice's tongue slips between her lips, just for a second. Black and glistening, a slug. Her voice is deeper, harsher.

"I know what you did, *Meens.*"

That's what does it, hearing my brother's nickname for me in her mouth. I stare at Alice, eyes flared wide, heart pounding in my chest. It feels like something inside me is working loose, blackened as a rotting tooth. She looks up at me from beneath the spikes of her lashes, her mouth stretched into a slick and queasy grin that shows too many teeth.

"Is that her?" I say quietly, bending down and leaning toward her. I make sure her gaze is fixed on me. "Is she in there, Alice? The witch?"

Alice doesn't respond but there is a deep clicking sound from the back of her throat, insectile and frightening. She peels her lips back farther.

"Can I talk to her? I'd like to ask her some questions."

Clickclickclick. A bubble of saliva bursts between her teeth.

"You see, witch—I know something about you that Alice doesn't." I can hear the slow creak of the floorboards under my feet as I lean in close, the *click*-ing ratcheting in Alice's throat, faster and faster, a sound like bones knitting together. I keep my voice to a whisper. "I know what you are. You're a thought.

You're shame and guilt and repressed emotion. You're not a hook in her brain, you're just some bad memories and I'm going to help her scrub you away. You. Aren't. *Real.*"

The clicking stops so abruptly I almost forget to breathe. I can feel the blistering heat of Alice's skin, can see the flare of her nostrils. She is breathing like a gored bull, shoulders flexing as she sucks in air, looking past me. Toward the fireplace.

"Alice?"

"Mina," she whispers, barely moving her lips. "Don't move."

Her eyes are huge, gleaming white saucers. The hairs on the back of my neck prickle. The urge to turn around and look over my shoulder is overwhelming but I am frozen in place, muscles stiff. Alice is shuffling slowly backward until she hits the wall, head shaking. Something scrapes in the chimney breast and then there is the sound of a low, meaty chuckle. I think of that old glass bottle stuffed with hair and pins and balls of dimpled wax.

"Alice, listen to me. There's nothing there, all right? It's a bird. Okay? A bird that got stuck in the flue."

Alice's head stops shaking but her eyes are still luminous and wide with fear. She draws her knees toward her, fingernails digging into her skin. I jut out my chin, defiant.

"There's no witch. No curse. She's a crossed wire in your brain, a delusion, that's all. Okay?"

The scraping sound deepens, as if something is clawing through the brickwork. I can smell that rich, animal odor again, heady as incense. Paul is hammering on the door, his voice loud and strident. "Let me in, let me in." I lift my voice, trying to keep it steady. I can't let her see that I am afraid.

"It's okay. Look at me. It's okay, Alice."

I'm trying to reassure her and yet I can't bring myself to glance behind me in case the witch comes creeping from the hollow throat of the chimney, limbs bent and twisted, face tilted at an upside-down, inconceivable angle, smile slit so wide you can see her teeth all the way back to the molars with the stump of a tongue moving in the gory hole of her mouth. There is a rain of hard blows against the door so heavy that the wood bows inward. Alice's eyes find me. She looks numb with fear.

"You're going to die, Mina Ellis."

Alice's tongue is black and bloated and long. Her teeth chatter together beneath round, haunted eyes. Then the door bursts open and Paul stumbles into the room, his cheeks red and hectic, shirt damp with sweat. I have just a single moment of utter, terrible clarity—*"my daddy sometimes thinks about taking his deboning knife to one of us kids"*—and then his furious expression slides away, face paling. He, too, is looking over my shoulder.

"What the fuck is going on?" he bawls, fists clenched. He looks as though he could start a fight in an empty room. "What *is* that stuff?"

Something unlocks in me. My muscles, rigid and unmoving, suddenly loosen and I slowly turn around to see what they are both staring at behind me.

At first I think it is blood. The dark and viscous liquid oozing sluggishly through the brickwork of the chimney breast certainly appears to be blood. It trickles slowly to the lip of the fireplace where it gathers and swells and begins to drip onto the hearth beneath, forming a fat and glossy puddle of thick, black ichor.

"What is it?" I say, voice cracking slightly. "What's happening?"

Alice is still sitting with her mouth hanging open. Paul looks as if his eyes might bulge out of his head. I take in the scene, the inky goo leaking through all the cracks and crevices like syrup—*molasses,* my tired brain supplies, *it washed away the horses*—and pattering to the tiled floor in large, coin-sized droplets. I crawl over the bed to where Alice, pale and shocked-looking, is staring at the black rivulets as they dribble down the brickwork. I put my arm around her the way Eddie used to do with me when we were kids and I'd had a nightmare, rocking her slightly back and forth, comfort in warmth, in a touch. In keeping the bad things at bay.

TWENTY-THREE

As Alice takes a shower, I fill a bucket with sudsy water to help Paul scrape the worst of the black substance from the wall and carpet. We work silently, avoiding each other's eyes. The room is stiflingly hot, suffocating. I keep thinking about Alice saying *"I know what you did, Meens,"* and fear passes over me like the shadow of a raptor.

"Soot and rainwater," Paul keeps saying, wringing his cloth out into the bucket. "Must have been trapped up there over winter, just collecting into a pool."

We both scrub at the carpet, stained an ugly dark color.

"There's probably a cavity in the bricks. Maybe that's what's been making all these tapping and gurgling noises, eh? Maybe the heat forced it out of the walls."

I don't reply. I don't know precisely what the liquid is but it is gluey and black as tar. Paul sees my hesitancy and gives me a sick grin.

"Some investigator you are. The look on your face when I came in!" He gives a mean little laugh. "You looked like you'd been hit with a fish."

I was frightened, I want to tell him. She knows about me, your daughter. I don't know how, but she *knows*.

"Is Sam back?" I lean back on my heels, wiping my forearm across my brow. Paul shakes his head, lighting the cigarette that hangs out the corner of his mouth.

"Done a runner, I should think. Don't blame him. I wish I'd thought of it first."

"What about Lisa?"

"Tomorrow. The kids will stay with their grandparents a bit longer. Just till all this is over, like."

"I might sleep in here tonight. In Tamsin's bed. Keep an eye on Alice."

Paul frowns.

"You still think she's delusional."

"What did you mean when you said 'this town is built on witches' bones,' Paul?"

I see his brief hesitation, as if pulled up short. He grunts, flicking ash into the fireplace.

"You getting married soon, Mina, that right?"

I hesitate a fraction too long. Just thinking about it feels like shards of glass are being pushed into my chest but I don't feel like admitting to Paul that actually no, my fiancé has almost certainly been cheating on me with his lab assistant, so I make an effort to keep my voice steady when I say, "Yes."

"Heh. He's some sort of scientist, isn't he? Must be rich doing such an important job. Must make a lot of money. Own home, own car. All that'll be yours one day, too."

I frown.

"I suppose."

"Then you'll forgive me for saying that you don't know what it's like to be broke. To be so desperate for money that you dent tins in the supermarket so they'll sell them to you cheap. To bring home the meat that no one else wants eating—offal and chitterlings and bones to make broth. Desperation makes you inventive, Mina. I just think it's important you know that."

I think of the rabbit corpses, skinned and gutted and glossy with blood.

"Every day in this family it feels like we're sinking. I mean, look at this"—he indicates the wall, smeared with black sludge—"the house is falling apart. We're putting food on the table but the kids are growing fast and I don't know how much further we can make things stretch. Do you remember me talking about the Enfield poltergeist? All over the news it was, how them little girls were haunted."

I have a vague memory of a photograph of a young girl catapulted into the air above her bed by what was described as an "unseen force." I nod.

"It was serialised in all the papers at the time. What they called 'supernatural events.' There were photographers, television crews—it was a big thing. Reckon that family made a fortune off it."

He sighs.

"When I called Sam at *The Herald,* Alice had been ill, and although there were some things going on we couldn't explain, I might of made more of it than it was. Elaborated on a few things, maybe."

"Because desperation makes you inventive?"

"I didn't lie, Mina. I just wanted to catch Sam's attention. That's all. That stuff about her puking up the hair and pins, I got the idea from a movie. But everything else—her hearing voices, seeing things—that's all real and now it's gone too far. I'm scared for Alice. It's superstitious, 'round here. You asked me about Banathel being built on witches' bones—they used to drag them onto the green and cut their tongues right out of their heads so they couldn't speak their spells no more. Riddance, it's called. A lot of these women—girls, really, barely more than teenagers some of them—were left to bleed out like cattle. Think about it. All that blood over the years, soaking into the earth. Banathel's foundations are rotted."

"That's horrible."

He turns to look at me over his shoulder. I can just make out the curve of his stubbled cheek and the glint of one dark, suspicious eye.

"It's *tradition*, Mina. You can't outlast it. Best you can do is outrun it."

I wait for Sam to return but by half past nine there's still no sign of him. I eat cold pizza and gladly take Paul's offer of a beer, sitting with the cold bottle clamped between my knees while I write in my little moleskin notebook. I need to find some order, and recording it this way helps me forget how Alice leaned toward me and hissed, *"I know what you did, Meens,"* in a rich, thick voice so unlike her own. I write down how she looked, with her head lowered and her eyes glaring at me through slotted lids. I write about how she said, *"I hear her voice all the time now,"* and then something occurs to me. I set down my pen and rub my temples. Paul is doing the washing up in cold, greasy water, a cigarette jutting from his mouth.

"Hey, Paul, do you have any batteries?"

"What size?"

"Uh, Walkman size."

Paul grunts, wiping his hands dry on the front of his jeans.

"Gone dead, has it? I'm not surprised, the amount Alice listens to it. I said to Lisa that it's cost us more in batteries than it did to buy the bloody thing. We ought to sell it, I told her, we'll save ourselves a fortune, but she won't hear of it. Said it'd be cruel. Tell you what, though, she won't be laughing when we have to have them headphones surgically removed from Alice's bloody head!" He laughs coarsely and nods toward the dresser behind me. "They'll be some in those drawers. Bottom ones, not the top. Have a look. I'm off to watch the news. Apparently they pulled some local kid out the quarry this morning."

My head snaps up. "Dead?"

"Yup." He sighs, shaking his head. "Dumb fucking kids. Everyone knows that quarry's a death trap."

"Who was it?"

Paul shrugs. His face is drawn tight. "Don't know. Just some kid, I heard. Probably trying to cool off in this bleddy heat."

I think of Tuff Shit saying *"coming to set your hair on fire,"* his face creased with tears. Buzz Cut with his thick neck and flat, mean face. I feel that worry again, deep-set and squirming in me like a clew of worms. I rub my hand over my dry lips.

"Can you find out who they are?"

Paul nods. He appears disinterested, nonchalant, but I think it's an act. I think he's thinking the same thing I am. Another one of Alice's tormenters has gone. I close the notebook and turn to the dresser, pulling open the top drawer, the one Lisa seemed to try to hide from view when she found me the map. I forgot about that moment till now and then I see what's in there, and I understand. I reach in and pull out a clump of letters, held together with an elastic band. The first morning we were here, Lisa told us the phone had gone down but I think she was skirting the truth there. It hadn't gone down, it had been cut off. All these envelopes are official-looking, marked IMPORTANT or FINAL REMINDER or DO NOT IGNORE. I pick up one of them and read *Legal Action Has Commenced* through the little plastic window.

"Shit," I hear myself say. I remember Paul saying *"desperation makes you inventive,"* and my stomach sinks. Just for a moment I entertained the idea that this could have been a genuine haunting—that long pale hand I thought I saw retreating into the chimney, the way Alice spoke about Maggie, that clicking in the back of her throat like insects building a nest there. Just for a moment I allowed myself to consider the possibility that it was real—because if it *was* real that meant Eddie might be out there, somewhere. But these bills, this desperation. That changes everything.

I give the batteries to Alice who takes them gratefully, sliding the headphones up over her head with a look of silent relief. I brush my teeth and change into my pajamas, climbing into Tamsin's empty bed with the *Garfield* covers and array of small stuffed toys beneath the pillow. Even though it's nearly ten, it isn't quite full dark and in the dusky light I can just make out Alice sprawled on her covers, can hear the muffled beat of her music and her soft regular breathing as she falls asleep. She looks so peaceful that it's hard to equate her with the same girl who said just hours earlier, *"You're going to die, Mina Ellis."*

I close my eyes and press myself as far back against the wall as I can. Some deep, primal reflex means I am unwilling to turn my back on that fireplace with the black, soot-streaked stains and the holes through which it's all too easy to imagine a glaring eye staring back out at you. I let my mind drift, returning to Oscar and inevitably to Lucy, the girl with the stud pearl earrings and citrusy perfume who sometimes took rides to work with him in the car. Lucy, who probably knew the right way to hold a lump of meteorite in her hands, who could tell the difference between nebulae and galaxies and who knew that once someone got dead they stayed dead.

I fidget miserably, sadness pressing like a concrete block on my chest. It stung earlier when Paul told me *"You don't know what it's like to be broke,"* because there *is* a truth to it, isn't there? Oscar has a good income, disposable wealth, a long future in an ever-expanding field of study. Without that support I'm going to flounder.

"Flounder," Mina? that internal voice sneers. *Sweetheart, you're going to fucking drown.*

I look down at the engagement ring on my finger. I feel like the coyote in the *Road Runner* cartoons who cycles in empty air in the moments before he realizes he's gone over the edge of a cliff. I reach for a frisson of excitement at the new possibilities opening up for me, the endless small changes I'll be free to make once I'm single. I'll be able to take those evening classes I've always wanted to do. Pottery maybe, or jewelry making. I've always thought I had a creative side, but never explored it. Maybe now is the time.

TapTapTap.

I sit upright, suddenly wide awake. My head turns very slowly toward the fireplace. Alice is asleep, lips parted, hands slightly curled by her head.

Tap. Tap. Tap.

It's a very deliberate sound. I slide my legs out from under the covers and stand up beside the fireplace, horribly attuned to the slightest noise. My blood roars in my ears, my pulse frantic. I'm almost dizzy with the anticipation.

TapTapTap.

No, not the fireplace. I move toward Alice's bed, my eyes drifting to the wall above it. I take a couple of steps closer and lean over her carefully, putting my hand on the wall and then pressing my ear up against it, listening. The wallpaper is green with small pink balloons on it. It must have been hung when Alice was younger, before Tamsin was even born, maybe. It feels cool beneath my touch. I curl my fist. I rap back, three times. The tapping comes back right away, urgent, as if they have been waiting for a response.

Taptaptap.

Pause.

Tap. Tap. Tap.

Pause.

TapTapTap.

"Are you kidding?" I whisper to myself, almost laughing. "Ess-o-ess? Really?"

Oscar loves Morse code. He actually bought one of the old machines from the Second World War at an auction, displaying it proudly at home. He's fond of telling anyone who listens that the term "SOS" doesn't, as is commonly believed, stand for Save Our Souls. It is simply a useful sequence designed to be easy to communicate in an emergency. I pull back from the wall, frowning. That's Bert and Mary's house there, I'm sure of it. Could one of them have had an accident? I knock against the wall again but this time there is no reply and when I press my ear to the wall there is no sound at all.

"Shit," I say, my hands on my hips. I'm going to have to go

around there and check. I glance at my watch as I pull on my jeans, cursing the heat and the knot of anxiety in my stomach, pulling tighter and tighter.

God, I'm so thirsty. My throat feels stripped dry. I reach the bottom of the stairs and turn back toward the kitchen, thinking I might just grab a drink before I go. Might, in fact, just skip using a glass and stick my whole head under the faucet, letting the cold water run right into my open mouth. I push the kitchen door wide and there is a figure sitting there in the dark, hunched over a little as if in pain. As their head turns toward me I'm sure for a moment that the eye sockets are empty.

An empty, eyeless head.

I slam the lights on with the heel of my palm.

"Fuck, Sam! What the hell are you doing?"

His eyes have a feverish luster, his jaw speckled with beard growth. The chair creaks beneath him as he leans back.

"What time is it?"

"Coming up to eleven."

"Can't sleep?"

His voice is croaky and damaged sounding. I shake my head, explaining about the tapping coming from Bert and Mary's house. He smiles, but there is not much humor in it.

"I've just been speaking to Bert outside. Maybe five, ten minutes ago. He's fine. I'm sure Mary's fine. Do you want me to come with you?"

"Are you sure? There was definitely someone tapping on the wall."

"I'm positive. We just talked right out front. Bert's worried about the graffiti out there. Have you seen it? All the stuff about witches? He said it feels like a threat. He was asking if he should call the police."

"What did you tell him?"

Sam lights a cigarette, waving out the match with a flick of his hand.

"I said wait till the morning. Things always look different in daylight."

My heart rate is slowing now, just a fraction. Maybe I'm being stupid. Overreacting. Sam gives me another of those barely touching smiles as I turn to the sink and fill a glass with water.

"Morse code." He laughs softly. "Were you a girl guide, Mina?"

"No," I say sulkily. "But I recognize an SOS when I hear one."

"It's probably the pipes, hon. These houses aren't old but they're badly built. Most postwar estates were designed for efficiency, not longevity. Sit down. Have a drink."

"Can't you sleep, either?"

"Not sure I'll ever sleep again. I feel like I've taken a load of speed." His leg is jittering under the table as he knocks the tip of his cigarette against the ashtray.

"Brandy?"

He tilts the bottle toward me. I shake my head and he pours himself a large measure into a plastic beaker. I gulp my glass of water down, almost breathless with thirst.

"Where have you been?"

"Walking. Down into the valley and past the stone circle. Almost made it as far as the coast. I had so much adrenaline feels like I could have kept on going right into the sea."

His gaze drops and he rubs the pad of his thumb against the tabletop, fidgety and anxious.

"Alice was right. I did abandon Maggie." He takes a sip of his drink. His expression is of a man in shock, pulled from the twisted wreckage of something. "She had measles, but we thought she'd brush it off, the way kids do. Only Maggie got sicker and sicker, couldn't eat, couldn't drink. They put her in an adult bed on an adult ward. It made her look so small, like a little doll. In the bed beside her an old man was coughing till blood came out his mouth in a mist. I tried to draw the curtain and my hands were shaking so badly I couldn't manage it. I remember saying to the nurse, 'How long till we get out of here,' and she said, 'As long as it takes.'"

I wait. I can hear him gathering his breath, the way the tears threaten, rising in his throat.

"I told Carla—that's my ex-wife, Maggie's mum—'I can't do this. I can't watch her die.' She said, 'Running away won't stop it happening, Sam.' She thought I was a coward and she was right. The last thing I said to her was 'Call me when it's over.' That's the last thing my little girl ever heard her father say. 'Call me when it's over.' Jesus Christ."

His voice is shimmering, but doesn't break. There are no tears but his mouth works silently for a moment as if warding them off. I reach out and take his hand.

"Sam, is there any chance you told Alice about Maggie, even in passing? Any chance she saw the picture of her you keep in your wallet? 'Hair like autumn leaves,' Alice said. Remember what you told me about cold-reading, Sam. It's clever, but it's still a trick."

"No." He's shaking his head, wiping his mouth with the back of his hand. "No, it was her, it was Maggie. The thing about the shoes squeaking? I hear it every night. Every single night." Now his voice does break, his breathing heaves ragged.

"Sam." I reach out a hand and touch his own, his skin warm and dry. "Sam, it's all right, it's all right."

"It's not fucking all right," he says, rubbing his eyes angrily. "It'll never be all right."

He falls silent, playing with his glass.

I lean closer, my voice low. "I spoke with Paul earlier. He admitted he'd elaborated some of what he'd told you about Alice—and you know what I found in that dresser drawer? Overdue bills. Lots of them. The phone's been cut off. The gas will be next. Things like this don't go away if you ignore them, they just get worse and worse. How long till they lose the house? Three children to feed, only one parent working? It must be a struggle."

"Why are you telling me this?" His voice is weary and sad. It's heartbreaking.

"Because it's money they're after." I think of Tamsin saying *"My dad says when we get our new house we can have a bedroom each"* and add, "Maybe even getting rehoused. All this stuff about Alice, it's just to get their story in the paper. You were right, Sam. You were right all along."

I'm not sure what I'm expecting. Satisfaction, perhaps. A nod, an indication of understanding. Sam doesn't even raise his eyes to me, simply stubs his cigarette out before lighting another.

"Sam?"

"I don't care." He shrugs. "This isn't about the story anymore. I need to ask Alice to talk to Maggie and tell her that I was afraid. I need Maggie to understand, Mina. I need her to forgive me."

I don't know how to respond.

He looks at me, eyes hooded in the dark. "What about you?"

"What about me?"

"I mean, put your skepticism aside for a moment, Mina. You were at the séance today. You heard those sounds at the door and the way Alice's voice changed. That wasn't pretend."

"We don't know that. Hauntings are faked all the time, it's not impossible."

A silence spins out as fragile as an eggshell. Sam leans across the table until our heads are nearly touching. His voice is rough, dry.

"Why are you here, Mina? Why are you really here? Can you answer me that?"

I open my mouth to tell him about my degree, the long hours of study, the weight of it on me. How I need experience, a foothold. But Sam is shaking his head as if already anticipating my excuses, swirling the brandy around in his glass.

"No, be honest. Tell me the truth, Mina."

"Eddie," I say abruptly, so sudden and honest I'm shocked at myself. I instinctively want to clamp a hand over my mouth but I resist. "I want to find Eddie."

"Why?"

"To tell him I'm sorry." My voice has started to shake. The air shimmers as tears prick my eyes.

"Sorry for what?"

Sam's voice is soft but it still feels like hands are squeezing my lungs into knots. I inhale shakily.

"Mina," he says, "tell me what happened to Eddie."

So, I tell him. I tell him how the air smelled like metal, so cold it burned my nostrils. It snowed in the night and the next morning the schools were closed. We ran, Eddie and I, through the lanes and down toward Brewer's Pond, skidding and laughing, our cheeks flushed red. I tell Sam how I saw the lake with its thick layer of glittering ice, how I ran out onto the middle of it with my heart and laughter soaring in the frosty air and how the cracking beneath my feet was suddenly too loud, the world tilting, the snap of Eddie's voice, *Mina! Don't move!*

I stood very still, not even daring to breathe as the ice began to split beneath my feet, cold water seeping up through the cracks, numbing my toes through the flimsy canvas sneakers I was wearing.

"Eddie, I can't swim."

"I know, Mina, just stay still, stay cool. Like a cucumber. I won't let anything happen to you." He inched out onto the ice on his stomach, cheeks glowing red, that long lick of hair he hated so much hanging in his eyes. He reached out his hand and his little voice was shaking, he must have been so cold.

"He knew exactly what to do," I tell Sam, wiping at my eyes with the tips of my fingers. "Eddie saved my life."

Something aches inside me, deep in the hollows. Bones and rubble. I was alone with Eddie the day he died. By that time my father had become heavily involved with the church. My mother was out walking the dog. When she came home and I told her he was gone, she said, very quietly, *"Well, that's that, then."*

When I finish the story, Sam is looking at me with a tenderness which almost takes my breath away.

"Mina, we can save Alice. If you're right, and this is all a scheme to get some money or a new house, then she's being manipulated just as much as we are. We can't leave without exposing that. But if *I'm* right, then she has a gift, and we can't ignore it."

"What are you saying?"

My voice is trembling. I have a bad feeling then, a sensation as though my insides are melting like rubber. Slippery and slick. I know what Sam's saying. He's saying we can try to reach Eddie, and even though I've waited so long, even though I've come all this way cradling hope like a flame in cupped hands, I feel sick at the thought of it, because what if Alice *can* reach out to my brother and he comes through the way Maggie did, his corporeal form shed, his bones light and hollow and filled with ice? That would be bad enough but what if he told them what I'd done? What, then?

TWENTY-FOUR

Sitting around the table in the kitchen downstairs, all of us crammed together shoulder to shoulder like stuck pigs. There's Oscar with a poinsettia in his lap, and Bert and his wife, Mary, who is wearing an oxygen mask over the lower half of her face, misted with condensation. Alice is opposite me and, when no one else is looking, she slowly and deliberately pokes her tongue out. It is blackened and bifurcated like a lizard's. Here's Paul, bringing a dish to the table, saying, *Here's your chicken, just how you like it*, only when he puts the plate down the chicken is still alive, struggling. Everyone's smiling and acting normal and Paul is sharpening the carving knife and Oscar squeezes my hand and when he smiles at me he says, *I love you, Mina, so much,* and the chicken's claws are feebly scratching as Paul says, *Leg or breast?* and no one can hear me as I scream, *It's alive, look at it, it's alive!*

I wake with my legs twisted in the covers, choked with a soft, frightened whimper. I lie there for what feels like a long time but is probably only a few minutes, dry-mouthed and flushed with fright, the sweat cooling on my skin. By the time I'm heading downstairs, the dream is fading and I'm thinking about Mary next door again. Sam assured me last night that both Bert and Mary were fine, but the noises were so precise, so deliberate. Save Our Souls. Or not, as Oscar would remind me.

When I check the sitting room I'm surprised to find the sofa is empty, with Sam's blankets rolled up neatly at one end. The room is foggy with smoke and the empty brandy bottle lists on its side next to a full, choking ashtray. The video camera, the one with PROPERTY OF THE WESTERN HERALD stamped on it, is sat in a nest of wires and cables, hooked up to the television. I wonder if Sam has slept at all or simply sat smoking and finishing the bottle until daylight slipped quietly between the curtains. In the kitchen there is only Alice, eating toast and listening to the radio with the volume up so loud the windows are rattling. I join her, and by the time I've washed the dishes I've persuaded her to join me in visiting Bert and Mary. I can't help but notice that she's lost that haggard, sleepless look and seems to be in better spirits. I even manage to convince her to leave her Walkman at home. We're laughing at something as we walk out of the door into the humid, soupy air and it's only as we're opening the gate leading onto Bert's pathway that Alice sees the writing there, the looping scrawl along the fence that had once read *bE Not afrAId* but now reads *Burn The Witch*. She stares at it a long time.

"Do they mean me?" she asks. She turns to me, her eyes wide and guileless. "Mina, are they talking about me? Am I the witch?"

"Don't be silly." I give her a big smile, but it's empty. "It's just graffiti. It's meaningless."

In one of her interviews Lisa told Sam that when the graffiti had first appeared she'd tried washing it away, but more would always appear the next morning. After a while she'd given up altogether. I remember Stevie's hands again, dusted with chalk, but dismiss it almost immediately. Fern likes the Webbers. She said so herself. Still though, I wish Alice hadn't seen this particular message. Her face looks pained as she steps cautiously around it.

"Bert says they never burned witches anyway. Not in real life. They tortured and hanged them or drowned them in the pond."

I frown.

"That sounds gruesome. I'm not sure Bert should be talking about those things with you."

"Nah. He says history *should* be taught by telling stories. When me and Tamsin were little, he told us all about his ancestors in the seventeenth century. He'd traced them all the way back to the Puritans in Suffolk. That's why we have the Riddance with the costume and the bonfires. We have to keep all these old customs alive, he reckons."

"Does he?" I say, thinking of the hagstones and Paul saying *"They were left to bleed out like cattle."* "I'm afraid I disagree. Some old customs should be better left to die in obscurity."

"Aw, don't say that to Bert, Mina. He'd be gutted."

Alice knocks on the door of Bert's house, grinning. It strikes me in the moment before Bert opens the door and welcomes us inside that she looks bright and happy, almost beautiful. It's the first time since I arrived that her face hasn't been clouded in misery and suspicion. It makes me hopeful, in a way, that underneath it all there is still a normal girl.

Bert's house is cool and clean and quiet. The hallway smells of polish and detergent and potpourri. I can hear the soft *tick, tick* of the clock on the mantelpiece, the gentle bubbling of a fish tank on a shelf near the television. It's no wonder Alice liked coming here when she was younger. Compared with the chaos of her own home, this must have felt like a safe harbor. Alice sinks into the overstuffed floral armchair, kicking off her sandals. I study the framed newspaper clippings from *The West Briton* and *The Morning News* that hang over the sofa, all crediting Bert Roscow in the byline. I can hear him whistling in the kitchen. He seemed delighted to see us both and was insisting on making a jug of iced tea.

"I'm so pleased you decided to drop by," he tells us, putting coasters onto the coffee table. "And look what I found hiding behind the biscuit barrel!"

He holds out his hand to reveal tiny paper cocktail umbrellas. Alice accepts a tall glass choked with ice and amber liquid, grinning when Bert opens the paper umbrella and puts it behind his ear. The other he puts in her drink, beside the straw.

"No Bertinis?" she asks.

"I'm afraid not. If I'd known you were coming I could have had some prepared but we're all out of tinned pineapple. This curfew is playing havoc with my shopping habits, I tell you."

"I was just admiring your work, Bert," I tell him, pointing to the framed clippings behind me. "I notice you wrote a piece on genealogy."

"On what?" Alice asks.

"Lineage." Bert smiles. "I spent a lot of time tracing my family tree. I even managed to do one for Mary. We discovered her ancestor had sailed on the *Lady Penrhyn* to the penal colonies in Australia. She'd been charged with assault and theft. It's fascinating stuff."

"Is Mary not around?" Alice asks hopefully. "I feel like I haven't seen her in forever."

"Ah, no. I'm afraid she's still asleep."

"Did she have a rough night?" I ask, putting my glass back on the table. The cold drink has made my teeth hurt but, God, it tasted good.

Bert frowns. His shirt is freshly pressed and his hair combed so neatly you can see the furrows in it.

"Not that I know of. On the contrary, this new pain medication is putting her to sleep more hours than she's awake. Come eight o'clock she's out like a light."

"Is that her?" I'm pointing to a framed photograph on the table beside Bert's armchair. It is a black-and-white wedding picture of a young couple dancing together; the bride in a floor-length gown, bridal train held in one of her hands, the groom in top hat and tails grinning at her. Bert reaches past the old record player and stacks of LPs to pick it up, smiling.

"That's right. Our wedding day, July 14, 1953. We were dancing to Billie Holiday singing 'Blue Moon.'"

"It's a lovely photo."

"She's a lovely woman. We've been married for thirty-odd years. And they really have been 'odd' years hah!" He laughs, seemingly delighted with his joke, then his countenance softens as he leans toward Alice.

"Talking of odd—Alice love, I don't know what to tell you

about those people that have been gathering out there. Do you know what the word 'tricoteuse' means?"

She shakes her head.

"It's French. It means 'knitter.' Historically, it was used to describe the women who would sit beside the guillotine and knit to keep their hands busy while heads rolled during the Revolution."

"Urgh." Alice pulls a face. "Why?"

"For many reasons, but mostly for sport. They would often sit so close they would get splattered with the blood of whichever unfortunate aristocrats had met the blade. That's who they are, these gawkers. They're like vultures, circling."

I help myself to another iced tea as the conversation washes back and forth. I'm surprised to find myself close to tears—it's that wedding photo, I think, the two of them brimming with hope and optimism, glad-eyed and joyful. The way Bert is looking at Mary in that picture, the way his face lights up. I don't think Oscar has ever looked at me that way.

"Hey, Bert. Do you mind if I use your bathroom?" I say, hoping my voice stays steady.

"Top of the stairs. There's a sign on the door if you're not sure which one."

Alice laughs again.

"'If you sprinkle when you tinkle—'"

"'—be a sweet and wipe the seat!'" Bert finishes and the two of them grin at each other.

Once upstairs I draw a few deep breaths with my back pressed against the bathroom door, hand clamped over my mouth to stop the tears spilling out of control. It's hard to know if I'm upset because of Oscar's affair or because I'm so afraid of what I will be once I have lost everything. I've barely known my adult life without him. There's fear there, of course, but I also feel a guilty spark of excitement, at the thrill of rediscovering who I am, the things I like. After a few moments I inhale shakily and splash my face with cold water, patting the skin beneath my eyes with a folded tissue.

I find myself hesitating before heading back downstairs. Along the hallway are three doors, and if I'm calculating correctly the middle one will border Alice and Tamsin's bedroom next door. That's where it came from. SOS. It's like an itch I can't resist scratching.

Forget it.

I almost do. Instead, at the last moment, I walk very quietly to the second doorway and stand outside it, listening. Downstairs I can hear Bert and Alice talking animatedly, voices overlapping, laughter. Fern was right, this is good for her. I put my fingers around the doorknob and it turns so easily I am almost sure it was already open. I tell myself I will just check on Mary because it's the responsible thing to do, and if she's asleep, then no harm, no foul.

"Mrs. Roscow?" I whisper. "Mary? Is everything all right?"

Silence.

"Mrs. Roscow?"

Inside the bedroom the light is bright and clean and it takes a moment for my eyes to adjust to the glare. I take in the primrose-yellow walls, the soft watercolor paintings, and the rounded, velvet headboard. They are in stark contrast to the commode chair in the corner and the nebuliser on the bedside table, the crisp smell of sanitation. In Eddie's last days the smell of his room was like this—clinical, disinfectant and bleach, the dry heat of the oxygen pump, rubber bed sheets, latex gloves.

"Mrs. Roscow?"

The figure in the bed is turned away from me, facing the window. I can hear the rasp of her breathing, how wet and painful it sounds. One pale hand lies on top of the covers.

"Mary?"

She must be asleep because she isn't reacting to the sound of my voice. I am about to slip silently back out the door when something draws my attention. I edge slowly around the bed, discomfort tightening like a metal band around my ribs. The net curtains flutter slightly as I brush past. I'm no longer looking at the sleeping figure in the bed. I'm staring at the wall above the bedside table where the nebuliser sits with its bulb of yellowing rubber the color of nicotine.

Black smudges on the paintwork in crescent moon shapes, a few inches long. Scuff marks. As if made with an object, perhaps a walking stick or the heel of a shoe. Someone *has* been hitting the wall. Tapping out a message, maybe. That discomfort pulls in another notch. I look down at Mary and that's when the floor seems to fall away from me, fear squeezing my throat so tightly I see stars.

She is looking right at me, pinprick pupils floating on irises the pale gray of snow clouds. There is no surprise on her face, no nervousness or fear. Just a simple weariness, mouth unhinged and hanging open, showing stubs of yellowing teeth. Her skin is very pale and creased as crumpled linen.

"Mary! I didn't mean to wake you. Are you okay? Do you want me to get Bert?"

Nothing. I step closer, pointing to the marks beside the headboard.

"I heard tapping last night. On the wall. Was that you?"

The slightest movement, a nod. The starched pillow rustles beneath her.

"Do you need help? Do you need me to call someone?"

She watches me with those arctic eyes, mouth working. She is trying to speak. Her chest heaves with the effort.

"Bill—" she drawls, her voice gluey. "Bill—"

"Billy?"

She nods, eyes close, open. She is so weak, trembling with the effort.

"Billy? What about him? Is he in trouble?"

"Billy," she whispers, then her voice disappears completely and she just mouths the word at me. Her eyes seek me out like searchlights, pleading with me to understand. *Bill. Eee.*

Mary's eyes close, her hand lifts. She is so pale and bloodless, like a vampire. Her jaw works uselessly, her breathing too fast, too labored. Her teeth are long and rooted, discolored in her pale gums.

"Mary, don't exert yourself. And don't worry about Billy, don't worry about anything. He's with his grandparents, him and Tamsin both. They're safe."

Her eyes are half-open, revealing narrow slits of white. The nightdress hangs on her bones as she lifts her hand and reaches it toward me. I don't want to take it. I'm too scared, too cowardly. What if it feels cold like Eddie's had? What if it feels like ice?

SOS. I lean a little closer to Mary, close enough that I can see the rich blue veins that run beneath her thin skin. I keep my voice low.

"Mary, are you in trouble?"

Her eyes slide to the doorway and her breathing begins to hitch wetly, spittle building in the corners of her mouth. I turn and see Bert standing there, looking from me to Mary and back again.

"What's going on?" His brow is deeply furrowed. "I thought I told you, Mina, she needs her rest."

I'm caught. I pin a smile to my face, keep my voice bright.

"I heard something. I thought she might need help."

"Mary, love. It's me. It's all right."

He leans over the bed and the concern that tightens his features makes me feel embarrassed and ashamed, caught sneaking around like a kid. Mary's eyes roll back toward me and Bert strokes her hair back from her forehead with a touch borne out of infinite tenderness.

"Bert, I'm sorry. I just—"

He waves me away.

"It's her suffering, Mina. I can't bear it. I just want it to end. Do you understand how that feels?"

He lifts his gaze then and his eyes meet mine and there's a moment when I feel utterly weightless. I have to reach out a hand to steady myself on the dressing table behind me.

"You'd better go downstairs." He turns back to Mary, waving me away. "Alice will be wondering where you are."

I do as he asks without another word, closing the door gently behind me. The binding in my chest is a constrictor, a deep and sinuous flex that tightens, tightens.

TWENTY-FIVE

As we leave Bert's house I tell Alice that I have something I need to do. She looks at me, concerned.

"What about the curfew?"

"I won't be long. Just go inside, okay?"

Overhead the sky is a vast, soaring blue. Sunlight glitters on chrome and glass, the air dusty in my throat. The news report this morning said two hundred and thirteen people had been treated for heat exhaustion in a traffic jam yesterday, with four people pulled dead from their cars. The words "You are advised to stay indoors" flashed up on the screen, bookended by red exclamation marks. No wonder everyone is so jumpy. Even the weather is against us.

Billy. Why had Mary talked about Billy? As far as I knew, he was the only one of the children that hadn't spent a lot of time with Bert and Mary when he was growing up. I wonder if I'll get the chance to speak with him. Paul said Lisa would be back today. I resolve to try.

The video store is open, dark and cool inside. There is a faint odor of incense and damp carpet and the ripe, fruity smell I recognize from my first year in a student flatshare: weed.

"Fern?" I call out to the empty shop. I turn to the hagstones stacked on the knotted string which hang in the doorway. The pebbles are washed smooth and streaked with veins. "You here?"

There is a doorway opposite, standing ajar. Beyond, it is dark. I move closer, trailing my hand along the ice-cream freezer that drones noisily like a swarm of bees. *Or wasps*, I think.

"Fern?"

The doorway leads to a narrow staircase that crooks out of sight. Upstairs I can hear the rustle of movement. Had Fern told me she and Stevie lived above the shop or had I just assumed it? I lift my hand and knock at the door. Outside, a car engine backfires and I jump skittishly. *What's happened to you, Mina?*

"It's this town," I whisper to myself. "That's what it is. It's all the bloody witches in it."

"Mina?" I look up. There's Fern at the top of the staircase, peering down at me. Her face is a study in concern; puckered brow, pinched, frowning lips. "You talking to yourself?"

I give her what I hope is a reassuring smile.

"Only way to get a sensible conversation," I reply. "Can I come up? I just need five minutes."

The stairs are narrow, the floor not quite level. I follow Fern through another doorway that opens into a large, open-plan room with oriel windows that look out over the green and the peat-colored hills beyond. The floorboards are covered with a patchwork of rugs and a tiny kitchenette has been sectioned off with a small bamboo divider. A little table sits in front of the window and Fern leans across to unlatch it, looking at me curiously.

"You sure you're all right, Mina?"

I smile tightly.

"People always ask that, don't they? But they're never really interested in the answer."

"Maybe you're just talking to the wrong people."

I stare at her. Kindness will undo me. I don't have time for it. I feel another wave of tears and I swallow against it, the backs of my eyeballs tingling and burning.

"I'm fine. Just had some bad dreams."

"I'm making coffee. Do you want one?"

"Yes. Thanks, Fern."

I take a seat at the table. On it is a scattering of drawings—child's drawings of little chubby animals and tall stick people in crowns and robes all sketched out in chalks of pale green, pale pink, a soft baby blue.

"Those masterpieces are Stevie's," Fern tells me, looking over the door of the fridge. "She's decided she wants to be an artist when she's older so now I'm finding chalky fingerprints and blobs of paint all over the house. Just put them to one side."

I do so, letting my gaze drift toward the green. It is empty of course—no dog walkers, no picnickers, no children playing by the pond. Fern seems to read my mind because she looks over from the hob and says, "Weird, right? How quiet it is out there. Summer holidays and not a soul around. I'm starting to find it a bit creepy."

"Bert said the curfew is playing havoc with his shopping."

"Tell me about it. No milk yesterday, this morning no bread. It's a worry."

I brush aside a sprinkle of tobacco into my cupped palm and scatter it into the ashtray. Upstairs, a thud and Stevie's voice exclaiming, "Kabloo-hoo-hoo-hooey!"

"She's got them all," Fern tells me. "Michelangelo, Donatello. The whole bloody set. It's cost me a bomb but it keeps her busy and what price a little freedom for her mother, huh?"

"I like your place."

She looks at me over her shoulder, one eyebrow perfectly arched as if judging whether I'm being sarcastic or not.

"It came with the shop. Used to be just for storage before I bought it. It's a pit, but it's *our* pit."

"I think it's great. Cozy."

"Huh." She passes me a mug of coffee and sits opposite. "I bet you've got one of those houses with fitted carpets and double glazing, haven't you? A double garage for both your cars."

"One car," I correct her. "I don't drive."

"I'm right about the house, though?"

I nod. *Oscar's house,* the voice says primly. *Not yours. Nothing in it belongs to you and now it never will.* I swallow my coffee. It's so hot it burns but it dissolves the lump in my throat.

"Is that what I look like to you? The sort of woman with a big posh house?"

Fern looks me up and down.

"To level with you, Mina, what you look like is shit. That's why I asked if you were *really* all right."

I put down my cup and point to her cigarettes.

"Can I get one of those?"

"God, yes. Help yourself. Misery loves company."

I take one and light it, blowing a long stream of smoke up toward the open window. I haven't smoked since university and almost never since I met Oscar. He used to take great delight in telling me the grave effects each inhalation had on my lungs.

"How is it?" Fern asks.

"Making my head swim."

"Ooh, that's the best part."

We smile at each other and just in that moment it's as if all the horror is bleached and faded away. We are just two women in a messy room full of rugs and plants on a bright sunny morning, talking the way I've seen friends do. It's nice. I wish it could be like this always. But it's a bubble, and like all bubbles, it has to burst.

"Fern, I've got to ask you something. About Bert."

"Uh-huh." She tips her head to indicate that she is listening. "I thought this was coming."

I stare at her in confusion and surprise.

"What do you mean?"

"This is about the basement, right? At Bert's house?"

I'm so confused I can only shake my head. I was going to ask her about Mary, about their relationship. I planned to tell her about the tapping on the wall but now, my interest piqued, I lean forward in my chair as she continues mildly, "Only Sam came by early this morning and asked me the same thing. 'What does Bert keep in the basement?' Tamsin said something in her interview and he said it's been worrying at him ever since."

I think of the video camera hooked up to the television. It's too easy to picture Sam, a man who appears to be coming undone at the seams, cigarette burning between his fingers, watching the taped interviews over and over all night, face lined with concentration.

"Go on."

Fern shifts uncomfortably. In the golden light her hair shines a dark, polished auburn.

"Well, it-it's just that. He came and asked me and I told him what I know."

"Which is?" I roll my hand to encourage her to keep talking.

She sighs. "I'll tell you exactly what I told him which is that I don't remember ever going down there. That's the truth. It was a long time ago, Mina, and you have to remember I wasn't in a good place. I was a teenager and I was *angry*. I was taking a lot of speed, a lot of pills. So much of that time is just darkness in here, you know?"

She taps the side of her temple with a polished nail.

I nod, but I'm not done. "Did they ever argue? Bert and Mary? Did she ever seem as if she was frightened of him?"

Fern takes a sip of her coffee and leans back in her chair. "You know what, I think there *was* something. Yeah. Mary was telling Bert he couldn't have them in the house."

"Couldn't have what?"

Fern screws her face up in concentration. "God, I tell you— motherhood softens your brain, don't let anyone ever tell you any different. I honestly don't remember. Or maybe they just never told me, and I overheard. It was nearly ten years ago after all. I *do* remember Mary saying to Bert, 'I won't have those things in the house.' She sounded angry, like properly *mad*. And Mary never got mad. Not with Bert."

"You don't know what 'they' were?"

"I don't, hon, and even if I did it might have nothing to do with Alice or the basement or any of it. It just stands out to me because, like I said, Mary never got mad at Bert. She's a sweetheart, really."

"Oh," I say, visibly deflated. I stub the cigarette out in the ashtray. Fern puts her hand on my arm, leaning toward me so close I can see the freckles on her skin under her pale, creamy makeup.

"Listen, Stevie told her teacher once that I had a pet anaconda that I kept in the bath. Kids say weird things, don't they? Their brains are all glitter and explosions. Maybe Tamsin is just repeating something she heard or saw on the television?"

I'm struck by an idea then, straightening up in my chair.

"Could I talk to her?"

"To Stevie?"

"Yes! She's at Bert's a lot, isn't she? Maybe she'll know something we don't."

Fern's whole expression changes. Her eyes flatten, narrowing a little. Her mouth is drawn in a sharp, tight line.

"Absolutely not. It's out of the question. She's seven years old for fuck's sake. Don't drag her into this."

I realize I've gone too far, even as Fern snatches up the coffee cups and stalks away to the kitchen. Alice is tainted and even if I can knock the supports out from under her delusions, the town will remember. That's how superstitions thrive, after all.

"Fern, I'm sorry. Of course. I wasn't thinking."

I push my chair back and grab my bag, suddenly keen to be out in the cleansing sunshine, hotter than fire. Another thud from upstairs rattles the windows and Stevie cackles a big, full laugh.

Fern studies me, unsmiling, seeming to be bracing herself against a fall. Then her eyes soften a little and she releases a long, shuddering breath.

"No, I'm sorry. I overreacted. I just don't want her swept up in all this, you know?"

I nod, stepping forward to shake her hand. Ignoring me, Fern grips me in a tight, clammy hug, pressing me to her close enough to whisper into my ear.

"Mina, I meant what I said. I really am interested in how you are. If you ever want to talk about it, you know where I am."

The mind can turn on you, can't it? That's what Paul told me. I try not to think about poor Terry bleeding out in his beloved Ford Escort, try not to think about those white, groping fingers hanging from the chimney in the dark of the fireplace. It's just fear, making my brain play tricks on me. It's not real. None of it is real.

TWENTY—SIX

That afternoon, the news report confirms something I had already begun to suspect. The young boy found drowned in the quarry is Simon Pascoe, local to the town of Banathel. When his picture flashes up on the screen, I recognize him immediately as the squat, muscular boy with the buzz cut and furry upper lip who held Vicky up on his shoulders. *"Where's your broomstick to, Alice?"* he yelled, in a voice hard and coarse as winter soil. Alice made a gulping sound as his image appeared behind the newsreader and left the room at a run. Sam and I had exchanged a brief, horrified look. We both know this means the stories about Alice will get worse.

By eight o'clock that evening, there is no one gathering outside the Webber house, no assembling mob with pitchforks and torches, and I let myself relax a little. The hot air clings like static, a feeling of a current moving over the skin. Alice is subdued, lying on the floor with her ankles crossed, watching a game-show. Lisa isn't due back from her parents' until nine and Paul is working another night shift on the killing floor. Sam and I are in the kitchen, playing cards. He is heavy-eyed, his voice scratchy. There is a three-day growth of beard raking his jaw and throat. As I lose yet another hand, he looks at me suspiciously.

"Come on, Mina. You're not even trying."

I sigh, leaning back in my chair with my arms folded over my chest.

"Can I ask you about something?"

"Sure." He nods, shuffling the cards.

"What does Tamsin say on the video, about Bert's basement?"

"Huh? Oh, that." He sniffs dismissively. "I thought it was something, but it was nothing. There's a point where Tamsin says something like 'I'm scared of Bert's basement' so I thought it might be worth chasing it up. It wasn't."

"You went to Fern."

"Yes. I went to Paul, too. Then I went to Bert."

This surprises me. He must see it on my face because he laughs, fanning the cards out in his hand.

"I got there just after you and Alice had left. Busy day for Bert, by all accounts. I asked him about the basement and he let me in to take a look around."

"What's down there?"

Sam holds the fanned cards out to me. "Pick a card."

"Sam!"

"All right, all right. There's nothing down there. A worktable, lots of boxes. It's well-lit and tidy. A few cobwebs, maybe. I think Tamsin might just have a touch of little sister syndrome."

"You mean she's feeling jealous of Alice?"

Sam nods, proffering the cards to me once more.

"That's right," he says, as I finally give in and slide one toward me. I peel it up to look at it. Two of hearts. "She wants the attention. You can't blame her really."

A sudden knock at the door startles us and I drop the card I'm holding. Sam curses, leaning back in his chair so he can peer down the dark hallway. That strange comet shape—the apotropaic mark that appeared outside and on the rafter in the empty house—is still horribly visible, carved deep and ugly into the wall.

"Should we get that?" I ask. Glimpsed through the reeded glass of the porch door, the figure standing there looks distorted, almost dreamlike. I suddenly feel that same creeping dread that I felt in Alice's bedroom. I almost reach out to Sam as he stands awkwardly and moves to answer the door. I almost say to him, *No, don't!*

"It's me, you daft sods," a muffled but familiar voice says on the other side of the door and Sam's face breaks into a relieved grin.

"It's Bert."

I release a long, shuddering breath as Sam unlatches the door. We're all on edge, jittery. Bert and Sam have a brief, murmured conversation and then Sam begins fishing his car keys out of his pocket.

"What's going on, Sam?" I ask. It's Bert who responds, standing in the hallway with one hand on the newel post at the bottom of the stairs.

"Bit of an emergency I'm afraid, Mina. Lisa is stuck at the garage near High Cross. The car has run out of petrol and she, uh, she doesn't have the means to get home. She's asked if I can go and collect her but I'm heading to the big supermarket out of town about nine miles in the other direction. Have you seen the news? Turns out there are food shortages all over the country. The local shop has bare shelves. Panic buying, they're saying. It's worrying, is what it is."

Sam looks at me with his eyebrows raised. "Mina, you'll be all right with Alice won't you, if I go and get Lisa? I'll only be gone an hour or so."

"Actually," Bert says, meekly, "I was hoping Alice would be able to sit with Mary for a spell while I'm out. She's asleep at the moment but if she wakes it could frighten her to find an empty house."

"Do you want me to go and sit with her?" I ask.

There is a beat, and I can actually see Bert's face change. Good humor to distrust. I don't blame him. Not after yesterday, when he found me creeping around the bedroom.

"Well, that's a nice offer, Mina, but I wouldn't be comfortable leaving her with someone she doesn't know. It's hard to say these days what might upset her. I'm sure you understand."

He looks at me meaningfully.

"Not at all. I'm sure Alice won't mind."

He smiles, relieved.

"Thank you, Mina. That puts my mind at rest."

I keep smiling until the door closes behind them. I wait, standing alone in the hallway, listening to the sounds of the cars pulling away from the house. Just to be sure, I wait a little longer, feeling the darkness pressing in around me like a living thing, like a snake's coils. Then I call Alice out from the sitting room.

TWENTY-SEVEN

Alice and I step out into a world of heat and soft color, a sky washed pink and gold and purple. Insects skate and dart in flickering nimbuses. Midges and biting gnats, crickets chirruping in the grass. At Bert's front door Alice stands on her tiptoes and gropes along the lintel until she finds the spare key. As she unlocks the door my tongue turns to clay in my mouth, soft and wet and heavy. I reach out for her, suddenly afraid.

"What's wrong?" she asks. Her eyes are flecked with gold, open very wide. "Are you all right, Mina? Are you sick?"

"No, I—" I don't know what to say. It's a feeling of dread, of something impending, like dark clouds gathering, heralding something ominous, something wicked with a forked tongue.

"Mina?"

"It's fine." I smile, but she doesn't look reassured. "Honestly. Go inside."

Inside, again; the soft ticking of the clock, the sofa, the beeswax polish. I try to shake off the feeling of dread, the slow creep of ice. Alice switches on the television and helps herself to a yogurt from the fridge.

"Do you want anything, Mina? They've got jelly, choc ices—whatever you want."

I stand beside her. The fridge is full of soft foods: bananas quickly ripening to black, Angel Delight, cream cheese. Rice pudding and applesauce. I think of Bert and his dentures, sitting alone in front of the television spooning runny yogurt into his mouth. It's a thought that is both sad and unsettling. I wonder if he gets lonely.

"Mina? You coming? *Cagney and Lacey*'s on in a minute."

"Give me five minutes and I'll be with you. You going to check on Mary?"

"Yeah. I'll do it when the commercials come on."

I thought I'd have to invent an excuse but Alice doesn't seem to give a shit if I'm present or not. She just wants to eat her yogurt and watch cop shows. Thank God for self-absorbed teens, I think as I head back into the kitchen. I know Sam told me there was nothing down there but I want to see the basement for myself. I've already seen the door, set as it is in an alcove beneath the sloping roof of the stairs. I try the handle but of course it is locked, of course it is. I poke my tongue into my cheek, thinking. Would Bert have the keys on his key ring? Probably, but—I reach up to the top of the doorframe the way Alice had outside, feeling my way along it until my fingers chance upon a small silver key. Stunned, I let it drop into my open palm. I hesitate, but only for a moment, before sliding it into the lock and gently, calmly, pushing the door open into the darkness.

The only cellar I've been in previously belonged to my paternal grandparents. It flooded a lot and as a result smelled like dank water, an odor that was somehow deep green and vegetative, like soft black mud. It was always cold down there and my grandmother had lined up jars and jars of pickled vegetables on the shelves, the sour tang of brine making our eyes sting as Eddie and I peered into the cloudy liquid and the strangely mesmerizing shapes within; warty cucumbers and the soft, cranial folds of cauliflower. Eddie would call Grandma a mad scientist and said one day we'd find body parts down there.

Bert's cellar is nothing like my grandparents' cellar. Just like Sam told me, it is clean and well-lit and, although it smells a little musty, I don't feel the same sense of trepidation going down the stairs as I had into the cellar at my grandparents' house. There's no dirt floor and no tube web spiders hiding in the corners—just boxes neatly stored on metal shelving and a long workbench running down the center of the room. I approach the boxes, reading the neatly typed labels fixed to them. PHOTOGRAPHS, PRESS CLIPPINGS, BOOKS. I lift the lids of a few of them and find exactly what I'm expecting to find—the scraps of a long life lived; memories and journals and scrapbooks. Old Ordnance Survey maps of Cornwall tinged yellow with age. I feel a sour sort of disappointment bloom in me. Tamsin said she was frightened of the basement but she's just a kid, isn't she? Seven years old and trying to emulate her big sister, maybe in more ways than I'd realized. Perhaps she wanted a secret of her own to divulge, perhaps she wanted some of that attention from her parents aimed at her. I pull my fingers through my hair and my eye catches on something on the shelf toward the back of the cellar in the place where the recessed spotlights don't quite reach.

"Urgh," I groan as I approach the object, wrinkling my nose with distaste. "Gross."

It's a stuffed red squirrel, balancing on its hind legs on a base of polished teak. The black glass eyes glitter, the fur moth-eaten and patchy, almost bald in places. Little yellow teeth jut out like tusks. I lift my hand and touch the tufted tips of its ears.

"Someone mangled the job on you, didn't they?" I stroke it gently, smiling. "You poor old thing."

I sigh. I was so *sure* that Bert was hiding something. I'm almost embarrassed at how nervous I was coming down here. I'll tell Sam after this and we can laugh about it. I lift my hand away from the squirrel's tawny fur and feel, just for a moment, the lightest draft kiss against the skin of my palm. I lean, notice the shelving unit isn't quite flush with the wall behind it. I press my face up to the gap. It's not a draft, not quite. It's a coldness, a sense of space, of opening up. Behind these shelves there's a gap about a foot across, maybe more. My stomach sinks like a stone. I squint along the back of the shelves but it's too dark to see what—if anything—is back there.

Jesus, Mina, calm down. Basement walls get cold and drafty. There's probably a damp problem, that's all.

Yeah, I tell myself. Maybe. But that strange, tickly feeling persists, tugging at the back of my brain, trying to warn me that something is wrong. I pull down one of the storage boxes from the shelf—it is labeled SLIDES-MASSACHUSETTS APRIL '83—and peer through the gap. I wish I thought to bring a flashlight with me. I don't see anything.

"This is nuts," I tell the empty room. "This is just fucking bana—"

Then, there. When I move, the shadows are positioned differently, and it just takes my eyes a moment to adjust. I experience a stomach-dropping moment of horror when I glimpse a shrouded figure almost as tall as I am before my brain catches up a moment later, recognizing it as an object covered in a dust sheet. It's an illusion. That's all. Like the dead, darkly transformed.

I edge around to the back of the shelves and ease myself into the space. It's so narrow I'm forced to do so sideways, pressing my back against the brick wall as I sidle in. There is just room for me to turn slightly so I can face the draped object in front of me. It's been well concealed, the dust sheet covering it almost the same muted color as the brickwork. I hesitate before tugging the material away, fear pooling in my throat as bright and sharp as cut lemon.

For a moment I am convinced Eddie will be under there, the remains of his teeth crystalized with frost, eyes sunk into his skull. Eddie, reaching up with one trembling hand, lips blue and slack. *Tell me about the ice, Mina,* he will say, and his voice will sound like rocks grinding together, like the rattle of thrown grave dirt. *Tell me about the ice.*

But it is not Eddie. It is a tailor's dummy about five foot tall, dressed in a white linen smock, very plain, with a long, full skirt that touches the floor. Above the headless neck is a cage of blackened metal, padlocked at the collar. It is bulky and crude-looking, with a sharp tab of spiked iron protruding inside of the neckband about the length of my finger. I press the spikes gently and my fingertips come away smudged dark. Something about it makes my insides curdle. The metal is old and well-used, an apparatus that has seen and tasted blood. Draped over the shoulders of the mannequin are rows and rows of necklaces, some short, some long, all strung with chunky beads in dark colors; brown and gray and black. I don't realize what they are until I try to lift one and find it shockingly heavy, cold to the touch. Stones. *Hag*stones. Dozens and dozens and dozens. They fall over the shoulders and between the white cotton breasts of the dummy, threaded on cord and leather and twisted old rope. One of the stones is as big as my fist, seamed with quartz. I run my fingers over them, hard little rocks polished by the motion of the tides. I step a little closer and my foot connects with something on the floor, something tucked at the base of the dummy, almost concealed by the long skirts. I have to lift the fabric to see what it is. Another storage box. This one also has a label.

It reads: THE DEVICES.

TWENTY-EIGHT

There is a sudden ringing in my ears, a rush of blood to the head as if I have stood up too fast. Heat blooms close to the surface of my skin like a surge of quick blood. I lift the box and carry it out into the basement, setting it on the workbench beneath the lights. I'm careful, brushing the fine scrim of dust from its surface. My hands are shaking and my heart is in my throat as I open the lid. Inside are two objects wrapped in tissue paper. I lift them out, feeling the dull weight of them, aware that sweat has started to trickle the length of my spine. Half an ear is pricked for the sound of a car outside, the slam of the front door. I have to be quick, I tell myself, but I make sure I unwrap the items carefully, laying them side by side on the table in front of me.

They look agricultural, like medieval farming tools. Crudely shaped but purposeful. One resembles a knife but thinner, like a darning needle with a long wooden handle. The handle is printed with writing in gold leaf, something in Latin. DAEMONIA EICERE, it says. The second is an ugly, industrial-looking tool, like something used by a blacksmith. As I stare at them, I realize what they look like—crucible tongs. I've seen them used in Oscar's laboratory, only what I'm holding aren't gleaming scientific instruments of stainless steel. They are fire-blackened metal, rough to the touch. The scissorlike handles are fixed to two long pincers that end in flat plates, crudely formed. Some inner revulsion forces a bubble of acid up into my throat. It burns like salt water. I hurriedly put the tongs back on the workbench, face twisted with revulsion. I turn back to the needle. DAEMONIA EICERE. I trace my fingers over the worn gold lettering, pressed into the wood.

Oscar would know what this means, the little voice in my head reminds me. *He's forgotten more Latin than you'll ever know.*

Overhead, the sound of a door slamming, footsteps pounding down the stairs. In my fright I bite my tongue hard enough to taste iron.

"Mina!" It's Alice. "Mina, oh God. Mina, where are you?"

"I'm here!"

I start shoving the items (*the Devices, he calls them "the Devices"*) back in the box, not bothering to wrap them, driven by the sound of Alice's frightened, desperate voice. I can hear her in the kitchen now, the clatter and thud of something heavy falling to the floor. In my panic I think it might be Alice, collapsed and convulsing, a wasp buried in her throat. But no, I can still hear her crying—hoarse, choking sobs.

"Where are you?" she croaks, and I answer, "Right here, I'm coming!" lifting my skirt so I can take the stairs two at a time, hitting the light with the heel of my hand and plunging the cellar, the dummy, and the Devices back into the darkness in which they belong.

There is a dining chair lying on the floor of the kitchen. Alice was moving at such speed that she was propelled into it, knocking it down and barely noticing. Her skin is ashen and when she looks at me she blinks rapidly, as if trying to make sense of what she sees. I move beside her, brushing her hair away from her face and forcing her to look at me.

"Alice, what is it? What's wrong?"

There is a tremor running through her. Her stricken face is damp with tears. I know what she is about to say before she says it, some ancient telepathy passing between us, can feel the answer in the heat of her skin beneath my hands, the sharp clockwork of her eyes moving left to right, wild with fright. I know, and I am afraid.

Adrenaline sends me flying up the stairs and into Mary's bedroom. My heart is a totem drum, a warning pounding out a rhythm to Alice's words, *she's dead she's dead.* Mary is sprawled on the bed with her face tilted toward the ceiling. Her body is askew, twisted slightly as if she were in the process of trying to stand and has fallen backward. Her mouth hangs open, lips stained a dusky, lethal blue. The bedside lamp has rolled onto the floor, casting shadows at strange angles.

"Mary?"

My fingers brush along the wall. The woodchip wallpaper reminds me of Eddie's bedroom. For a moment the déjà vu is so complete I can almost see him lying there in the bed, football scarves and posters on the wall, oxygen mask hanging from his narrow, pinched face. Headlights splash across the ceiling—a car driving past outside—and for a moment I see Mary's eyes, shiny glass orbs, blank and empty.

"Mary? Can you hear me?"

I approach the bed and lean over, resting two fingers on the underside of Mary's wrist. There is a line of spittle suspended between her parted lips. Tears sting the backs of my eyes but I keep my fingers there a moment longer, just to be sure. There is nothing beneath my fingertips except her skin, soft and cool and powdery. No pulse, no rattling breath. No telltale rise and fall of her chest. I sink onto the bed next to her and the movement cants her body toward me, head lolling bonelessly to one side. A skein of silver hair falls over Mary's brow and I instinctively lean over her to gently tuck it behind her ear. The movement reveals a redness that has flooded Mary's glazed and staring left eye. A capillary burst and spread like spilled ink. I pull away quickly, heart pounding.

"No," I say quietly, voice small as if it has curled up in my mouth. "No, no, no."

I snatch up the lamp and point the light toward her, making all the shadows of the room stretch and swell. For a moment it looks as if her mouth is yawning open and filled with (*molasses, it drowned the horses*) the same tarry substance that leaked through the cracks in the brickwork, but it is just a trick, an optical illusion conjured by shades. That's when I see the livid marks on her neck, the long, vertical furrows dug into the skin of her throat. It is as if she has raked her nails there, clawing for air. The thought sends a shiver through me, strong enough that I have to wrap my arms around myself to stop the violent shaking.

Bert will be home soon, that same voice says. Practical. Assured. *You need to pull yourself together.*

Yes. Yes. I force deep drags of air into my lungs. I need to focus. Alice is just downstairs. Alice, I think. Oh God. I think of Vicky Matherson with her heels beating on the soft tarmac, the scratching in the chimney breast. I think of Simon Pascoe pulled cold and bloated from the still quarry waters and Alice saying *"The dead become transformed."* I wonder what shape Mary has taken, what strange vision she has become. Flame and eyeballs floating over strings of nerves.

You see it, Mina. You see it, don't you? That eye. That bloodshot void.

I lean against the wall, my strength seeping from me, down, down, subterranean behind my ribs. I think of Eddie, how weak he became, how quickly he let go.

You know what it means, don't you?

I turn and run out the door and down the hallway, bouncing off the walls like I'm drunk. I burst into the bathroom and fall to my knees in front of the toilet, one hand clamped around my stomach as all my dinner comes back up, spattering into the bowl. The sour smell makes me retch again as I grope for the flush and it's only as I sit there, spitting out long spindles of drool, stomach fluttering, muscles sore, that I hear it.

There is music playing downstairs.

TWENTY-NINE

I walk trancelike into the hallway. My voice—"Bert? Alice?"—weak from puking. The piano is lilting, delicate. The woman's voice smoky, with a texture both rich and lethargic, like a stretching cat. I float slowly downstairs, feeling as though I have been filled with helium. The front door is standing open. Outside, the streetlights are halos against a crescent moon in a cloudless sky.

"Alice?" I say again. Silence. "Hello?"

Trembling legs threatening to spill me over. The music rises and falls, sonorous in the living room. The television is still playing although the sound has been muted. An advert for toothpaste, everyone smiling as if at gunpoint. The curtains are open. Alice's can of lemonade sticky beside the record player. I stand there, swaying slightly, black roses blossoming in my vision before I collapse into the chair. There's a voice in my head that won't stop talking.

You know what that bloodied eye means, Mina. It's a sign of asphyxiation, isn't it? You know what asphyxiation means, don't you, Mina? Don't you?

I pick up the remote control and switch off the television set, then turn to the stereo and lift the needle from the record. *Billie Holiday*, the label reads. The cover is leaning against the wall and I pick it up and oh wow, there she is, the white gardenias in her black hair, her poise, those striking features. I lift up the sleeve and turn it around. There, right there, is the song Mary and Bert danced to on their wedding day, the song Alice said that Bert often played when Mary was having her hair cut. "Blue Moon."

Maybe Alice played it to her, Mina, while you were preoccupied in the basement. Maybe she played it so Mary could hear it one last time as Alice took the life from her.

I shut out that voice. I can't listen to it right now. I need to move. I need to tidy up before Bert gets back. He'll have a terrible shock when he hears about Mary. My hands are shaking so badly that the record glides through my fingers as I try to slip it back into the sleeve and only sheer luck stops it from falling to the floor. I try again to slide it in, but something is blocking it. Frustrated, I jerk the record out and look inside the sleeve, thinking the obstruction is an insert or tissue paper. But it's not. There's something stuck there, all the way back. Taped to the cardboard. I reach in for it, hearing the soft ripping sound it makes as I pull it free. It is an envelope. The paper is thick and creamy, expensive. No writing on the front and when I turn it over, I notice the back is tucked in but not sealed shut.

It's called petechiae, Mina. That redness of the eye. It's a result of physical trauma. But you already know that, don't you?

"Mina?"

I turn slowly, staring at Bert who is standing in the doorway with a box of groceries, smiling at me in a puzzled way that creases his eyes. "What's going on? Where's Alice? Why is the front door open?"

I stand, shoving the envelope into my pocket and push my hair away from my face. I can still taste bile at the back of my throat.

"Bert—"

"I managed to get the last pint of milk. We'll be back to rationing if this carries on. In the war my mother had to cook with powdered egg."

"Bert."

He pauses and then he must see something in my expression or in the way I step forward as if to take his hand. He takes an automatic step away from me.

"No." He is shaking his head. "No, don't. Don't tell me, Mina."

"Bert, I'm so sorry."

The words seem to ambush him, making him stoop in agony, his face cruelly lined. The box slides slowly out of his hands as I go toward him, putting my arms around him, feeling his frail shoulders begin to shake with hoarse, helpless sobs. "I'm sorry, Bert. She's gone. I'm sorry." Over and over.

THIRTY

For the second time that week, emergency vehicles make their way to Beacon Terrace. This time, though, there are no pulsing lights, no paramedics rushing to the scene—just the stately progress of the undertakers and Mary's doctor, his hat respectfully removed as he enters Bert's home. Even though it's late, the air is sticky with heat, almost tropical. Sam says that storms are forecast over the next few days, breaking the back of this hot spell. I've always hated storms. Eddie loved them. He would hide out in our spot in the attic to get the best view of the lightning, me squirrelled beneath a coverlet in the dark, him with his eyes wide, face lit up with exhilaration. Eddie would count the seconds between the lightning and the thunder and tell me if the storm was moving away. He'd laugh at my fear, making sure to squeeze my hand when the thunder got too loud. *"It's just opposite forces, Mina,"* he'd say. *"Just warm air meeting cold air, that's all."*

I stayed with Bert as the private ambulance took Mary away. The vehicle was low and dark and close to the ground, the undertaker and two young men barely out of their teens, their gangly frames hung in black suits like crows. Bert looked stunned, as though someone had knocked the air out of him. He kept saying, *"I hope she didn't suffer,"* and putting his head in his hands. I did not mention the burst blood vessel in Mary's eye and, if Bert noticed it, he didn't, either. He had simply drawn the bedsheet over her body and shaken his head sadly. I had to help him out of the room when his knees buckled.

Sam brought Lisa home just as the doctor arrived to certify the death. As soon as she realized what had happened, Lisa had started to sob and she hasn't really stopped since. I remember Fern telling me that Bert and Mary had taken Lisa in when she was pregnant and homeless, and my heart sinks a little deeper.

I'm brushing my teeth with my head hung tired and heavy over the sink when Sam slides in, softly closing the door behind him. I get a shock when I see him in the bathroom mirror. He looks as if he has aged a decade overnight, washed-out and shaken. He scratches at the skin of his neck idly, waiting for me to spit and swill water down the sink before asking, "Are you all right?"

"I was just going to ask you the same thing. You look awful, Sam."

"I've just got off the phone to the hospital."

I stare at him, eyes widening in horror, because I know what's coming, I *know.*

"Vicky passed away this afternoon. She never regained consciousness. Brain death, they called it. Imagine that, from a tiny sting no bigger than a pinprick. You can imagine the state her parents are in."

I remember the way that wasp had crawled over Alice's fingers and shudder as if suddenly cold.

"God. They must be devastated. Does Alice know?"

"Lisa went in and told her just now. She said Alice barely responded. It was as if she already knew."

We are both silent a moment, deep in thought. My mind keeps circling back to Mary's eye filmed with blood, the bluish cast to her lips that hinted at a protracted struggle for breath. My hands are gripping the cold porcelain of the sink so tightly I can feel my pulse under my nails.

"That's three people dead in as many days and Alice was with two of them when it happened," Sam says. He is choosing his words carefully, as if picking his way across a minefield. "I don't need to tell you what people are saying, do I?"

"She didn't do it, Sam."

"Have you tried telling that to all the people outside?"

"I've been trying to avoid them," I say truthfully. It started with a handful, about half past ten. Now, at nearly midnight, there are dozens out there, stumbling around and catcalling, looking at the Webbers' house with suspicion and a bright, bristling hostility. "Someone must have seen the undertaker take Mary away. She's barely cold and the whole town knows about what happened."

I turn on the tap. My hands shake as I soak a cold flannel and wipe it over my face. Sam watches carefully and I realize he is waiting for me to say something.

"What?" I ask.

"What *did* happen? In there?"

"I've already told Lisa and Bert this. I spent half an hour with them going over it."

"Humor me, Mina." He palms sweat from his forehead, voice low and conspiratorial.

"Alice went upstairs to check on Mary and found her dead. Alice was—*is*—traumatized. This whole thing has been awful for her and now she's lost her best friend as well."

"Ex-friend, remember? But here's the thing, Mina— according to her parents, Vicky had been stung by a wasp before a few years ago and had no reaction at all. Not even a rash. Don't you think that's strange?"

"I suppose."

"I want to show you something. Lock the door."

He is reaching into his pocket as I flick the lock on the door and turn to face him. I catch sight of us both in the clouded mirror. Sam's eyes are shuttered, without light. His hair is tangled and raked through and I can tell he hasn't been sleeping. Beside him I'm vampiric, skin sallow-looking and hung with shadows, eyes darkly hooded. *What a grim sight we both are,* I think.

"I meant to show you yesterday but, well, with everything that happened—"

"What is it?"

"Here." He hands me a matchbox. "Look inside."

I slide open the little cardboard drawer but there are no matches inside. Instead, I see the tiny wax balls that were inside the witch's bottle. Each one has been carefully slit open to reveal the curled husks of dead wasps.

"I know you told me not to open them but once I started I couldn't stop. There's nine in total."

"Yes, but that bottle was created two, maybe three hundred years ago. We've already established that. It has nothing to do with what happened to Vicky."

"You know what a familiar is, Mina? Bert was telling me

about them last night when we were looking at that graffiti out there—'Burn The Witch,' it says—and he told me how witches kept pets that would do their bidding for them. Toads and rats and imps. It was often thought the familiars were given to the witch by the Devil. I know, I know." He holds his hands up as if to ward off my protest. "If I'd heard myself saying this a few days ago, I would've wondered what was wrong with me."

"Bert told you about familiars?" I lift out one of the small wax balls and hold it up to the light. It has been pricked so many times with a pin it looks like a pomander. "Did he mention anything about a Riddance festival at all?"

"A what?"

"Riddance. Some old custom Alice was telling me about. Something to do with bonfires, I think."

Sam frowns.

"No, I don't think so. I'd had a good bit of brandy by then, mind you. Heh. Bert could've danced a conga and I'm not sure I would have noticed."

Something about that image, the absurdity of it, makes me snort with laughter. Sam grins as he leans his head against the cool glass of the window and peers out into the dark.

"I have to call this story in tomorrow. My editor wants it filed by Monday. What will I say?"

I nestle the fossilized wasp back into the matchbox beside the others and slide it closed. I can understand Sam's consternation—three people are dead, and all of them are somehow tied to a girl who believes she is possessed by the spirit of a long-dead witch. To sensationalize it would be a body blow for Alice. She'd never get out from under the shadow of a story like that, even if she moved away. To downplay it would mean this has all been for nothing, and nothing would be solved.

"I don't know, Sam. I honestly don't."

"The thing is, Mina, it's not over. You can feel that, right?"

I know exactly what he means. The heavy air feels incendiary, ready to combust. Raised voices, fireworks, chanting. Alice in front of the chimney, rocking. Mary with her single bloody eye. Outside, the wind is picking up. A storm is coming.

THIRTY-ONE

I'm back to sleeping in Billy's room. It's a relief, really. I'm restless and paranoid. Alice won't let me into her bedroom, won't let anyone in, not even her mother. She pushed the chest of drawers against the door and turned up the volume on her Walkman. Tamsin and Billy are still with their grandparents. That's a relief, too. The atmosphere is heavy tonight, barbed with suspicion. I sit on the bed, massaging face cream into my skin and looking at the photograph of Eddie propped up on the table beside the bed. I snatched it back from Alice the day before and even now I'm unsettled by how possessive I feel of it, even though all it really depicts is a blurred figure with blank eyes, half turned toward me. Somehow though, it feels like all I have left of him.

I become aware of the sound as I'm settling on top of the covers. The curtains are closed but the window is open and I can hear people milling around in the street outside, the occasional raised voice. The sound which grabs my attention though is just outside my closed bedroom door. It's the one I heard the night I'd arrived, the same sound that had sent Sam running during the séance. Guttural breathing, the grunting and panting of a big animal searching for a way in. I stare at the door, suddenly dreadfully afraid as I lever myself slowly out of bed. Sweat sticks my clothes to me as I cross the room, heart sailing into my throat. My pulse is soaring like a rocket. The door shudders in the frame. Outside on the street, someone is howling and singing in a strangled, thick voice. I stand in front of the closed door with my hands pressed against the plywood. Under my fingers it creaks and groans and a wet, sucking breath huffs through the keyhole. I reach out with numb hands and twist the handle, pulling the door open and expecting to find nothing there except that long, empty hallway filled with shadows.

But this time there is something there. Alice. She is standing in her nightie, her skin a deep, painful color so dark it is almost purple. Sweat coats her like grease. As I watch, her mouth opens helplessly and black foam bubbles out, sliding down her chin and her neck, soaking the front of her nightgown. I cry out, reaching for her arm. Her skin is so hot I snap my hand away. She is making a wet, ugly sound, *guck! guck!* as more foam erupts from her wide mouth. Thick curds of it, a black froth. Like a rabid dog, like a rabbit addled with myxomatosis. She looks at me with round eyes and I think I hear something then, her voice or something close to it, saying, *Help me, Mina. Help me.*

I call out for Lisa who comes at a run, with Sam charging up the stairs only moments later. In the dark, wearing that long blue nightgown, Alice appears to be levitating. She looks otherworldly, transformed. If someone were to ask me right now whether I believe she is possessed, I would tell them without hesitation yes, completely. Her hair hangs around her shoulders in knots and tangles, skin slick and shining and bruised looking. Black bile seeps between her lips and trickles down her chin, eyes so white and round they are rolling marbles. She makes that noise again— *guck!*—and that's when Sam steps up behind her, hands locked beneath her ribs. I hear Lisa cry out, "What the hell are you doing?" but I know what he's doing, he's saving her. I grab Lisa, pulling her back as she charges at Sam, her teeth bared. I have to lock my arms around her but still she struggles, calling Sam a bastard, telling him to keep his hands off her daughter. Sam pulls Alice toward him sharply and she jolts backward, white eyes gazing sightlessly toward the ceiling. Sam locks his fists together and thrusts them toward Alice's diaphragm again and again, the cords on his neck straining, his mouth drawn down with effort. Alice grunts wetly with each upward thrust, her head thrown back, mouth open and drooling thick globs of foam.

Finally she makes a wet hacking sound and something flies from her mouth, hitting the wall opposite with a sharp *clack*. Alice slumps against Sam who staggers back against the wall behind him, almost tripping over his own feet in an effort to stay upright. Lisa runs to her daughter, cradling Alice in her arms and searching her face for injury. I crouch down beside the object Alice expelled with such force, hesitant to touch it, but too intrigued to leave it alone.

"What is it?" Sam's panting, one hand against the wall to support himself. His face is a deep, vivid red.

"I think it's—" I hesitate. I'm loath to go near it, especially covered in all that stringy black bile, so I slide my hand inside my T-shirt and use the fabric as a glove, picking up the small round object and weighing it in my hand. "It's a hagstone."

I carry it carefully past Sam, who is massaging his chest with an unsteady hand, and down the hallway to the bathroom, tossing it into the sink where it clatters onto the plug. I swill water over it, surprised at how big it is, the skin of the pebble the color of old leather. The hole is off-center but the stone is almost perfectly round and almost as big as an egg. No wonder she was choking, I think, looking up as a shadow falls over me. It's Lisa, standing in the doorway with an ashen, shocked face. Her arms are folded against herself and she can't seem to stop shivering. I can hear it all through her voice.

"Do you think she needs the hospital?"

"I don't know. Whatever it was is out of her now."

"Is that it?" She nods toward the sink, her eyes narrowed. "Is that what was in her throat?"

"Yes."

"I thought I was about to watch her die right in front of me. I thought"—her voice falters and she heaves in a jagged sob before continuing—"I thought the witch had got her."

"Lisa, listen to me—" I begin calmly. She immediately brushes me away.

"Oh I know, I know. I sound mad, don't I? Maybe you would, too, if you'd lived the last few months that we have. Fevers and witches and those horrible noises coming from that chimney. It's enough to send anyone up the wall!"

She snatches at the toilet roll, pulling off enough to blot her eyes. I watch her soberly, wishing I could think of something to say that would take the weight off her, even just a little.

"The day I arrived I told you I'd help you. I meant it, Lisa. Me and Sam, we're not leaving till we know what's going on."

"I think we're beyond your help now," she says, sadly. "There's going to be a Riddance, you mark my words."

I switch off the tap, drying my hands on my pajamas. That word again. "Riddance." It chills me.

"What is that? A 'Riddance'?"

Lisa glances quickly back down the hallway, as if fearful of being overheard. In profile I can see the strain on her face more clearly; the fine lines sketched around her lips and netted at the corners of her eyes, her lips chapped and blistered.

"It's a tradition, Mina. Banathel has always had a Riddance. It sweeps away the bad."

Lisa's honey-colored hair has worked free from her ponytail, curling around the jut of her collarbones. She tugs at it nervously.

"How will that help Alice?" I keep my voice low.

"By driving the Devil out."

"You mean like an exorcism?"

"I mean like a ritual."

I stare at her for a beat before Sam's voice cuts in from down the hallway.

"Lisa? Alice is asking for you."

"I just want to save my daughter, Mina," she tells me, hooking her gaze onto mine before turning away. I stare after her, feeling a slow horror forming in the pit of my stomach, something which burns dull and painful and as blunt as superstition.

THIRTY-TWO

In the morning the sky is a soaring cobalt blue, the heat layered so thick it is hard to breathe. I take my coffee outside and stand in the shade of the tall privet hedge, studying the writing that has been scratched into the pavement among the stubs of candles and empty wine bottles. The same two words appear over and over and over, creeping all the way to the Webbers' front gate in bright paint and pastel chalks.

Good Riddance! Good Riddance!

My mind circles back to Lisa telling me that the Devil needed to be driven out of her daughter. It's such a strange, archaic thing to say, yet almost entirely in keeping with this strange town with its hagstones and offerings and "Devices" in boxes. I wonder what Sam will make of it when I tell him. I lift my head at the sound of approaching footsteps, smiling over the rim of my cup when I see Stevie running toward me. She is wearing a Ninja Turtles T-shirt and baggy corduroy shorts, her tongue pink from the ice lolly slowly melting in her hand. She stops right in front of me and very gently threads her hand into mine. Her fingers are cold and sticky.

"Mary's dead," she tells me. "Mummy's been crying *all* morning."

Fern is wearing oversized sunglasses and a pinched expression, her usual sunny demeanor noticeably dimmed. She carries a small posy of wildflowers in her hand.

"I've been dreading this day." She sniffs loudly, dabbing at her face with a handkerchief. "I don't know what Bert'll do without Mary. She was his whole world."

"How did you hear about it?" I tip the remainder of my coffee out into the hedge. It's gone cold anyway.

"The same way all news spreads in Banathel. Yesterday afternoon I bumped into Karen Archer who had spoken to Matthew Tregurra who had been working at the hospital when Vicky Matherson had died. Then last night I had a call a little after ten-thirty to tell me about Mary. It was just rumor at that point, of course. Someone had seen the undertakers arrive. They're Glenn Richards's boys, by the way. Twins, but not identical. It's a family business. They deal with all the deaths 'round here. It must take a hell of a toll on them."

"Why?"

"Because we all know each other, Mina. Those boys went to church with Simon Pascoe and now they're dressing him for his burial. It's a hell of a thing."

Fern slowly lowers her sunglasses. Her eyes are red rimmed and swollen from crying.

"Everyone talks around here, Mina. Simon wasn't an angel,

we all knew that. We all knew he'd wind up in trouble one day, probably find himself in jail or something. I don't think anyone expected him to—" She glances down at Stevie who is looking up at her mother with big, round eyes, ice lolly dripping down her arm. "Hey, kiddo, why don't you give Bert these flowers? I think he'd like a hug from you. Go on and knock, I'll be there in a moment."

She waits for Stevie to run up the path to Bert's front door before pushing her glasses back up her nose and straightening up. She sighs.

"People have been talking about what happened to Simon the same way they've been talking about Vicky. Pretty soon they'll all be saying the same thing about Mary. Some of them have already started."

"And what is it they're saying?"

"You *know* what. About Alice. That she hasn't been right since she broke that witch bottle. You can't tell me you don't see it."

Her voice lowers.

"You'd do well to get away from here, Mina. You and Sam both."

"Is that a threat?"

Fern looks down at the ground for a few breaths, staring at the writing beneath her feet. *Good Riddance!*

"I know you had good intentions in coming here. Maybe you thought it would almost be fun—a little trip away, some spooky goings-on—'cos everyone loves a ghost story, don't they? Everyone loves to look into the darkness."

I think of the car wreckage Oscar and I drove past, the way I twisted in my seat to see it, even though it frightened me. I think of the basement with the Devices in the box hidden away at the back of the room. *Yes*, I think, *everyone loves to look into the darkness.*

"Thing is, this story, it's grown teeth, hasn't it? It's mutated. It's not cozy anymore, it's not a story about redemption or ghosts. You can't wrap it up neatly and give Alice a diagnosis and pills to fix what's broken. It's a mess and it's going to get worse before it gets better. I know this town, I know these people. There has to be a penance."

"God, you sound like Lisa."

Fern nods, smiling. "She's another one. A Riddance girl. She knows what's coming. Look, I'd better go or Stevie will be trying to get poor Bert dancing or something. I haven't had any sleep and I'm sad as all hell so maybe I'm not making sense. I just want you to be careful, Mina. Things'll settle here one way or another but you might end up doing more harm than good."

Just for a moment her hand moves over to her arm and runs her fingers over the fine lines of scars there, stroking them distractedly. She sighs again before turning away and walking toward Bert's house with her head down. Chalk rises in rainbow-hued dust about her feet.

THIRTY-THREE

Shortly before curfew begins, I leave the house to call Oscar. Inside, the phone box is stifling with the reek of warmed metal and urine. I'm forced to stand with the door propped open so that the air can circulate. It is almost unbearably hot. I feed the coins into the slot and the phone rings in my ear—I'm trying the laboratory again because given the choice Oscar would always opt to be there—and it is picked up on the fourth ring.

"Baldhu, eight-nine-four."

It's him. I swallow, suddenly unable to speak.

"Hello?" He's impatient. *I don't have time for prank calls, I have to study the known universe.*

"Oscar? It's me. It's Mina."

"Mina?" There's no softness to his voice. It digs under my skin. "This is a terrible line. Speak up."

"I'm in a pay phone."

"Why?"

His voice sounds dry and tinny and distant.

"Long story. How are you, Oscar?"

I want him to tell me I'm wrong. That he misses me, that Lucy is a figment of my imagination, I want him to make me feel weightless.

"I'm at work, Mina. Been busy. You know how it is."

I stare at the heat haze rising off the green. The water in the pond is a silver mirror.

"I just want to— I just wanted to talk to you. I miss you. So much has happened, so much weird stuff. I've been feeling"—*strange, like I'm falling into a void*—"lonely."

His response is curt. "When are you coming home?"

"Do you love me, Oscar?"

A beat. She's there, of course. Lucy. I tighten my grip on the phone.

"Oscar?"

"Of course I do, Mina. Let's talk when you get back."

"Say it. Please."

He sighs and I think—this is how it ends. I hear the rustle of movement at the end of the line. Perhaps he is switching the phone to his other ear, perhaps he is moving out of her embrace. I change the subject, voice croaky with the stifling heat.

"Can you translate something for me, Oscar? It's Latin."

"I'll try."

"*Daemonia eicere.* I can spell it for you—"

"No need. It means 'cast out devils.' You mixed up in something you shouldn't be?"

"I don't know. I really don't."

"Because you can't say I didn't warn you. I did try." He

sighs again, and the edge of his voice blurs, just enough for me to know he is disappointed. "I knew this would happen."

"What do you mean?"

"Just come home, Mina. Come home and rest. You've got a wedding to arrange."

I trace a finger over a crack in the plastic window, warm to the touch. I wonder what Lucy's thinking, hearing this. Has she left the room? Is he turning his back on her, still plowing ahead with a wedding I don't think either of us wants anymore? His tone gives nothing away.

"Oscar, do we have a song?"

"A what?"

"A song. One that makes you think of me when you hear it?"

He pauses. His throat clicks. "I don't know, Mina. Do we?"

"I've met an old couple here who've been married forty-three years. They had a song. 'Blue Moon' sung by Billie Holiday. In their wedding photo they're dancing to it. They look so happy, Oscar. Mary, her name was. She died yesterday and it was me who found the body. I don't know why I'm telling you all this, I just—I wondered if we had a song."

A beat.

"I don't think we do, Mina, no."

"Ah. Well, then."

Silence. I let it expand. The timer tells me I have a minute of the call left. I scuff my feet against the concrete. Oscar's voice then, amused sounding. A ripple of static on the line.

"Interestingly, it's called a 'blue moon' because it comes from the Old English word 'belewe.' 'Belewe,' meaning 'betrayal' because the blue moon disrupts the lunar calendar."

"Is that right?"

I'm thinking about Bert and Mary dancing to a song about

a lunar rock so powerful it can induce madness. The same song that was playing the previous night on the record player after I'd discovered Mary's prone, dead body. That eye, rich with blood. Blue moon. I straighten up. A belewe moon. Billie Holiday. *Bill-ee.*

"Oscar, I have to go."

"When are you coming home? Mina?"

I hang up the phone with fingers I can barely feel. The handset slips from the cradle and swings on the end of the cord. There is an electrical arc in my head, spitting sparks. Mary was saying "Billy" but she'd meant "Billie." Billie Holiday. She was talking about the record, not the boy. Sos. SOS. S-O-S. She *was* trying to get my attention.

I think of the envelope I discovered, the one that had been taped inside the record sleeve. Hidden there, right at the back. I run.

THIRTY-FOUR

I walk into the house with a strange sense of foreboding hanging over me. There is a pressure at the back of my skull as if something is pinching the nerves there. I peer into the sitting room as I kick off my shoes, heart pounding with the exertion of running all the way from the green. Sam is sitting on the sofa with the curtains drawn. There is a frame of video frozen on the television, warped by lines of static. I hesitate. I want to go and find the envelope but something in Sam's demeanor gives me pause. Even though I can't see his face, I can tell from the slope of his shoulders, the way his head hangs slightly, hair scraped back from his temples, that something is wrong.

"Sam?" That feeling increases as I step inside the sitting room and glance around. It's gloomy, full of dust motes and a pall of thick cigarette smoke, but it's tidier than I've seen it in days. Sam's blankets and pillows have been cleared away and his suitcase is sat neatly in the corner, sunglasses and car keys on top.

"Sam?"

"Why did you do it, Mina?"

His voice is trembling. I stare at him in genuine confusion.

"I don't know what you m—" That's when I see what he is holding in his hands. A flash of yellow stitching, the gleam of a silver buckle. It's the little shoe we found in the fireplace, the one he reached for, saying *Maggie had those.* "Sam, where did you get that?"

He looks down at it with mild surprise, as if he has forgotten he is holding it.

"Tanner's Row, Mina."

"You went up there on your own? You should've waited for me!"

"I can't trust you."

I throw my hands up in frustration.

"What's going on?"

"I'll tell you what's going on, shall I?" Sam's eyes are suddenly slitted in anger, voice filled with a quiet, furious heat. "You went into Mary's bedroom, even though Bert asked you not to. You did it not once but twice! *Twice!* He said you were questioning her. Harassing her. She was eighty years old for fuck's sake, Mina. She was sick and you knew that and you went up there anyway."

"I just wanted to check on her. Because of the knocking on the w—"

"Oh yeah, that's right. The SOS," Sam spits, shaking his head. "I told you to ignore it, but you had to go and see for yourself. If you'd just asked Bert he would have told you."

My voice is high with confusion, heart punching my chest. "Told me what?"

"That since Mary's stroke a few years back her mind's not been right. Sometimes she thinks there's still a war on. More than once she's accused him of trying to kill her. He told me all this and he would've explained it to you, too, if you'd only asked him."

I open my mouth to respond and snap it closed again. As far as I know Sam never actually met Mary so he can only take Bert's word for how sick she was. He has no idea how vulnerable she was at the end. I could tell Sam about the marks on the wall and her bloodied, gory eye but if I start contradicting Bert now I'll only infuriate Sam more so instead I ask, "When did you see Bert?"

"Today. He came over and spoke with Lisa and Paul. They've asked us to leave, Mina."

"What?" My knees feel suddenly weak. That sense of dread swells and clings. "Why?"

"They said you can't be trusted." Sam wipes his nose along his arm and I realize he is crying. "I was so close, Mina."

"Sam, there'll be other opportunities. You said yourself ghost stories these days are ten a penny."

He looks at me in genuine confusion, face crumpled with disappointment. "I meant Maggie, Mina. I was so close to contacting her, and now you've ripped it away from me."

Pain radiates from him like heat from an oven. He hugs the grubby shoe against his chest, so small in his big hands. I stand very still, head down. Thinking.

"Okay. Okay, listen, Sam—I'll speak to them. I'll speak to Bert. I'll make it right, okay?"

Sam isn't listening. He is shaking his head, still talking. "Bert said if we go quietly he won't ask for an inquest."

"An inquest into what?"

Mary's eye, muddied with blood. The claw marks on her neck. I swallow dryly.

"You weren't meant to be in her bedroom, Mina. Bert told you not to go in."

I stare at Sam, jaw fused with shock. I want to speak but the words won't come. Black spots dance in front of my eyes.

"They want us out by four. I'm already packed. You should make a start."

"Sam, you can't possibly think *I* had anything to do with Mary's death."

He looks up at me and I'm frightened by the lack of feeling in his gaze. I lower myself in the armchair beside him, reaching for his hands. He flinches but doesn't pull away.

"I wasn't even in the bedroom when she died. I was—" I stammer, suddenly feeling sick. What can I tell him? That I was poking around in the basement instead? It might absolve me of suspicion in Mary's death but Sam and I will still be asked to leave. There is a buzzing in my ears like a soft electrical charge, a static I feel all over. I wasn't even meant to be in the house last night, only Alice. I remain silent for so long that Sam sighs and picks up the remote control, pressing Play. The video jerks into life, so sudden and so loud that I jump, turning toward the television.

It is footage from Sam's video camera, the image grainy, laced with static. The ambient noise is a sound like rushing water, slightly muffled. The camera has been positioned in the center of the room directly between Alice's and Tamsin's beds. The focus is on the dark arch of the fireplace and the red-bricked chimney breast but to the right, seated on the edge of her bed, Alice is visible in profile. She glances at the camera warily, tucking the waves of her hair behind her ears before turning back to the object on her lap.

"When did you film this, Sam?"

"Early this morning. I went to Tanner's Row first thing and when I got back I found Alice in the kitchen. What happened last night really scared her, Mina. She swears on her mother's life that she doesn't know where that hagstone came from—that she's never seen it before, let alone tried to swallow it. She doesn't remember standing outside your door, only that she dreamed she'd been watching herself sleep and that something liquid and black had slid out of the chimney and into her open mouth. She only fully woke up when I grabbed her."

"Good thing you did. You probably saved her life."

"Yup, and that's why she agreed to try to contact Maggie for me again." He points to the screen. "She said even though her ribs hurt and her throat is sore, it's better than being dead like the others."

"What others?"

Sam gives me a look and I know instantly he is talking about Vicky, Simon, and Mary. Still though, it's a strange thing for Alice to acknowledge and I file it away, turning back to the screen as Sam keeps talking.

"Alice said the witch wouldn't show herself if I was there so I gave her the shoe and set the camera running. It's about twenty minutes of footage, give or take. She sits like this for nearly fifteen minutes with nothing happening. I've watched this over six times now and I still can't figure out how she does it."

"Does what?"

"Keep watching, Mina."

Sweat dampens the collar of my T-shirt and gathers in the folds of my stomach. I watch the screen carefully, my pulse climbing. My saliva dries up, sticking my tongue to the roof of my mouth. Sam presses the remote control again and a little green bar appears in the lower left corner as he increases the volume. There is a low, static hiss. Alice is swaying a little, her head moving like a snake about to strike. I glance at Sam. He is chewing his thumbnail nervously and I feel my pulse spike again, the friction of fear shooting up my arms and beneath the thin skin of my neck.

A fine scrim of dust begins trickling from the chimney space. The tape crackles. I see Alice flex her toes like a dancer, as if she is stiff from sitting for so long. Briefly, a dark, blurred object appears on the lens like a smudge. It obscures the room a second or two before darting away. I look at Sam, eyebrows raised.

"A wasp landed on the lens. I asked Alice about it. There were a few flying around when I went in afterward."

My eye keeps trailing back to the soot pattering into the grate. For a moment it looks as though the hollow of the fireplace is filled with a blackness so rich it has become a living thing, a bloated shadow grasping for the light. I blink, wiping sweat from beneath my eyes. I feel nauseous. Acid rises in my throat. The tape must be corrupted, I tell myself, plucking at the hem of my shirt, it has to be, because that darkness appears to be swelling and bulging as though it is pushing through a membrane.

"Why is she still sitting there?" I hear my voice, plaintive. "Can't she see it? Why doesn't she *move*?"

Sam doesn't respond and after a moment I see why. Alice's face is turning slowly toward the camera, only it isn't Alice's face anymore, it has—changed, somehow. Her eyes droop as if her face is wax left to soften in the sun. I almost scream when I see her smile, the corners of her lips pulled desperately upward as if by fishhooks. Her skin is oily and yellowy-white, eyes stunned-looking, witless. *Rattling teeth in an empty, eyeless head*, I think hysterically, and the darkness filling the hearth looks about to burst like a blackened, rotting fruit and there is a sound then, a noise on the tape like the *whumph* of ignition and the footage abruptly ends.

I realize I am digging my nails into the fabric of the chair, hands hooked into claws. I force myself to breathe, taking in big gulps of air as I turn to look at Sam with wide, wondering eyes.

"Did you see that? Did you see her change? Holy shit, Sam!"

Sam lights a cigarette, tipping his head back to blow smoke at the ceiling. I'm fidgety, feeling as though someone has put fire-crackers under my chair. I keep seeing the way that Alice turned her head, the absent, mindless look in her eyes, as if all sense were knocked out of her. It's chilling.

"Did that look like a fit to you, Mina? Some sort of seizure, maybe?"

"No. No, it didn't, although without more footage it's hard to say one way or the other."

"I can rewind it. Freeze-frame."

"No," I say immediately, with real feeling. The idea of look-ing at that face static on the screen, flesh sagging and somehow wet-looking, makes my stomach hurt. "But I need to speak to Alice. Where is she? Is she okay? What did she say when you asked her what happened? We should be writing all this down."

"You can't talk to her, Mina." His voice is flat, eyes dark and almost pained. "They won't let you, remember?"

"But we're so close, Sam!"

Sam sighs and rubs at his temples. He looks frustrated and

tired and strung out and I don't blame him. I stare at him, thinking. I need to put this right.

I hear voices behind the kitchen door as I enter the hallway.
The low rumble of a man speaking, the clink of coffee cups.
I hesitate as I raise my fist to knock, tapping lightly, but loud
enough to be heard, and push the door open as Lisa's voice calls
out, "Come in!"

It's Bert I see first, standing at the sink. He is clean shaven
but looks tired, with pouches beneath his bloodshot eyes, a
slight tremor in the hand holding his cup. He glances at me with
his chin lifted, face flat and without affect, giving nothing away.
Paul is leaning against the fridge with his arms folded, hands
tucked beneath his armpits. It's a shock to see him after a night
working on the killing floor—his mouth chiseled into a hard,
straight line, face gray and gaunt. His eyes are dark, hard glints
of metal. Iron nails in wood. Lisa sits smoking at the table with
her hair scraped back from a face which is taut and shiny. Her
gaze flickers coldly as she looks me up and down. Beside her is
Alice, her features mostly hidden beneath the long curtains of
her hair. I experience a sensation then, like I am floating out of
my body, as I remember the way her flesh distorted in the video,
becoming rubbery and soft. For a moment no one speaks. The
open door stirs the smoke hanging in the still air. I catch that
scent again, of iron and minerals and thick, clotted blood.

"Mina." Bert's voice is hoarse and dry. "I thought you'd be
packing by now. Long drive home."

"I just wanted to explain." I hear my voice creeping up an oc-
tave. It's nerves. I don't like the feeling in this room or the jolt of
anxiety in my chest. "My intention was never to upset you, Bert,

and I shouldn't have gone into your bedroom without permission. I hope you understand that I did so only out of concern for Mary."

Paul grunts indistinctly but when I look at him he glances away. Bert smiles, however, speaking gently.

"Be that as it may, Mina, the damage is done. Trust is delicate, and easily broken, after all. How can you ask this family to trust you with their daughter when you can't even be trusted to follow instructions?"

"I never meant for any of this to happen, Bert. I was just trying to help."

"Yet Alice is still suffering and I find myself a widower. Three people have died since your arrival, Mina. I think you've helped enough."

Bert's voice is wary as he sets down his cup.

"With all due respect, Bert, Mary was very sick."

"Yes, she was, wasn't she? But with her new medication the doctor said he thought there were a few more good years in her at least. She wasn't ready to die, certainly not yet."

"She was asking for help, Bert. She was tapping on the wall."

I can feel tears breaching my eyelids, making my vision shimmer. I try to blink them away as Bert continues. "The only help my wife required was peace and rest, as I believe I told you more than once. I failed in my duty to her, but I don't intend to fail in my duty to Alice."

"Oh? What duty is that?" There is a tremor in my voice and Bert smiles as he hears it.

"We need to break the spell." Lisa's voice is hard and cold. It shocks me, how different she sounds to the woman who stood in the bathroom last night, saying *"I just want to save my daughter, Mina."*

"A Riddance, Mina." Bert is moving to the table, behind

Alice's chair. I think suddenly of the gravelly voice on Sam's Dictaphone, the writing outside on the pavement. *GoodRiddance. GoodRiddance. GoodRiddance.*

"Are you joking?"

"Mina," Paul says warningly, but I ignore him. I laugh bluntly.

"A 'Riddance' is just more superstition! You might as well cover her in leeches. I came here to offer you proper answers, empirical support. All right, well, you wanted my opinion so here it is—Alice would benefit from some observations and assessments outside of this house. My concern is that she's being overly influenced by her surroundings and the people in it."

"The Riddance is a tradition, Mina," Bert tells me, quietly. "It's important we follow the old custom. It's expected."

I stare around the room in dumb silence. Alice is still wearing the crumpled T-shirt—POBODY'S NERFECT!—and now a tear draws a line down her cheek, followed quickly by another. Her voice is husky and pained.

"I don't know how to make her stop, Mina."

"Who? Make who stop, Alice?"

"The witch," Bert says pleasantly, as if he is talking about the weather. "That's who she means. She's spread in Alice like a bad seed and we have to rip her out at the root."

I wince at how violent the words seem, how brutal.

"There are a lot of Riddance girls in this town," Bert continues, his hands settling on Alice's upper arms and working their way up to her fleshy shoulders. "Although they are mostly women now, of course. Lots of girls who needed help to find their way out of the dark."

"A 'Riddance girl'? What is that, like a May Queen? Does she get to wear a crown?"

I'm bristling with anger and a sense of keen injustice, sharpened by seeing that tear rolling down Alice's face. Bert's gentle, restrained tone makes it worse, makes me want to hit the table with my fist.

"Riddances have been performed here a long time." Bert's hand squeezes Alice's shoulders gently. I feel a wave of something—disgust, fear—that I quickly swallow down. "I've seen it described as 'a noisy ritual to cast out devils.'"

Daemonia eicere, I think to myself. Printed on the handle of that needlelike instrument. *The Device.*

"But Alice doesn't need a ritual, Bert. She needs real help. Practical help. Therapy, maybe something on prescription to get some sleep. Am I going mad? Why are you all even considering this?"

"Think of it as a cauterization." Bert's voice is heavy, his thick fingers brushing Alice just beneath her collarbone. "Sealing a wound so the infection can't spread."

"Alice?" I say, hearing the urgency in my voice, the alarm. Why are they all being so *normal* about this? "Alice, is this something you want to do?"

She stares at me.

"I don't want to end up in St. Lawrence's, Mina. I don't want to be mad."

"You're not, I promise you, you're not." I hold her gaze with my own. "Alice, if you want, I can get you away from here. Somewhere safe. There are places, you know. For children having problems with their families or their schools or even in their own heads. Places where you can be alone and get better."

"She'll follow me," Alice whispers, her eyes swiveling in their sockets, "and I'm so tired of fighting her."

"Alice, *I* can help you. That's why I came here."

"No, you didn't," she says simply. "You came here because of Eddie. Because he died and you didn't."

That cracking sound again, that rift in the ice—only it's not in the ice, it's in me, somewhere where the blood flows thick and dark and sluggish, where secrets stagnate and grow long, fibrous roots. Bad seeds. I feel my face grow hot.

"Alice, my brother died because he got sick."

"He died because of you." Her face is pale. "You put your brother in the ground."

I stutter in shock, turning my gaze to Paul who looks away from me quickly, eyes dark and miserable. I feel suddenly panicky, like the walls are closing in. I think of Alice turning toward the camera and the darkness in the grate, the eyes swiveling in the brickwork. Sam, holding that grimy shoe like a drowning man. I look beseechingly at Lisa, palms held outward, tears coming finally, frustrated, hot, guilty.

"Lisa, please. Let me make this right. We just need a few more days."

"What you *need* is to stay away from my daughter, Mina Ellis." Lisa sucks on her cigarette and I see how angry she is, vibrating with it almost. She doesn't seem mousy and downtrodden anymore. Her jaw is stiff and her mouth so sharp I'm surprised her lips aren't bleeding. "An' you need to get away from this town. No more. Just leave us be."

THIRTY-FIVE

I storm upstairs, my head spinning. My jaw is clenched, teeth grinding together until I hear the squeak of enamel in my ears. I shove open the door of Billy's room and kick it closed so hard it bounces off the frame and swings back open again. Outside, someone is letting off firecrackers. I crawl over the unmade bed and open the window, leaning out on the sill. There are people in the road, clustered together, talking and laughing. The atmosphere seems anticipatory, even excited. Some of them are carrying slabs of timber taller than they are, old knuckled branches, broken wooden pallets. I remember Alice saying *"That's why we have the Riddance with the costume and the bonfires"* and wonder if they will build them up on the green, flames so high they lick the tops of the trees. Outside, the air is so heavy you could swim through it. It smells like burning plastic and warm metal and in the east, out toward the hills, dark clouds are massing. Sam had said the weather was going to break, hadn't he? It's a long drive back to Baldhu. I hope he's still talking to me by the end of it.

Sighing, I reach down and grab my case, hauling it onto the bed. I hadn't brought much with me, and most of what I did bring is crumpled on the floor. Oscar always bemoaned my messiness, reminding me I wasn't a student anymore so I should stop behaving like one. I sigh again. I don't want to think about Oscar, either. Right now, the world feels full of people who don't particularly like me very much. Propped on the desk next to my toiletries is the photograph from Crete, the one with my dead brother in the background, eyes silvery and wide. I smooth out the creases in it with my fingertips, tears pinching my sinuses and burning the back of my throat. I say his name, just once in the empty room, let it be swallowed up by the hot, soupy air.

It was raining the day Eddie died. It made a soft hushing noise at the glass, like silk moving over polished floors. The light was hazy and gray and the ice had been black underneath and Eddie was in the bed, face gaunt and skeletal, eyes too big for his skull. *"It hurts, Mina,"* he said. *"Let me put the blanket over you,"* I whispered and Eddie put his hand on mine—God, he was so cold! *"Tell me about the ice,"* he said so I told him the story of the night of heavy snow and the morning of the frozen pond and how cold and blue the water had been and how he'd saved me, even though he had been so afraid and by the time I'd finished telling it he was gone.

I gulp, wiping tears away. It's nearly four. I have to pack. We'll be leaving soon, me and Sam. I drag my suitcase toward me and that's when I see the shorts I was wearing the day before, exactly where I left them in a heap on the carpet. I think of Oscar telling me about blue moons and the Old English word "belewe," meaning betrayal, and then I remember the envelope I found in Bert's record sleeve. A sensation of cold prickles over my skin. I reach into the pocket and pull it out, slightly crumpled. I hesitate for a moment, thinking about Mary sending an SOS to the girl on the other side of the wall, and then I slide the envelope open with the tip of my finger.

I don't know how long I sit there in that small, stuffy room, sweat coating me in a shimmering aura, making my hands slippery. I sift through the photographs feeling sick, feeling heavy. Young women. No, *girls.*

Riddance girls.

A dozen of them. Shaky Polaroid pictures, badly lit, lazy. Skirts lifted, shorts lowered to the knees. Tan lines on shoulders, intimate moles and sprays of freckles against pale skin, rib cages stark on narrow, adolescent frames. The eyes are always the same, slightly closed to show crescents of white, lips parted, slack, heads turned to the side. They are all lying down. They are all unconscious.

"There are a lot of Riddance girls in this town," Bert said, *"Lots of girls who needed help to find their way out of the dark."*

GoodRiddanceGoodRiddanceGoodRiddance. My mind loops back to the conversation I had with Alice in her bedroom. The smell of the chimney was ash and sulfur, wisps of smoke. *"He makes us funny little cocktails . . . he calls them Bertinis."*

Alice's skin is wan, caught in the camera flash, striped dress shoved upward to reveal a pair of yellow knickers, the shallow depression of her belly button. My stomach rises and falls like the swell of a wave. It's tidal, this feeling. Of being dragged and lifted, a sensation of overwhelm.

There is a glass half-visible in the foreground of one photo, slightly blurred. It's a cloudy pink liquid with chunks of pineapple floating on the surface. What had he put in them, these Bertinis? Rohypnol? Ether? Laudanum? That seemed like Bert's style. Something old-fashioned and melancholy, like a sober Victorian ghost. I'm sure the truth will be much more pedestrian; sleeping pills crushed into powder and weighed carefully on a dull afternoon, that clock in the kitchen *tick, tick, ticking,* slicing away the minutes of a life he was starting to despise. He would have been careful not to put too much in. He would have done his research, made sure of everything. Too much and someone dies or gets brain damage. Too little and they would be stumbling and slurring.

I think back to Sam saying *"Sometimes Alice gets sick, gets headaches."* How she had to take so much time off school her parents had pulled her out. I wonder if each period of sickness tied in with her visits to Bert and Mary, the after-effects of whatever he was spiking her drink with lingering for days.

Then I remember Lisa telling me how she'd passed on her rotten headaches to Alice and pick up the photo of the knocked-out young girl with the slightly rounded stomach and pink smock dress. I stare at it before hanging my head to my chest and forcing deep, muscular breaths into my lungs. The images are printed onto the insides of my eyelids, the walls of my skull. Fern telling me that Lisa was a Riddance Girl—*she's another one, she knows what's coming*—and there she is, her photograph shaking in my hand. Teenage Lisa, her blond hair looking fairer and finer in the camera flash, Alice inside her, gestating.

The final photograph is a young girl with pink hair and a bloodied ear that looks as if a piercing has become infected. Her face is obscured but the scars on her arms are visible, this time fresh, pink, and raw-looking. Lines carved into her arm, a way to feel something. To hurt. Fern. She would have been fourteen when she was staying with Bert and Mary so that would mean this picture was taken about ten years ago. The rest of the girls I don't know or recognize but I bet people around here do. I bet they all watched them have a Riddance, these troubled adolescents. All these young bodies stretched out like sacrifices. That same sensation persists of being dragged by a violent undertow that sucks the sand from beneath my feet.

"I was a troubled kid," Fern said. *"They took me in."* Did Mary know what was happening? I don't think so. Hadn't Alice and Fern both said how quickly she'd fallen asleep? I wonder if Bert was mixing her cocktails a little stronger, with a little more *kick*. No, I don't think Mary knew. At the end, maybe. When she had found the photographs. That's why she was trying to draw my attention any way she could. To rat that fucker out before she died.

A strange memory occurs to me. My mother, drying the flowers my father had given her for their wedding anniversary—big, blousy red roses, sweet and fragrant—she hung them upside down in the window of her bedroom. One afternoon, I was only about three or four I think, I climbed up there to get another smell of them, that delicate perfume that made my toes curl; like warm milk and honey and powdered Turkish delight. One of the brittle little heads snapped off in my hand and when I peeled it apart the petals at the center had blackened and grown rotten, infested with tiny crawling bugs. I screamed so loudly my mother came in at a run carrying baby Eddie in her arms. The dark hearts of things, riddled with worms.

I open my eyes and the room spins. I close them again and see the bloodied rabbit cadavers on the table, the bucket of leporine heads, black eyed and bucktoothed. Freckled collarbones and tiny flowers on the fabric of underwear, eyes slightly open, loose jaws, small teeth.

Something disturbs me then and I look up, my face streaked with tears. Bert is standing in the doorway, cast slightly in shadow. I don't know how he managed to sneak up on me so quietly. He must have crept up the stairs, glided over the carpet, maybe. I wonder when he noticed the photographs were missing, how soon he realized that I must have taken them. Last night, after the undertakers had left? This morning, as dawn broke? No wonder he wants me gone. No wonder he wants me to leave quietly.

"I'll call the police," I tell him flatly. It doesn't sound like a threat. I'm not brave enough. My voice wobbles with emotion. Bert smiles, not unkindly. He shakes his head.

"No, you won't, Mina. Not after what you did."

He pulls the door closed, and I can only sit and stare in astonishment as I hear the click of the key turning in the lock. I'm suddenly struggling to draw breath, a sensation of choking filling my throat. It's frightening, and I want to cry out for Sam, for help, but there is nothing I can do. Maybe this was how Eddie felt as the pneumonia clogged his lungs like molten molasses, the rain against the window, the pillow in my hands. The pillow in my hands. The pillow in my hands.

THIRTY-SIX

I have to get out of here. I consider hammering on the door or trying to kick it down; it's flimsy plywood and already perforated with holes, but I don't want Bert to come back up here. There is movement downstairs—the scrape of chairs, muted voices—and I wonder what he is telling them. I can't sit and wait to find out, I need to get to Fern. I need to find someone who is thinking straight and right now I don't trust anyone in this house—Lisa with her cold, hard stare or Sam cradling a child's shoe in his large, heavy hands—to do that.

I lean out the window and look down. It's broken concrete down there, stuffed with tall weeds that punch up through the cracks. It's a long way to the ground but if I can swing over to the right I can jump onto the porch roof, and then it's just a drop of a few feet. I start to clamber out, hooking one leg over the casement, hands holding on the frame. The wood there is rotten and spongy, black with mold. I don't think it can hold me, but what choice do I have?

I slide the envelope into my pocket, keeping my eyes fixed on the porch roof below. Then I pull my other leg through until I'm sitting on the sill trying not to think about the way it creaks and shifts beneath my weight. If I jump, I might land on the porch and just go right on through, breaking a few bones in the process. If the cheap rubber roofing is as rotten as this window-sill, then it's a real possibility. I swallow. I can already see smoke rising from the green. The early evening air bristles with voltage, charged with it. I can feel it against my skin like static.

Another creak and I dig my nails in. Wood splinters beneath me. Shit. Shit. I lean out into space, bracing my feet against the brickwork and pushing against it, releasing my grip, arching forward, the ground a long way down. Almost immediately I realize I have not jumped nearly far enough, that there's no way I'm going to reach the porch, no way, and then I hit something solid, hard enough to knock the wind from my chest and my hands grope blindly, frantically for purchase. I hang on, I hang on so tightly my nails draw blood into my palms. I look down, realizing my feet are about four feet above the ground, kicking in the space. I'm clinging to the satellite dish, the metal groaning under my weight, feeling the give as it bends slightly, nails coming free with a screech of metal and brick dust. I don't give myself any more time to think about it. I let my fingers go and my body drops to the ground.

A dull pain flares in my right ankle as I land awkwardly, rolling onto my side. I don't scream, but my jaw snaps closed and I yelp in fright. When I stand and try to walk, the pain intensi-fies, throbbing a little. I manage though, limping toward the gate with my heart in my mouth. I expect to hear Lisa or Bert yelling my name any minute, expect to hear running footsteps behind me and a hand clamp down on my arm. I picture Lisa hauling me back to the house with a wide, sick grin, saying, *Time for your Riddance, Mina Ellis, we need to break the spell.* I keep going.

It's busy down by the green. I'm shocked at the amount of people. The bonfires have already been lit, smoldering in the half-light, the wood not quite catching yet. It is a carnival atmosphere, voices high and rowdy. A woman with a long throat is laughing with her head thrown back. A man I recognize as having been out-side the house right at the beginning, holding a placard with GIVE THE DEAD THY TONGUE painted onto it, is standing on a bench and singing at the top of his voice, one hand placed over his heart. Children are running amok as the first stars begin to prick the sky. I don't know how long I've got before Alice will be brought down here. Maybe they are already heading this way. Maybe the Riddance has already begun.

The video shop is shuttered and two words have been spray-painted messily over the grille. *Good Riddance.* I hammer on the door with the flat of my hand but there is no response. I step back and look upward, can see a light on in the flat above. I jerk as someone throws a firecracker at my feet, laughing, dashing away. Everyone has big, red smiles. It's disconcerting. I want to get off the street.

"Mind out!" a voice calls, and I'm shoved aside by someone moving past me at speed, their head down. My ankle sings in pain as I stagger sideways. They approach the door of the video shop, hands groping for the keys.

"Fern?"

She turns and looks at me and I'm startled by her expression. She looks stricken, almost panicked—wide-eyed and breathless. It takes her a moment to really see me.

"Shit, Mina! Come on in."

Inside it is dark, muted evening light filtering through the grilles pulled down over the windows. From the flat above comes the sound of the television loudly playing cartoons and the strobing light of the screen projected onto the stairwell. Outside, another muffled bang as a firecracker explodes somewhere out on the green.

"Bet you wish you'd stayed at home now, right?" Fern says, pushing her bag onto the counter. I can hear the clink of bottles inside.

"You can say that again," I say, and I mean it. I wish I'd never met Sam Hunter or heard that tape of his. I should have made that appointment with the caterers, I should have stayed home with Oscar and left that photograph of Eddie and his silvery eyes buried in a drawer. But then I think of the Polaroids in my pocket, Mary's eye spiked with blood. I think of how she deserves justice, how all these Riddance girls deserve justice.

"I've got to talk to you."

"I don't have long. Stevie's upstairs, and she'll be needing dinner and a bath before it all kicks off tonight. I'd been hoping she'd be a bit older before being confronted with all this, but it is what it is, right?"

Fern laughs, and I think of the clinking bottles in her bag, wonder if she's been drinking. She seems hectic, like she can't settle. A prey animal with fast-moving blood.

"I'm not going to pretend I know what's going on in this town, Fern. I don't know about hagstones and Riddances and all the rest of it, and right now I don't trust anyone to tell me. You know what happened earlier? The Webber family asked us to leave. Sam's sitting in the dark with a shoe in his hands and Alice looks like she's on the brink of a fucking breakdown." I tug at my hair, pushing it away from my face, feeling frantic. "When I went to pack my bags, Bert locked me in the bedroom. I had to climb out of the window to get here. It feels like everyone is losing their minds."

She laughs, a small, soft disbelieving sound.

"The Riddance is a form of madness. I've always thought it. Purification through chaos. It works though, Mina. It works. I should know."

We stare at each other a long time. The light coming through from outside changes texture, becomes warm and golden and flickering.

"How old were you?" I ask gently.

"Thirteen. June 1977, baby. Last full moon of the spring. The Native Americans call it the 'strawberry moon.' I was out of control, the whole town said so. I got into trouble setting fires—what's it called? That urge?"

"Pyromania."

"That's it. Pyromania. You know, if they don't want kids starting fires, they shouldn't make it sound so fucking *cool*, you know? Anyway, that's when Bert and Mary took me in. I had a Riddance two weeks later. Fighting fire with fire, I suppose you'd call it. I'd damaged a bunch of property and was looking at ending up in a youth custody center—a 'Borstal,' as it was known back then. It felt like the whole town came out to see me. The bonfires were twenty feet high. And the noise! Loud enough to drive the Devil out of me. I went to my knees in that grass and I've never felt lighter. I can't explain it. I never set a fire again. No more stealing, no joyriding. I stopped cutting myself, went back to school—I mean, you can say it's horseshit all you like but there are girls in this town who are proof of . . ."

She trails off. I feel frayed, as if I am coming undone. Panic, gnawing at me. Outside, firecrackers, a man shrieking at the moon.

"Of what?"

"I don't know. Magic? Power? I'm not the best person to ask. Bert would know."

Bert. I reach into my pocket, for the envelope.

"Actually, Bert's why I'm here."

"Oh?"

From upstairs, Stevie's voice floats down, "Mum-ee, I'm hun-gree!"

"In a minute, baby!" Fern calls back. She is still looking at me. "Is this about Mary?"

That ruptured eye full of blood.

"Partly, yes. I saw her before the undertakers took her away. Did you know that?"

Fern nods. Outside, another firework. The windows rattle.

"I don't think that she died naturally, Fern."

She regards me for a moment. Her gray eyes are luminous, gleaming with tears.

"Don't. Don't, Mina."

"The way she was lying, the position her hands were in. Her fingers were hooked, like she'd been clawing at her throat." I swallow, scrambling over my words. Fern takes a single step away from me as if I am infectious. "There were signs of a struggle in the room. A lamp had been knocked over, the bedcovers were on the floor. It wasn't right."

"Mina. Be very careful about what you're saying."

"I haven't told anyone else about this. Just you."

"Listen, Alice Webber is an oddball, okay?" Fern laughs uneasily. "We all know it. But Mary was like a grandmother to her—"

"I'm not talking about Alice. I know everyone thinks she had something to do with it but I was *there*, Fern. Alice found Mary that way. I'd bet my life on it. I'm talking about Bert."

I watch Fern's face switch slowly from shock to affront. Her mouth springs open, her head shakes.

"No, no, no. Bert wouldn't do that. That's absurd. It's fucking *offensive*."

"Fern—"

"He loved that woman. You ever hear the way he talked about her? Saw the way his eyes lit up just at the mention of her name?"

"I'm not suggesting he didn't love her. But she was very ill. It's hard looking after someone who isn't going to get better. Sometimes you just want to—"

"What?" she snaps. Her T-shirt slides down to reveal a round shoulder, freckled and pale. "Sometimes you want to what? Murder them? Are you listening to yourself?"

I swallow. *The hush of the rain, the gasping breath.* The grille rattles as if someone has fallen against it.

"You should go, Mina. I've got my kid to look after." Fern picks up the bag and I realize how angry she is, how much I've misjudged this. I grab her arm and am surprised at how quickly she pulls it away.

"You should go, I said."

I pull the envelope out of my pocket, feeling sick, feeling afraid. Right now, Fern is the only friend I have and I'm about to lose her, too.

"I found this at Bert's house. Mary was trying to tell me

about it. It was hidden away in a record sleeve. Billie Holiday. 'Blue Moon,' remember? It was their first dance."

Fern turns to me, her face set. She doesn't even look at the envelope.

"He, uh—there's photographs in here. Polaroids. That's a self-developing cam—"

"Jesus, Mina, I know what a fucking Polaroid is."

"I don't know how long he's been doing it for— I don't-I don't have any answers for you. I just know that he isn't the man you think he is, and this is why."

I can hear my voice starting to fracture, strained sounding. I'm begging now.

"Take a look. Please, Fern. You're in there."

Fern squares her shoulders, jaw lifted.

"Bert took me in when I had nothing and no one. He has helped a lot of people in this town, Mina."

"A lot of girls, you mean."

"Huh?"

"Girls. Riddance girls. Like you, like Lisa. Like Alice." I swallow, because this is it, I'm pulling the pin. "Stevie, too. You ever think about that?"

"Out," she snarls. I actually see her lip curl, teeth bare. "I won't ask you again."

Something twists painfully inside me in a secret, deep chamber. Some emotion, straining for release. This is not how I imagined this conversation going. I wish I could think clearly. Fern takes a step toward me and I back away, hands up, palms out in a gesture of surrender.

"I'm going," I tell her, because I am afraid. There's real anger in Fern's expression, her eyes glittering like mica, the heat of it searing and boiling. I try to take the Polaroid out, the one of

Fern at age thirteen (*"June 1977, baby!"*), with her pink hair and her scarred arms, nails bitten all the way to the cuticle, but she slaps the envelope straight out of my hand and shoves me out through the door. I stumble into the street, injured ankle flaring painfully like a tendon is ruptured, lurching against someone who immediately pushes me away against the wall so hard I crack my head and see stars. I am dry-mouthed and breathless, feeling the heat of those bonfires even at this distance, like standing in front of a furnace. The smoke makes my eyes water and it stings. It hurts.

THIRTY-SEVEN

I walk back to Beacon Terrace in a daze. The streetlights are wavering, spinning almost. I feel like my legs might give way any second. I can't seem to think straight and so perhaps that's why, after walking through what seems like a tunnel made up of shadows and winking lights, I end up outside Bert's house. I find myself barefoot on the cool grass of the lawn, staring up at the darkened windows. I don't know what the Riddance involves but I'm almost certain it will have something to do with the things Bert keeps in his basement. The dress, the Devices. That head cage blotted with rust and old blood. I look around me to make sure no one is watching and then I stand on tiptoe just the way Alice had and feel along the lintel until my fingers chance upon the silver door key hidden up there. I pull it down and look

around me again. I feel watched. No, not watched. Hunted. I
open the door and slip inside.

Down, down to the basement. No key needed this time, the
door is already open. I turn on the lights with caution but am
greeted only by an empty room; immaculate, tidy, well-kept. This
time, however, I know exactly where to go. I pull the dust sheet
once again from the tailor's dummy behind the shelves and stand
back, staring at the Riddance dress. I run my hand over the heavy
fabric, lifting the folds of the skirt and letting them drop satisfy-
ingly back into place. I thought it was a drab, concrete-colored
linen but now as I start to untie the waist straps, peeling it from
the mannequin, I can see it is a faded Florentine blue. The color
of spring flowers; love-in-a-mists and forget-me-nots. I hold the
dress against my body, enjoying the soft rustle of the material as
I move. It's mesmerizing. There is the lightest scattering of stains
on the chest, like rust spots. When I brush at them, they don't
come away.

"Put it on."

The voice startles me and I utter a short scream, clamping
my hands over my mouth as a figure steps out of the shadows
under the stairs, blocking my exit. It's Bert. In the harsh overhead lights the hollows of his temples look like pools of ink. He
is wearing a long, purple robe fastened at his neck with a golden
clasp, silvery hair swept back from his head. He reminds me of
a Las Vegas magician and I almost blurt out a shrill, panicked
laugh, not quite sane. Bert notices my expression and dusts his
fingers down the velvet.

"Ah yes. My ceremonial robe. A touch grandiose, I'm afraid,
but these things are worth doing correctly if they're to be done
well, don't you think? And people do expect these traditions to

be performed a certain way. I see you're getting into the spirit of things." He points to the dress. "You want to see how it feels to be a Riddance girl, don't you? Put it on."

Mina, some soft internal voice says warningly, *be careful.* I keep my eyes fixed on him as I back away toward the far end of the table. Bert must have already been down here when he heard me come into the house. It's unnerving to think of him stepping into the shadows and watching me in silence. It's predatory. A wild animal hiding in the dark of a cave.

"I know you came down here yesterday, Mina. You left traces of yourself everywhere. Smudges on the glass, the banister, footprints on the carpet. Did you really think I wouldn't notice?"

"Bert, I just wanted to—"

He keeps talking, voice smooth and unruffled and almost idle sounding.

"You made a mess down here, though. Left everything out for me to find. I thought you were cleverer than this but you're too far gone, aren't you? You're already bewitched."

I think back to how I dashed out of the basement the previous day when Alice was screaming. I meant to come back down and tidy everything away but, of course, I never had the chance and in the chaos that had followed I'd forgotten all about it. Bert flashes me a sly grin, all dentures and pink gums. "Let's see now—breaking and entering, trespass, theft. *Murder.* You're building up quite the record, aren't you?"

"I didn't murder Mary, Bert. You know I didn't."

He gives a soft, dry chuckle. Another of those long, vulpine smiles.

"I wasn't referring to my wife, Mina."

I feel suddenly weak. Fear runs through me like ropes of mercury, slippery and poisonous.

Bert smiles again and nods toward the dress. "But! Accusations and recriminations will have to wait. We have a Riddance to attend, don't we? The question is, *whose?*"

I stare at him, heart ticking in my throat. Bert's old, but fit. I don't doubt he has a certain wiry strength, even if he can't move fast. But that's the other thing, isn't it? My ankle. I hobbled down here by leaning on the handrail but to run past him, up the stairs, and out the door? Not a chance. So if I want to get out of this basement, I have to play along. Get upstairs into the kitchen where there might be knives and scissors and meat cleavers, long steel skewers for barbeques. More important, there is a phone in the hallway. I've seen it there on the wall and I know it works because Lisa called Bert only the previous night when she'd been stranded. All I need to do is disable him long enough to get to the phone. But I can't do that down here. Down here I'm cornered like a rat.

"Okay, Bert," I tell him, holding up my hands. "I'll put on the damn dress."

He graciously turns away as I peel off my clothes, stained and crumpled and stiff with sweat. I catch a glimpse of my ankle, swollen and starting to bruise. I don't like the look of that bruising, don't like it *at all*.

The dress is designed to open up like an apron and be wrapped around the body, secured with long straps of material about the waist. I step into it, strapping it around me. The pale blue fabric drops away from my breasts like liquid and when I move, turning slowly around so the full skirt circles out, the material whispers to me in delight. My fingers carefully tie a bow

at my waist, cinching it in. I almost gasp at the sensation of con-
striction, it's muscular somehow. Color flares in my vision, the
room seeming to take on a clarity that is almost supernatural.
No wonder so many girls wanted to wear it, I think. It's magical.
The throb of my heart is slow and steady as I lift the necklaces
one by one from the dummy, taking care to hang them from
the shortest to longest so they don't tangle around my neck. It's
heavy work, the stones rattling against each other with a sound
like dice being thrown. By the time I lower the last one over my
head, I can barely stand, yet it is a peaceful, almost meditative
feeling, the weight bearing down on me. At the far end of the
room is an old fly-spotted mirror, silvery with age. I stand in
front of it and my breath catches in my throat. I look like a paint-
ing, some old master rich in shadow and shade, my hair coming
undone, high spots of color in my cheeks. I am a pre-Raphaelite,
bruised and heavy with love. I am strung with the bones of the
earth around my neck. I am beautiful.

In the misty reflection a subtle movement catches my eye.
Just for a second, I think I glimpse something pressed into
the farthest corner of the ceiling; tilted, grinning face, bruised
knees, blackened tongue. Then, gone. I catch that sweet scent
again, iron rich; candied almonds and spoiled meat. It curdles
in the air like bad words softly spoken. When Bert's hands slide
around my waist, I almost scream. They wind around the straps
and begin to adjust the knots, his breath rasping in and out of
him, his exhalations hot against the back of my neck. I am suddenly mute with dread. Bert pulls the knot so tight I clutch my
stomach, sucking air in. I'm forced to lean forward, trying to
create a space for my ribs to expand.

"You're hurting me! Bert!"

"The combined weight of those stones is precisely five point seven kilograms," he whispers, as if I haven't said a thing. "That's how much it took to weigh down the original witch back in the seventeen hundreds."

"Weigh her down? For what?"

"Her Riddance, Mina." His eyes glitter dangerously. "Those women didn't want to stand still."

I stare down at the dress. The rust spatters are a fine spray, a constellation across the soft blue fabric. A spray of arterial blood, perhaps. Something is caving in inside of me, some vital prop shaking loose. I can feel it. I force my nails into my palms until they dig bloody grooves there, pain lighting up my brain, forcing my eyes wide open. I need to be thinking clearly if I'm getting out of this.

"I need some air, Bert. I feel like I can't breathe. Please."

Bert steps aside with a gallant sweep of his hand and I have a moment to consider just making a break for it, figure I can maybe get as far as the hallway before he brings me down, but as I turn, my injured ankle makes a sound like grating rocks and a shard of pain races up my leg. The hagstones clatter against my chest as I make my way up the stairs and by the time I reach the kitchen, one hand propped on the doorpost to prevent myself from collapsing, I'm sweating, my teeth gritted in effort. My heart sinks when Bert closes the kitchen door behind him before crossing over to the dining table. There, three boxes are laid out with the lids removed. The Devices have been unwrapped.

"It's a shame you didn't think to come to me and ask me about these, Mina," Bert tells me. "I would happily have shown them to you. These Devices belonged to my ancestors, a long time ago. They were used as instruments of righteousness. The scold's bridle and the heretic's fork, the witch pricker and the pincers. They were all necessary. They all had their place."

The hagstones anchor me to the spot, unable to move. Bert's eyes are dark with desire, or something akin to it, as he plucks a grape from the fruit bowl on the table and tosses it into his mouth with a practiced flick of his wrist.

"Your wife didn't like them, though, did she?" I surprise myself by saying. "Mary didn't want the Devices in the house. That's why you had to hide them down there in the basement. Turns out you became quite adept at hiding things from her, didn't you? For a time, at least."

He spits grape seeds into his palm, still holding on to that soft, wry smile—but is it becoming slightly strained or is that my imagination? I hope some part of him is starting to squirm. The thought makes me feel braver and I step closer toward him.

"Mary had the measure of you at the end, didn't she? I can't imagine the effort it cost her to try to get my attention."

Bert looks up at me, one hand sliding behind his back. *Uh-oh*, I think.

"Mary was very sick. Her death is a blessing in many ways. I'm sure you understand that more than anyone, Mina. Sometimes you have to be cruel to be kind."

"But that's not why you did it, is it? You didn't kill her to alleviate her suffering. Because you *did* kill her, Bert, that much I knew the minute I saw her. The way she was lying, her eye filled with blood—that's called 'petechiae,' by the way. That's the scientific term for it. I'm told it's useful when diagnosing the cause of death in choking or strangulation cases."

My voice is steady but inside I'm screaming, *Run, Mina, run, RUN!* My eyes scan the kitchen for something I can pick up to use as a weapon, a doorstop, a frying pan, *anything*. I keep talking, keep letting my mouth run. I need to keep him distracted.

"That's why you asked Alice to come over here last night—so that fingers would point at her when Mary was found dead. You knew it would be easy, especially so soon after the news about Vicky and half this town already convinced there's something wrong with Alice Webber. Only I messed that up for you, didn't I? I wasn't meant to be here, but I was. I was. And I found out so much about you, Bert Roscow."

I take a step away from him. I want to be out of range whenever he comes out swinging. Because he will, I know that much.

"How do you think Mary felt when she discovered the photographs, Bert? Do you think she was shocked? Surprised? Or do you think some awful part of her had known it all along?"

I watch his face twist sharply, his chin pull back into his chest. He is silent and frowning. I keep going.

"You know, you'll go to prison for this. All these girls were underage."

"The problem with Riddance girls, Mina, is that they're liars. Thieves. Runaways. The Riddance isn't a panacea, it can't fundamentally change who they are. Under the skin they are still rotten."

I blink, stunned. Because he's right of course. The pyromaniac, the pregnant teenage mother, the girl hearing voices? Who *would* have believed these feral young teens? Who would have listened? And who would have cared enough about them to do anything?

"You wouldn't have made a Riddance girl, would you, Mina? Or maybe you would. There are so many ways a person can be out of control, don't you think? Appearances are so often deceiving.

Take Mary for instance. When we first started courting, I called her 'dollybird' because she was so fair and blond and tiny, just like a little doll. She was perfect, God, she was perfect. When the police brought her home three weeks after we were married, I naturally thought there'd been some sort of mistake. When they told me she'd been caught stealing, I'd laughed at them. The idea of it was so absurd! My Mary? In the pharmacy, they said. They'd made her empty her bag out onto the counter. Hair spray, perfume. A bar of soap. Later I asked her why and you know what she said?"

I shake my head.

"That she couldn't help it. She told me it was as though something had taken over her. I wasn't too worried then. About the Devil. About the way he makes some girls act up. He wouldn't do that to my Mary, I thought. Still. I kept an eye on her and sure enough it happened again. This time she was charged. An eight-pound fine for taking a one-pound lipstick. I didn't know what to do. We had the money to buy the things she was stealing but it was like she had no control over it. It was a compulsion. Well. I knew all about that. Knew all about how the Devil works when he worms his way in. I pleaded with her to stop. I told her she'd end up in prison. I thought the shame of it would kill me. What broke me was finding the shoebox under the bed full of all the things she'd stolen and got away with. A hoard. Books and records and jewelry, makeup and stationery. There was even a key ring in there from Majorca where we went on our honeymoon. She'd taken it right out of the gift shop while we'd been walking around. She couldn't look me in the eye when I found it. Tried to tell me she had a condition, that the doctor had told her she needed pills. But I knew we were past that. I knew what she needed."

His eyes have darkened, glittering dangerously.

"Mary had her Riddance, right out on the Green. The whole town came out to watch. I remember seeing the flames of the bonfires reflected in her eyes, big and round as mirrors. She wore flowers in her hair and rings on her fingers and she never stole a damn thing again. We chased the Devil right out of her, we drove the witch away. All these Riddance girls, I tried to warn them what was coming. I tried to tell Lisa, when she was pregnant with Alice. She was a good girl, very athletic. So much promise. You wouldn't have known she was a whore, how easily she gave it up as soon as she realized the power she had over those poor boys. Fern was manic, uncontrollable. Starting fires just to watch things burn. She frightened me and it was wonderful. I was almost sorry to have to force it out of her."

Bert reaches out and picks up a peach from the fruit bowl, pressing it to his nose, inhaling.

"But Alice—Alice *is* different. There's something almost otherworldly about her. People making pilgrimages across the county just to stand outside her door. There's witch blood in her. My ancestors would've strung her up and watched her dance till her neck snapped."

He takes a bite from the peach, huge and greedy. The juice slowly runs down his chin.

"This is what I love about the summer, Mina. Everything is so *ripe*."

I catch the fragrance of the peach; that bright, clear scent like running water. Bert squeezes it in his hand until his fingers dent the flesh.

"So soft," he continues, in his gentle voice. "And look how the juice runs, Mina, when you break the skin. You could almost crush it completely. They bruise so easily. They all do, in the end."

His tongue flicks out—wet and pink and quivering—and licks peach juice from his wrist, watching me carefully. Another step forward. Now he could reach me, if he swings what he is holding in that hand. A paperweight maybe. A hagstone. A short, stubby blade that will rip into my neck. I brace myself to move.

"You have something of mine, Mina Ellis." He looks at me calmly. "I'm going to need those pictures back, there's a good girl."

"I don't have them."

He sighs with something like regret.

"Where are they?"

I hold on to his gaze, even though it feels as though my insides have turned liquid, even though it feels as if my voice is small and lost and frightened.

"I don't know. Maybe I lost them."

"Mina, being a journalist taught me many things. One of those is how to tell when a person is lying. I learned that very quickly. Another was that there isn't a policeman who doesn't have a price. Any idea how many contacts I have in the force? How many old friends owing me favors? All it took was a single phone call."

Distantly, a boom. Thunder. The heat is building, stifling as a damp flannel over the mouth.

"They questioned you, didn't they? After your brother died."

"It was routine," I say automatically. My heart is beating an erratic rhythm in my chest.

"Oh, Mina. I think we can dispense with all this"—he flaps his hand idly—"*politeness*. After all, you've accused me of killing my wife."

He steps up to me, putting the peach gently to one side. His hand slides out from behind his back. He is holding one of the Devices, the one which looks like a long, slender needle with a worn wooden handle.

"This is the witch pricker," he tells me. "It has broken stronger women than yourself, Mina Ellis. When I introduced it to Alice, she cried out like a wounded animal. Do you know what it's used for?"

I shake my head.

"This particular pricker was used by one of my Puritan forebears as a test for witches. I'm told he drove it through the skin all the way to the bone. In the old days it was believed that a witch had a place on her body that was devoid of feeling and nerves and would not bleed when pricked. Let's see if we can find it, shall we, Mina? Let's find out. Let's see how deep it goes before you confess."

He grips my wrist in a surprisingly strong, manacled grasp, resting the tip of the pricker against my forearm. I can see the dent it makes in the skin as he applies slow pressure.

"Your brother, Eddie. He was quite the star pupil by all accounts. Very bright. Very driven. It's no wonder he held out as long as he did toward the end. That tenacity is inbuilt in some people, isn't it? Such a shame he was robbed of that future."

"Pneumonia killed him. It was"—I gasp in pain as the needle draws a bead of blood—"th-the ice."

"But why was he *on* the ice, Mina?"

I stare at him. There is a tingling sensation in my hands and the backs of my eyes, a feeling of pressure surging. I have to bite down on my tongue to bring the room back into focus. A voltaic flicker of lightning and all the lights lower for a second. That buzzing, is it in my head? I don't know. I don't know.

"It wasn't my fault. Dad said Eddie would have gone to save

anyone. A squirrel even, if it was stuck. That's just who Eddie was."

"But it wasn't just 'anyone' and it wasn't a squirrel, was it, Mina?"

In that long, heavy cloak Bert seems bigger, heavier somehow. Like he could crush me underfoot. He puts his forehead against mine, the witch pricker cold on my skin, slicing me open. "It was *you*."

It's as though I've swallowed a shard of ice and it is sliding down my throat, lungs crackling with frost. I'm shivering. *Slow down Mina the ice is black,* Eddie had shouted, but I hadn't listened, had I? The crack beneath my feet so loud that rooks had risen into the wintry air like burning leaves.

"I'm told in the police interview you were very nervous. You shook all the way through it. No tears, though. No sadness. Funny, that."

"I was broken. I was beyond tears."

"I'll bet you were. Like I said, it hurts to see the ones we love suffer. So much better sometimes to do what we must to ease their pain."

I'm crying. I can feel the tears swell and sting, the soft, velvety punch of emotion in my chest and throat, that rising sensation like I'm lifting off the ground despite the hagstones tethering me. My mouth moves but no sound comes out. Bert nods, his voice gentle.

"Oh, Mina."

My knees give way, suddenly and completely, and I slide bonelessly to the floor. The sound of the stones around my neck is a rattling applause. *Bravo!* Bert stands over me, his head tilted to one side.

"Ah-ah! No tears, Mina. Eddie wouldn't want that. Come on. Up on your feet."

"I can't."

I hate the way my voice sounds. Weak and needling. Bert eases himself into a crouch beside me. I can hear the joints in his knees pop, the long sigh. His eyes bore into mine with an agitation that borders on excitement.

"Now we could sit here all night and blackmail each other, but I rather think we've reached a stalemate, don't you? Besides, I'm old, Mina. Old and widowed, with no family. I've lived in this town my whole life and I've helped a lot of young girls who've strayed off the path."

He leans closer, smelling like incense and metal, like the thuribles they use in my father's church, speaking in a low, rough whisper. "I'll be a long time dead before this town turns on me, Mina Ellis. Now give me the photographs before I do something you'll regret."

I spit. I do it the way Vicky Matherson had, through a V shape in my fingers, hitting Bert on the temple. A spew of white foam slides down toward the outer corner of his eye and his face darkens with what I first mistake as anger. It is only as he drives the pricker into my arm that I recognize it for what it is—loathing. Then, the pain. I see stars, blinding-white flashes. It feels as though the whole of my lower arm has been dipped in molten lead from wrist to elbow. I hiss through clenched teeth, eyes streaming as Bert pulls the pricker free and a fat droplet of blood blooms on my skin. Already I can feel the wound throbbing.

"They used to strip the witches naked but I don't think we'll go that far, Mina," Bert says, tugging at the knot on my dress. "I think once we find the right spot you'll remember where you put those photographs very quickly."

My skin crawls as I feel the cold press of his fingertips on my ribs. I try to pull away but Bert is wiry and strong and, with the stones around my neck and the hot throb of my shattered ankle, I can barely move an inch. He shushes me, feeling along the long lines of my ribs, hooking his fingers into my damp armpit.

I gasp as the cold metal tip pierces the skin there. It is a bright, exquisite pain that forms a collar of white heat around my shoulder. Bert shows me his teeth, his nostrils flared as his hand jerks and I curl up, winded. His eyes are hard and glazed like hagstones in the rain.

"Bert?"

It's a small female voice, coming from the doorway. Bert's head snaps up. His eyes seem to clear and focus. His hand loosens his grip on my arm and slowly, slowly he draws the pricker out from my armpit, leaving behind a hot, metallic sting. Blood is already oozing down my rib cage, the side of my breast. I clamp my hand there and look up to see Alice standing in the doorway. She stares from me to Bert, wide-eyed.

"What's happening?" She steps into the kitchen. "I thought you were bringing the dress to our house?"

"Change of plan, Alice," Bert says sharply, using the breakfast bar to straighten up. The pricker hangs from his loose fist, a fat droplet of blood swelling at the very tip. "I found the witch."

"What do you mean?" Alice asks. She is staring at me. "Why is Mina wearing the Riddance dress?"

"The witch is *in* Mina," Bert says, pointing the pricker at me. "It must have crawled inside her while she slept."

"Mina?" Alice's timid, cautious voice filters through the muffled waves of pain. "You all right?"

I look up at her, peeling my lips back into something approximating a smile. It doesn't reach my eyes, but that's okay, it's okay. I just need to get through to her.

"Alice, you have to go and get help. Find Sam. Tell him—"

"Did you hear what I said?" Bert lifts his voice, smoothing back his hair with his free hand. "The witch has found a way in. It's been using Mina all along."

My head switches around, sees Alice's mouth drop open into surprise.

"Don't listen to him!" I hiss, blood blooming on the side of the dress.

Bert talks over me, voice strident. "It's trying to trick you, Alice. It's what it does. It's what they all do."

My skin feels tight and hot and agitated, and I struggle to get to my feet, pressed back down into the earth by the heavy stone necklaces. My voice is high and hectic, striated with fear.

"Alice, go and get Sam, please! Bert's lying."

"Come on over here and see for yourself," Bert says, and I realize with horror he is holding out the witch pricker to Alice. "Don't be afraid. We've got it now. It's trapped."

His eyes rest on me, bright and hungry.

"Alice, for God's sake—"

"She's bleeding," Alice says, pointing at my arm. A thread of blood winds about my wrist from the puncture wound just below my elbow.

"That's because it is clever, and it is trying to trick you. But sooner or later we find the spot, don't we?"

I have a moment then, remembering the conversation with Sam in the café light-years ago, in a time when there was no curfew or witches or pyres on the Green. Sam, telling me that Alice had developed a 'pinprick rash.' How she'd complained of pains in her sides like needles being pressed there. How long had he been trying to convince Alice that she, too, felt no pain from the witch pricker? How long for her to start to believe it? I twist around, struggling to stand, but Bert puts a hand on my shoulder, pressing down hard enough to make the joint in my neck crack. The blood on my wrist is tracing a line down toward the tips of my fingers.

"Alice, whatever he's telling you, whatever he's done to you, he lies. He killed Mary, Alice. He's dangerous and you have to get help. Please!"

"Can you smell that, Alice? It's the witch, rotting Mina from the inside out. It's all over her. Can't you smell it?"

Alice's nose wrinkles. "I guess," she says slowly.

Bert nods, sadly. "I told you. It's taken root in her."

My mouth is very dry, vision blurred. I claw at Bert's restraint as Alice moves closer. I scuffle for purchase on the linoleum. He continues to hold the witch pricker out, his hand steady.

"I don't want to," Alice says quietly. "I don't want to hurt her."

"It doesn't hurt them. You know that, don't you?"

I watch with dread fascination as Alice reluctantly lifts her hand, hesitates, then grasps the witch pricker. Bert turns it carefully so the blade is pointed outward, mindful that she holds it the right way. The look of vacancy on his face is terrifying. I am frozen to the spot.

"She doesn't *look* like a witch," Alice says uncertainly.

"That's because it wears a human cloak," Bert replies. "You'll be next. In the night you'll wake and find the Devil in your throat. Do you want that?"

"No," Alice says tearfully.

"Don't listen to him!" I urge her, as pain radiates from my armpit in tight, muscular waves. "It's me, it's Mina!"

"Look at her, Alice. *Really* look at her."

Bert pulls my hair until my face is tilted up to the ceiling. I'm pale and breathless and wild-looking and something in Alice's face is frightening me. She believes him. Alice grabs the handle of the witch pricker with both hands as if she is going to drive it into my skull.

"It wants you to hesitate," Bert continues in the muffled silence, almost drowned out by my frantic, panting breath. "The longer you wait, the better as far as the witch is concerned. It has more time to think of all the ways it will dig into you when it has the chance."

I see Alice tighten her knuckles as she steadies her grip. Her eyes widen.

"I'm sorry, Mina," she whispers and then she drives the witch pricker into the top of my thigh. The shock makes me gasp and I twist violently. Bert's hand is tangled in my hair and there is a ripping sound as strands are tugged free at the follicles. I look down at where Alice has jabbed the pricker but there is something wrong. Different. *There's no pain*, I think calmly. *There's no blood*. Alice frowns, pulling the pricker out of my thigh. I lift the material slowly and study the place it went in. There is a small, red mark, barely visible. Nothing more. I rub at it, confused.

"You see?" Bert says with mocking triumph. "The witch's mark. I told you."

THIRTY-EIGHT

I'm thinking about the ice. Thinking about the pyres on the Green climbing toward the arch of the heavens. A flower crown is placed, Caesar-like, over my head. It makes me look ethereal; green-gray leaves of sage and sprigs of fresh rosemary studded with little purple flowers, cow parsley and borage with its pale, watery blues and star-shaped blooms.

I am a Goddess. I am an ascending angel. I am speaking in tongues.

Bert says, it is time for your Riddance, Mina Ellis.

THIRTY-NINE

My head is spinning and the stones around my neck are so heavy they pin me to the earth. My footsteps drag over the grass. I experience moments of strange clarity punctuated with flashes of nothing, lost time. A small, distant part of me knows it is a reaction to the shock. My mind is reduced to rubble, smoking craters and scorched earth. It retreats.

—FLASH—

The night is inky dark, humidity pressing close to the skin. Smothering us. Sam, running his hands through his hair, walking beside me, long shadowed, pleading. He is still clutching that shoe to his chest, glassy eyes deeply socketed. Distant thunder over the moors, a pall of hazy smoke across the green. The crackling PA system, which plays over speakers hanging from the branches of the trees; a waltz, the tune slow-moving and drowsy. Children running through the dark laughing and playing pixie in the dell, holding sparklers aloft and streaking embers like comets. The stones hanging around my neck are rubbing the flesh of my neck raw. Paul and Lisa beside the bonfire, their features corrupted by shadows so it looks as though they have holes for eyes.

—FLASH—

Bert is cloaked in smoke and darkness.

—FLASH—

Sweat warm and salty on my lips. The bonfire is a spirited wraith in veils of orange and gold, logs split and crackling and throwing up sparks and I've never felt more beautiful. I let the heat press against my skin, the fury of it. Crowds of people stare with wet, moony eyes: the woman with the dog that pissed on the gate; teenage boys on their bikes; young girls in tank tops and eyeliner, glossy lipped, unafraid; a man with a round face and upward slanted eyes shouting something, spraying spittle all over me.

—FLASH—

Someone shouts, "Good Riddance," and throws something at my feet. There is a bang loud enough to make my teeth rattle and a cheer goes up from the crowd. A scorch of lightning flickers blue and silver in the sky to the east. The dress billows around me.

—FLASH—

A sea of pale faces.

"What do we do with witches in this town?" Bert calls, dark and smoky. The reply, massed voices lifted to the sky, heads up.

"Run them out!"

"Run them out!"

"Run! Them! Out!"

The last is distorted by screaming, straining necks, heads lifted to the sky. The bonfire flames are sinuous, mesmerizing. The crowds are cheering and catcalling, voices so loud they drown out the crack of thunder. The wind is picking up, stripping petals from my crown. Someone is shrieking and clapping. Excitement or fear, it's hard to tell. People are holding hands and linking arms, lifting glasses of cider and cloudy beer, voices raised. There is Sam, standing slightly apart from the group, his face set miserably in the flickering light. He is looking at me with eyes like frozen puddles. I see a small huddle of children—the eldest can't be more than ten years old—running in circles around the fire, throwing handfuls of grass at each other. Faces shiny with excitement. A small figure detaches from the group and walks toward me. I know her. It's Stevie. She is holding the same plastic gun she'd had the day Sam and I had arrived. Her hair is tied in bunches and when she smiles I see she has lost another tooth. She looks up at me, pointing the barrel at my head.

"Bang!" she says, and pulls the trigger.

FORTY

The flames of the four bonfires shade everything in capering shadows and waxy orange light. I watch as figures begin to detach from the crowd and leap through the flames, landing on the other side of the fire like smoking, twisted wreckage. There is a chorus of cheers and yells as they emerge with their hands patting at their smoldering clothing, reddened faces twisted into howls and roars and a deep guttural barking. The air is boiling with noise, it *seethes* with it; screaming and whistling and the pounding of feet.

A hand on my shoulder, I flinch. It is Bert, looking twenty feet tall, teeth strong and white as marble tombstones, smiling wickedly down at me.

"It's time," he says.

I want to tell him no but my mouth won't work, my throat

locked. Some instinctive, primal part of me lights up with fear. His hand grasps my arm as I stagger under the weight of the hagstones, feet dragging over the grass, inhaling smoke and grease and sulfur. He is leading me away from the bonfires, moving into the shadows beyond, to where the rushes at the pond's edge grow as tall as my waist. People part to let us through, the crowd moving like a murmuration, sealing back up and blocking an escape. Even over the smoke I can smell the water; silt and copper and rich black mud. As he shoves me into the shallows, I can feel something essential slipping away from me, some hold on the situation, the danger spilling over. Bert knew all about witches, Alice had told me. They tortured them and hung them or drowned them in the pond.

"Bert, I—"

He shushes me gently, putting his mouth to my ear so I can hear him say, "You wanted an old-fashioned Riddance, Mina. You don't get more old-fashioned than a good tongue splitting."

The dark water shimmers. It is cold, brightly, lip-bitingly cold. The mud oozes and sucks at my bare feet. My dress is growing so heavy I can only stand helpless as the weight of it pulls me down as if the water is full of grasping hands. I'm trying to run but it's awkward, the mud too soft and viscous. Bert knows it, of course he does, how can I run with these stones around my neck. I'll only work myself deeper into trouble. Now the water reaches almost to my waist. He wades out toward me, lifting his robe slightly so he can reach beneath it. Behind him the fires are sending sparks into the sky on thermals of searing air. I am shivering, searching around for something to ward Bert off. He plants both hands on my shoulders and shoves me down into the water. I stumble and splutter, gagging at the taste. The hagstones drag at my neck, threatening to sink me.

"You need to open your mouth, Mina. The Devil's in there and I need to get him out."

Bert has produced something from beneath his robe. It's the pincers, the blackened forceps I found in the Devices box. I'm on my knees, sinking into the mud. Algae blooms around me, a thick green carpet. Bert's eyes blaze with some sort of faded glory, some long bygone triumph that died with the witches of Salem and Pendle Hill.

"You know in the old days people like me were valuable," Bert says, moving closer. "We were considered wise and knowledgeable. In a town like this, three hundred years ago, I would have been venerated, and girls like you would have been crushed underfoot."

The rushes bend and sway like nodding heads in the rising wind. *Yes,* they seem to be saying, *yes, yes.* Bert's hair is a silver corona, his eyes scorched holes in paper. He looms over me, resting the pincers against my cheek as he takes my throat with his free hand, squeezing. My stomach contracts like a fist. My hands are at the knot of the Riddance dress, desperately trying to untie it. I have to shed this weight. The mud is cold and thick as glue. The water seeps into the fabric as I sink down, down into the water. It is up to my chest now, cold, despite the heat. It is making me breathless.

"That's the trouble with Riddance girls, Mina. They think they're special. They think the Devil chose them. But it isn't the Devil. It's me."

Bert's hand tightens on my throat and my mouth bursts open, gasping for breath. He slides the pincers between my teeth, levering my jaw open. I taste cold metal, silt water sour as bile. I am flooded, pinned down. The fabric of the dress has grown so heavy I can barely keep my head above the surface of the water. I try to pull away and that's when the pincers clamp on my tongue, the pain instant and brutal as Bert jerks his hand back as if to tear it right out of my mouth. My head is propelled abruptly forward with an agony I feel zipping up the back of my skull like metal teeth. My tongue stretches like elastic. Bert's hand tightens at my throat and each breath is a drag, a thin, dusty suction. Filmy water seeps between my fingers. Bert twists the wrist of his right arm slowly and the pincers with it, and I see neon lights, sparks on the surface of the water. The root of my tongue is red-hot and burning. I can't move, I can't breathe. The water level has risen to my chin as I sink slowly beneath the surface. I slide my eyes away from Bert and his big, wide smile, his expression of captivation and something like disfigured joy. I don't want him to be the last thing I see when my bloated, swollen tongue rips free.

I force myself to look toward the heavens for Hydra and Orion's Belt and Venus. I want to watch beauty as I go under. Bert grunts with the effort and pulls harder on the pincers. Something tears, the warmth of blood flooding my mouth, copper in my throat, pain spreading roots through my nervous system. My blurry eyes find the nearest bonfire and the spiraling columns of flame, and I see the dark outline of a figure leaping through it, knees almost as high as their ears. They are trailing sparks as they land on the soft grass, their silhouette slightly smudged against the flames, a comet with a long, smoking tail. Then they are running toward us and I can see long flaxen hair, that dumb T-shirt that reads in big, cartoon letters—POBODY'S NERFECT!

My mouth is a mess of shredded muscle, tongue engorged and mutilated. I cannot speak, can only make a wet gargling sound in the back of my throat, but even with the pincers forcing my jaw open I still manage a gory, humorless smile. Blood seeps between my teeth and down my chin where it billows in the water like storm clouds. Perhaps it is the change in my expression or perhaps Bert feels the pounding of feet through the earth and senses the undertow of danger. Whatever the reason, his face suddenly contorts into an expression of confusion; nostrils flaring, eyes bulging. Shock drops his mouth to his chest. There is a moment in which his eyes meet mine and he makes a single, guttural sound—*urk!*—and that's when I notice Alice standing behind him, teeth bared, her hand slicing through the air.

Bert tries to twist around, hands groping for purchase. There is something jutting from his neck, a wooden handle with gilded lettering. I don't have to be able to see it to know what it reads: DAEMONIA EICERE. The pricker. Bert's hold on me falls away and his hands reach up to clasp over the handle, blood weeping through his fingers as he does so, staggering and turning and sweeping at the water. As the pressure on my throat is released, I draw in a gulp of air, blood gurgling in my throat. My tongue throbs.

Bert staggers out of the pond and across the damp grass, swaying from side to side. He has one hand clamped over his neck, the other reaching out in front of him as if blindly groping in the dark. Around him the cheering and the singing start to fade, slowly at first, then almost completely, like a siren winding down. Someone shrieks as he stumbles into them, his bloodied hand grasping for their face, trying to keep himself upright on trembling, weak legs. His purple robes swirl as he gracelessly staggers backward in a move that is almost comical—arms flailing, legs cycling uselessly beneath him—the pricker protruding from the side of his neck like a dart. It's beautiful. I will never forget it.

"Mina, come on." Alice is trying to help me to my feet but I'm too heavy. I'm pulling her down with me, like gravity, like a black hole. Her face is pale and beaded with sweat, her hair smelling of ash and smoke. "Hurry, Mina!"

I can feel her shivering beneath the thin cotton of her T-shirt as I bat her hands away. She looks down at me confused, her mouth working as if to find the right words to get me moving. But there aren't any. There are no words. There is only the ice. I pull her a little closer, blood sluicing as I try to speak, lips numb.

"Run," I manage. I push her away from me with all the strength I have left, watching her stagger backward in the claggy mud, almost stumbling in the shallows, just about righting herself in time to look back at me with an expression of confusion and sorrow. That's when Bert falls into the fire.

By now the only sounds across the green are those of the wind and the flames of the towering bonfires. The crowd is staring at Bert, open-mouthed. Good ol' Bert, beloved of Mary, fine, upstanding citizen of Banathel, historian, babysitter, witch-hunter. His steps falter as he manages to grasp the handle of the pricker, tugging at it until it works free, releasing a jet of blood in a liquid black arc. He looks at his smeared hands with a frown and then his eyes seem to roll backward into his head. Bert takes a few faltering steps back, his arms spread as if to receive a host. He sways on the spot for just a moment, long enough for me to think *hurry up and die you fucker* before he falls backward into the flames.

I look back for Alice but she is gone. In that moment of perfect, blurred confusion, someone screams high and loud and panic seems to spread across the grass as if it were the flames themselves. I lurch toward the banks, tugging at the folds of my dress but they're soaked through, the material so waterlogged I can barely move. My head slips under the water's surface, hands groping beneath me for something solid to hold on to but it's just black mud, slick and heavy and lethal as setting concrete.

My mouth fills with cold water. It tastes like swamps, like green things decaying. The pain of it against my ruptured tongue is as high and shrill as an aria. I manage to just lift my head above the surface, gasp in a lungful of smoky air. Blood and drool pendulums from my chin and stains the water around me in a fan shape. In the distance, sirens. That means there will be questions. More questions, just like before. The policemen leaning forward in their chairs and saying, *Tell us about what happened when your brother got sick Mina his eye was full of blood that's called petechiae and that's why we have to ask these questions, do you understand, nod if you understand.*

My lungs shriek as I'm pulled under, so heavy, the hagstones and the dress and the mud dragging me down, down. A trail of silvery bubbles leave my mouth and race to the surface of the water just over my head, a night sky full of orange flames. Flares of lightning illuminate the rushes which crowd the bank and hide me from view. My eyes are wide, the flower crown drifting away and floating on the surface like a marker, a buoy. Here lies Mina Ellis, she could not swim. My lungs squeeze and protest as I struggle to free myself from the necklaces and the bindings of the Riddance dress but Bert has tied the knot so tightly my fingers cannot dig beneath it. He has condemned me after all, struggling under the water as sediment rises like great dust clouds around me. I think of Eddie, of Sam. I think, too, of Alice and Vicky and poor Mary, of Simon Pascoe being lifted from the quarry. My lungs are screaming but I'm peaceful, the water bright and cool. Eventually my bones will soften and dissolve into the mud, stirred up by future winds and sticks in children's hands, the shimmering tails of fish.

FORTY-ONE

The pain is rich and seething, rolling like an undertow. Something is broken inside me. I feel it as I flex my fingers; the roar behind my ribs, lungs crackling like a torn paper bag. My tongue is so swollen that I can't swallow. There is a hospital smell, bleach and cleaning fluid. It's clinical, as am I. The needle, the cannula. I sleep. When I wake, there is a hand on my arm, and a voice I recognize says quietly, *"Hullo, Mina."*

"Am I dead?" I croak.

She laughs.

"What do you remember?"

"Nothing."

I have burned a hole in my memories so vast that light has not been able to get in. For a long time the memory of Eddie has been hidden down there, not dormant but growing and swelling like mushrooms in the dark. Fern gives me a tentative smile.

FORTY-TWO

"First things first, you're in hospital. Good news, huh?"

She holds her hand out to me; the skin of her arm embossed with that network of old scars, a road map in braille. Her skin is warm and soft. She is alive, and that means that by extension, I am, too. *Alive.* I blink slowly as she pours a glass of water from the jug on the bedside table.

"How long have I been here?"

Owong ave I binere?

"This is day six. You want the headlines?"

I nod. Fern holds the cup to my lips so I can take a sip of water. It tastes stale and warm and plastic, and it is so good she has to stop me gulping the whole lot down.

"Ah-ah," she says, "you'll be sick. How's your tongue?"

"Sore." I can feel it in my mouth, huge and puffy, throbbing in time with my pulse.

"Well, the good news is that Bert didn't manage to pull it all the way out. He just tore it. It'll heal, although you may lose a bit of sensation. He did, however, do some major tissue damage to your throat and he dislocated your poor jaw."

"How do you know all this?"

"I read your notes, Mina." She gives me a small, mischievous smile.

"What happened to Bert?"

"First, let's talk about what happened to *you*. You think you're ready for that?"

I nod.

"You sank. I thought you had to be dead. It was Sam who pulled you out. He waded right in once he realized what was going on, and he lifted you and carried you to the shore like the Swamp Thing. You looked like a fucked-up Ophelia. Your eyes were wide open but you weren't seeing anything. I thought you were a goner, for sure. Sam checked you for a pulse and when he couldn't find one he started doing CPR. They reckon that's what saved your life. He kept you going till the paramedics took over."

Her eyes are shimmering.

"You were clinically dead. Do you remember anything?"

I shake my head as much as the pain will allow. I remember the pond, the dark water, surface slightly ruffled by the building storm. Everything after that is a blank.

Is it, Mina?

Something stutters, like a short circuit in my brain. A hand-clap, there and gone in a moment. Eddie, smiling that goofy grin he did when he knew he was making me laugh. No ice, no oxygen masks hanging from bed frames. No cold, no rain. A warm patch of sunlight and the huge beanbags we had in the attic that smelled musty and old. An open book on his lap, *Mysteries of the British Isles,* dust motes in his hair.

Eddie had been there.

"I want to say I'm sorry, Mina. About Bert. I didn't believe you. I should have listened." She looks down at her hands, and a tear rolls down her cheek. "I was so scared when you mentioned Stevie—that he might have—he looked after her for me all the time, Mina."

She sniffs, swiping her tears away with the back of her hand.

"You know the first thing I thought of? How he used to call her 'Stevie-Beans.' She wouldn't let anyone else use it, do you remember? Only Bert. His special name for her. What does that say about me as a mother? That I let my daughter visit every day with that monster? I was angry when you said it but not at you, not really. I was mad at me and I just felt so sorry for who I was back then. That messed-up little girl in the photograph. I wish I could go back and save her."

She lifts her eyes to the ceiling, catching her breath.

"I don't remember picking up those Polaroids but I must have done because I took that envelope upstairs and threw it right in the bin. I tried to forget it but like the heart in that Edgar Allan Poe story, it just kept right on beating, reminding me it was there, so I pulled it back out again and then God help me I opened it. I looked at those pictures for a long time, long enough for Stevie's bathwater to get cold. By then I was shaking all over. It was in my jaw and in my legs, I couldn't stop."

Fern picks at the bedsheet anxiously. I can hear the tremor in her voice.

"After that I made Lisa look at them. I think I scared her. I admit it. I meant to, because she *had* to listen to me right the first time. I asked her straight out about the Bertinis and the headaches and the holes in our memories. I told her what you'd told me and her face lost all color, like she was about to throw up. She kept saying Bert wouldn't do this, he wouldn't, not Bert, until the tears started. I didn't hear when Alice came in but we both turned around when she said, 'Mum?' She had something in her hand. Something about it made me feel queasy, like I'd seen it before, only in a bad dream."

"The pricker," I mumble. She snorts.

"Is that what he called it? Horrible thing. I didn't know where Alice found it—I just know she held out her hand, palm facing up, and said, 'Mum look at this,' and then she drove the needle down hard into her hand."

I flinch. I remember how it felt when it had skewered into my side. I can even look down and see the wound on my arm, clotted over with a nasty scab.

"But here's the thing. The needle went into her hand—all the way in—but nothing happened. Alice just stood there, pulled it out, pushed it slowly back in. Lisa didn't get it, but I saw what it was straightaway."

I think of Alice driving it into my leg and how it had left no impression.

"Witches don't feel pain," I slur. I don't know if she understands me but Fern nods all the same.

"Oh, they do. But this was a trick. The pricker has a mechanism—a simple thing really, no more than a switch—that allows the needle to retract inside the handle. When Alice hit her hand, the needle disappeared, but the mechanism made it look as if it had gone right in. If you flipped the switch the other way, the needle locked in place. Lisa was staring at it with horror and I suspect she'd been on the blunt end of that instrument more than once while staying with the Roscows."

We both fall silent. I keep remembering the way Bert handed Alice the witch pricker, how carefully he placed it in her hand. He must have flicked the switch as he did so, mindful that when she drove it into me it would then retract, making it seem as if I were impervious to it.

"Did Alice see the photos?"

Fern nods.

"I hadn't meant her to, but it was like trying to hold back a tide. Something happened to her that night, Mina. She changed. It was like watching a Valkyrie rising. Something took over her."

My brain skips, skimming like a stone. I can see the expression on Alice's face as she drove that pricker into Bert's neck, the brutal, boiling rage. *Daemonia eicere.*

"Is Alice okay?" I manage. A runnel of spit runs out the corner of my mouth and I wipe at it, alert enough to feel self-conscious.

"The Webber family haven't been seen since the Riddance. At some point that night their house caught fire and carried on burning till morning. The statement from the fire department claims it was a chimney fire but that can't be right. No one was having log fires in the middle of a heat wave."

I think of the clicking of old bones, the pattering of soot. Alice saying *"She watches me through the cracks in the bricks."* I am numb, at the edge of sleep I think. Drifting.

"Where've they gone?"

I open my eyes and turn to face her, wincing at the throb of pain on my right side.

"The police say the younger two were picked up from the

grandparents about half eleven that night and then the family drove north. That's as much as I know. What remains of the house is boarded up but already a lot of ghouls have been in there taking photographs and souvenirs. Hey, that reminds me—this came to the video shop this morning."

She hands me a postcard and at first I think, *That looks like me,* and then I see it *is* me, me in my yellow dress in Crete a million years ago with Eddie reaching toward me. My photograph, slightly creased. When I turn it over, I discover it has been stamped and postmarked and the writing on the back is brief.

He 4gives U!

The photographs in Alice's bedroom, the writing beneath them in the same curved, giddy swirls. *Best M8s 4 Ever!*

He 4gives U!

I make a sound, somewhere between a laugh and a sob. Fern's eyes widen in alarm but I'm smiling. I take a look at the postmark but it is smudged and illegible. Probably just as well. I'm near the edge of sleep now. Everything is getting heavy. The lights are fuzzy, haloed. But I have one more question for Fern, one more answer I need.

"Sam?"

"I spoke to him yesterday. He's desperate to see you." Fern leans a little closer to me, whispering, "You didn't hear it from me but he calls the hospital every day to see how you are. He pretends to be your cousin."

"He's got form for that." I laugh, despite the way it sends sparks of pain into my damaged jaw.

"He feels terrible about what happened. He blames himself. I think once he saw Bert fall into the fire, he . . ."

Fern trails off. She doesn't finish the sentence but she doesn't need to. I know what happened. The spell broke. That's why he'd come into the water to save me. I think of how I last saw Sam only moments before, blank-eyed, wistful. That shoe, scarred and scuffed and tiny in his hands. I don't blame him. We were both lost, both unglued. The witch had got under our skin, just like she had with Alice.

"Tell him to come and see me when I'm better." I manage a small, exhausted smile. "I'd like that."

I close my eyes and feel my body, cushioned by painkillers. It's like being suspended in a cradle of stars. When I open my eyes again, Fern is still looking at me and I know there is something else and that I won't like it. The morphine will be wearing off soon and the edges of the pain will start to show through the thin blanket of protection and it's going to hurt. I hold my fingers up to her, *wait*. I have something to say, first.

"Oscar left me."

"I know, Mina, I'm sorry."

"Don't be. It was coming. He told me right after they brought me in."

I was half-conscious when Oscar walked in and took a seat in the chair beside the bed, the one Fern now occupies. He tugged at the knees of his trousers as he sat, an old Oscar affectation, one I still find warm and comforting. I suppose one day that will fade.

"I can't marry you," he said stiffly. "I don't even know who you are anymore."

It might have been the morphine but I like to think there was some relief for both of us. He went on to tell me he had already canceled the venue and rescinded invites.

"I called to cancel the caterers and they told me you'd never even made the appointment."

"I'm sorry, Oscar. I should have told you."

"My mother is furious."

"Oh."

As he walked out, I said, "Tell Lucy I said 'hi'." Perhaps he didn't understand me, with my tongue fat and heavy. He paused, but only for a moment. Then he kept right on going. Safe. Careful. A man who knew all about the heavens and nothing about love.

"It's for the best," I tell Fern, yawning. *Ish fordabesh.*

She nods, lacing her hands around her knees and looking at me steadily.

"I'm going to leave you to get some sleep, Mina. They think you'll be out on the ward tomorrow and discharged maybe the day after—and at some point the police will want to talk. Do you have someone to support you?"

I think about it for so long my chest tightens with sadness.

Fern notices, and nods. "Then I'll come. Every day if I have to."

"No, you don't have—"

"I do, Mina. For my own sanity, I do."

This reply is so funny to me in my dreamy, zoned-out way that I burst out laughing. Fern waits politely for it to fade away before saying, "I should tell you about Bert."

I stiffen, suddenly cold. From somewhere down the corridor, I can hear the hush of the nurse's footsteps, the beeping of a distant alarm.

"What about him?"

"He's here."

I immediately try to sit up, gasping at the flare of pain in my ribs.

"Settle down. He's not even on this floor. He's in intensive care. Been there since they dragged him out the fire and they brought you both in."

Silence. My heart is racing so fast I think I might be sick.

"He's going to pull through. That's what they reckon."

"Fern—"

"I'm just telling you, so you know. He's badly burned, and he'll never look like he used to. He'll probably be talking through a hole in his throat the rest of his life, but—he's alive."

She stands up as if preparing to leave, her face carefully composed.

"Which ward?"

"Uh, I don't know."

"Yes you do."

Yesh oo do.

Fern looks away from me, keeping her voice steady and low.

"He's in a private room. Trelawney Wing, second floor. Third door on the left, number nine. I went up there but I couldn't go in. Guess that makes me a coward, huh?"

She leans forward, kissing me gently on the head.

"I'll be back for you, Mina."

I watch the pneumatic door swing slowly closed behind her. I don't doubt that she means what she says, that she *will* return. It's a good feeling. I lean back into the pillows, feeling sleep overtaking me, the painkillers lifting me upward among asteroids and satellites and into the hearts of stars.

I dream of Eddie. Of my mother saying *"He's always been a sickly boy."* Maybe that's why no one was worried at first, when he started shivering, his temperature climbing dangerously high. Another cold, another sore throat. Two days after I fell through the ice, I came home from school to see Eddie with his feet in a bowl of hot water and a towel over his shoulders. A few days later he started coughing. Deep and guttural, like something was clawing its way out of him. He was tired all the time, shadows swimming beneath the surface of his skin. By the time the snow had melted and the rains had come in, Eddie was breathing in long, hard gasps, frame too bony and eyes too sunken to be my brother. *It's not him,* I thought, as I carried the pillow toward his bed. *It's not Eddie in there, just a sick imposter.*

"*Tell me about the ice, Mina,*" he whispered, mist fogging up his oxygen mask. "*So I'm not afraid while you do it.*"

The story always started the same way—"*Remember how the snow had smelled like metal,*" I said, "*how it was so cold it burned our fingers?*" I slipped the mask off his face, left it hanging from the bedpost. When I lowered the pillow, we'd reached the lane that would take us to Brewer's Pond, the ice cracking beneath my feet as his hands clenched and unclenched, hitting feebly against my own, the rooks taking flight as his heels drummed into the mattress, and by the time he stopped his feeble struggling he had saved my life and the lethal cold burrowed into the soft tissue of his lungs and ruptured an eye bloodred.

I don't take my painkillers that evening. I don't want to risk falling all the way asleep. I clench my teeth as the opiates wear off and the world swims into focus, raw and sharp edged. The nurse leaves a tray of food by my bed at six-fifteen. Soft things that my tongue and throat can manage. Warm soup, mashed potato, jelly. I eat the jelly.

At eight o'clock I sink into a fitful, sweaty doze infused with dreams of an abyss, a great gulf of space beneath my feet that cracks like ice. When I wake panting around midnight, I am in such pain I almost call for the nurse. Instead I force myself to sit up and drink a glass of water, swallowing against the burning in my throat, the jarring pain in my jaw that shortens my breath with every movement. I put on the television and watch old shows and the nightly news, stories of how the heat wave was broken in a series of storms across the country, flash floods in the Highlands. I watch the clock move past midnight, then toward one o'clock. By one-thirty I carefully, so carefully, swing my legs out of the bed and onto the floor, the tiles blissfully cool beneath my bare feet. It takes me a moment to stand and another for my legs to steady beneath me, and I walk a slow circuit around the room before I'm confident enough to open the door and slip out into the hallway, following the signs for the lifts and using the wall to hold on to when I need to catch my breath. My chest crackles noisily and my breathing is short and hard, making me dizzy. There is a pain all the way down the side of my neck like something has me in a metal vise, squeezing.

I take another step and another, and then I'm in the empty lift and pressing the buttons for the second floor. I'm shivering, feeling something rupture as I lift my arm. A spot of blood blooms on the bandage. My gown flaps around me like a winding shroud. The lift chimes as the doors open and a sign welcomes me to the Trelawney Wing. *"Third door on the left, number nine,"* Fern said. I can see it up ahead of me. I look up and down the corridor but there is no one around. Distantly I can hear the muffled squeak of shoes as the nurses pass along the wards. I wonder if Sam is still hearing that sound in the night. I hope not. I hope it's over for all of us. I stagger past the first two rooms, sweating heavily, gritting my teeth against the pain, one hand pressed against my side.

I can't do this.

Keep going, Meens.

My hand is opening the door to room nine and I feel like I'm floating away. Even the pain recedes briefly, like an ebbing tide. I see a figure on the bed wired up to machines that beep and flicker, an intravenous drip, blood bags glowing red in the low light. Bert's bandaged hands are folded on top of the coverlet. His chest is a slow rise and fall, head turned slightly to one side. Carefully, so carefully, I close the door behind me. I consider putting a chair in front of it but I need to conserve my strength so I have to just hope I can be quick. It's not like it's my first time.

There is a burn mask over his face—a rubbery, flesh-colored shield with tiny holes for his eyes and nostrils. The name on his notes reads *Albert Roscow* and when I lean close to his face I think I detect a shift in his breathing, a quickening perhaps. Deep in the mask, the eyes open. I smile at him as I slide the pillow out from beneath his head and I think he is trying to say something but it is muffled, made unintelligible by the mask. A wasp, striped bright yellow, is crawling over his raw pink scalp. I don't know where it came from. All the windows are closed. I think of Alice, of witches' familiars and heat waves and bright red wax. I lean closer, close enough that he can hear me when I whisper, "Goodbye, Bert. Good Riddance."

ACKNOWLEDGMENTS

A book is a collaborative process, and none more so than this one. Huge thanks to Jordan Lees for his unwavering support and guidance. Thanks to all at St. Martin's Press, especially Alex Sehulster for giving the book a home and knowing exactly what it needed, and to Ryan Jenkins for keeping it all in check. Thanks also to Cassidy Graham, for her patience!

As always, I couldn't do it without the support of my family and friends. Thank you, all.

To my daughter Poppy, my best pal and my North Star, always.

ACKNOWLEDGMENTS

ABOUT THE AUTHOR

Daisy Pearce was born in Cornwall, but currently lives in Sussex, UK. In 2015 she won the Chindi Authors Short Story Competition. Her short stories have previously been published in *One Eye Grey* and performed at the Small Story Cabaret. She has also written about mental-health issues for *xoJane*. She is the author of *The Silence* and *The Missing*. Specialist subjects include ghosts, poltergeists, and the perfect red lipstick.